OVERCOME

The Story of a Girl

M.E. REACH

outskirtspress

DENVER, COLORADO

Overcome
The Story of a Girl
All Rights Reserved.
Copyright © 2012 M.E. Reach
v1.0

Outskirts Press, Inc.
http://www.outskirtspress.com

ISBN: 978-1-4327-9070-7

Library of Congress Control Number: 2012908519

Outskirts Press and the "OP" logo are trademarks belonging to Outskirts Press, Inc.

PRINTED IN THE UNITED STATES OF AMERICA

Chapter One

August 13th - Monday

It's the beginning of another year here at Davis-Buckley High school, which means three very important things. First, the Buckley High Bucking-Broncos will be starting their much anticipated football season soon. After their undefeated season last year, I'm sure there'll be a lot more people at the games. Dad, Mom, and I went to every game last year to watch Ian sit on the bench with all of the rest of the freshmen. You name it, we were there. We even went to the ones way out in Lunsford and Deadwood. I didn't even know they had electricity out there, much less schools. Hicks! How could people live like that?

Whitney, Carrie, Kylie, and I are going to celebrate our freedom from the harassment of being freshmen. Thank God! I thought the year of cruel and unusual punishment would never end. I spent all summer with them, which was a little different than my old routine, but things change and people grow up. I used to spend the summers with my cousin Sarah down at my aunt's house in Hammond Falls. It used to be a lot of fun when I was a kid, but let's face it I'm not a kid anymore, and when you have friends who needs family?

And last, but not least, and *certainly* the most important of all, the big 1-6 is only two months away. I can't wait! Whitney said that her mom and dad talked to my mom and dad and the party is planned and underway. They better get me a car!

The halls were the same as always, dingy and old. I think the teachers get paid more if they're extra peppy on the first day or something, because they're all smiling and all excited to teach. On the first day of school everyone's always dressed to impress, too. It took me a little time to recognize some people. Joe Gregory sprouted about another foot in the air and started getting some muscles. It took me a minute to stop noticing.

Natalie Fletcher found out that she had breasts, and it showed! And apparently, by the looks of the crowd around her, the guys noticed too. My boyfriend from last year, Eric Stapleton was standing by one of his good buddies, the ever-annoying Charlie Anderson. I pretended like I didn't see him once I got closer.

"I think he still likes you," commented Whitney when I walked up.

"Nuh-uh…"

"He was scannin' the goods girl!" added Kylie.

As if it were her cue, Carrie walked up from somewhere behind me and slammed her back on the lockers. We all jumped, even Whitney who saw her coming. She looked up at the ceiling and lolled her head.

"It's only the first day and I'm already in love!" she announced.

"What?" I asked.

"Have you seen Joe Gregory? Oh-my-god! I wonder if he's doing anything Friday?"

Kylie shook her head, annoyed. "Yeah, *you*, skank!" she blurted. "White girls are always in *love* with the first thing they see. Girl, you gotta be patient! Look," she said, pointing at Dyson Edwards, "he's been in my sights for a year now."

She stopped eyeing Dyson as if he were a piece of dark chocolate and then looked to Carrie."You gotta aim girl! You can't be just laying down for anybody. I ain't gonna be friends with no skanky girl all year! Boys be all tryin' to get my number cause I hang out with you...Pssh."

Whitney and I held our hands over our mouths and laughed while Carrie descended from cloud nine. By lunch everyone had seen the majority of their required classes like history and English and all the rest of the boring ones. But the afternoon was packed with electives like computers and art; the classes we called, "the easy A's." Carrie spent all day ranting about the obvious. How well this guy filled out or how strong that guy looks after a summer working at his uncle's farm in Yellow Brooke. For some reason she was all about the muscle-heads now. I can't say that I blame her though. My brother did bring home some hot football players last year. As I thought of my brother, Ian walked up and sat down next to me. We were a year apart in school when we were younger, but he passed some test and got advanced a grade, which is kinda cool. We've always been sort of close anyway, so it worked out. Besides, he does my homework for me sometimes.

"Well if it isn't Mr. Mitchell..." teased Carrie.

Ian smiled shyly, "Hey, Carrie."

"How's it going?" he asked everyone.

Insert Carrie's lengthy gossip that lasted more than half our lunch period. Ian listened as if he cared, which I noticed he had become really, really good at. So much in fact, that if I didn't know any better I'd say he was wooed by Carrie. And who wouldn't be? Long, curly blonde hair, full lips, perfect in all the right places, flat rock of a stomach, she was every guy's dream girl. Well, every guy *but* my brother.

"So you *don't* like her?" I asked hours later just before dinner. Between the two of us we split the chores while gossiping about someone at school or complaining about homework or boring each other with our own personal things. For example, he would try to explain why he should be the starting receiver and not Jeremy Hale, while I would share with him the more important things like why Jessica Wilson should never, ever again wear a miniskirt.

"No...well...," he stammered a reply, before bearing his infamous 'it depends' expression.

I opened the dishwasher and started handing him the cups. He opened the cupboard and started shoveling them in all nice and neat. After all, our coffee obsessed household must have its shelves well-stocked.

"So you're telling me..." I looked around to make sure our mom was nowhere near, "that if she were upstairs right now, naked, that you wouldn't..."

"No!" he replied, almost disgusted. I laughed.

"See, that's exactly what I mean!" he added, "I knew I should've never opened my big mouth after lunch!"

"Ian, I get it, she's hot and all, but you can't just stare at her all the time. You've got to be braver, grow some..." I made the expression and thought that would suffice.

He only shook his head and placed another cup in the cabinet.

"What?" I asked.

He took another coffee cup. "I don't know. I'm just taking my time is all. You know, weighing things out like you did with Eric. I'm just not too sure about her."

"What do you mean?" How could he not be *sure* about her?

"She just...she's all about sex and things now. She wasn't that way last year. She was cooler and funnier and more into sports and movies and things."

"Yeah, but sex is like a rites of passage, Ian. It's like a part of growing up!"

He stopped and glared at me. "Do you really believe that? Or do your friends just have you believing it?"

I wanted to reply automatically with something real disarming, but I could only manage, "It's not what we *believe*, it's what we *know*!"

Ian scoffed and shook his head.

"Besides, those sorts of things never happen!" he argued, trying to change the subject.

"What sorts of things?"

"Her being upstairs..." he replied with a smirk.

"It's not like it *couldn't* happen..."

He looked at me skeptically.

"You know, your birthday *is* coming up..." I joked, "I could put in a good word..."

His eyes widened, "You wouldn't! Oh, Erin, I swear if you..."

"I'll never tell her!" I said slowly, rolling my eyes.

We could hear mom talking to dad as the two walked down the hall toward the kitchen. He leaned in close.

"Swear it!" he said, "You can't tell her! I'll be a laughed at... She'll laugh at me!"

"She wouldn't laugh at you!"

"Oh, yeah! Did you see the way she treated Dexter Brady last year when he asked her to homecoming?"

"Well...yeah, but you're better looking than him!"

"Better looking than who?" mom interjected, as she slid into the kitchen. I swear she has the ears of a jungle cat.

"Brad Pitt!" I answered quickly with a smile.

Mom's face scrunched up oddly. She looked to my father confused, who only kept walking through the kitchen to the garage door.

"Course you are honey," she replied with a wink to Ian.

Chapter Two

August 27th - Monday

Only two weeks into school and Mrs. Clark's already giving us a Geometry test on Friday. I don't understand why teachers have to make it so much harder than it already is. Carrie's going out with Joe Gregory on Friday night. She says it's only harmless, but Kylie doesn't think so.

"You crazy girl! Couldn't you keep your panties on till at least Homecoming? Dang, what's your thang, you on fire or something? He a fireman?"

Whitney and I would've loved to have hung around to see the outcome, but we started laughing so hard that we had to run to the bathroom or risk peeing ourselves in the middle of sophomore hall.

Buckley High is like a big square prison. It has two main halls lined with lockers that connect four wings used for classes. On one side you have the freshmen and sophomore lockers and bathrooms and then on the other, the junior and seniors. Its two stories, but only the juniors and seniors go upstairs for classes. The four halls are separated into the sciences, math, the nauseatingly boring English and history classes, and then the cool ones like art and shop. Away from it all, beside the gym and cafeteria was the band hall for the geeks. Of course, that term was used lightly around Whitney who was the most stylishly gorgeous geek of the entire herd.

"Band isn't geeky!" she'd attempt to argue. Fierce looks of skepticism made her falter every time and if that miraculously didn't work we would opt for the occasional point in the direction of Stephanie Howler or Derrick Jenkins, the geek representatives of Davis-Buckley.

By third period Whitney and I were staring numbly at the clock on the wall while Mr. Harper continued to ramble on about the Greek and some war where some guy yelled "Nike." He made the ultimate mistake by saying at the beginning of class that this lesson wasn't going to be on the nine weeks test. Once the words exited his mouth my mind was already wandering to what interesting gossip Carrie might bring to the lunch table.

"Tonya Hanks is gonna fight Terri Bush after school today, I think," she said first thing before she even took her seat. Her eyes were wide with excitement. Both girls were well fed and likely to have an actual throw-down as opposed to the usual name calling and head bobbing that regularly occurred.

"I bet we'll even see a few punches," she added.

"Ain't gonna be a fight," interjected Kylie, "Terri Bush gonna die! Tonya's tuff!"

"I don't know…" argued Carrie. She lifted her diet coke to take a sip before Kylie sounded, "Pssh. Girl, what you know with your diet coke drink'n self? Only thing you fight with is that hair in the morning! Hootchie! Where's your boy toy anyhow? Ain't you two s'posed to be make'n out or something?"

Whitney choked on a French fry just as Ian sat down.

"What's so funny?" he asked. He looked at his shirt, worried he had gotten something on him and then looked behind him. "What?"

"Nothing cutie pie," teased Kylie, "You just come on down here and sit your fine self next to me!"

She tossed a wink to Ian and he smirked.

"Hi, Kylie," he said, almost blushing as he took the empty seat beside her.

Kylie looked at me and winked. I glanced to Whitney who was still laughing.

"What you got next?" Kylie asked.

"Tanner for government and then Mrs. Erickson for Biology II," I replied.

"Man, I think Mr. Tanner's racist!" she replied.

"Racist?" echoed Ian, "but he's black!"

"Oh, so you think just cause a man's a brother that he can't be racist?"

"You mean against white people?" asked Whitney.

"No, I'm talk'n about a brother who's racist against his own kind girl," she clarified.

Everyone sort of looked around at one another.

"I don't think I've ever heard of that," chimed Ian.

"Course you haven't," blurted Kylie, "Cause ain't no brother gonna be accused of racism against his own kind! That's like a white boy hanging another white boy...it just ain't something that happens!"

"Why do you think he's racist?" asked Whitney.

"Well, for one he's teaching government and ain't no black man should be teaching government unless they preaching about welfare or how those crusty ole' crackers upstairs are holding us down in the ghetto... And don't you know that man gives every black kid in his class extra work all the time too."

"Yeah," laughed Ian, "but it's extra credit work!"

"Oh, and you some expert now, huh cutie-pie? Take your fine self on up and get me another milk!"

Ian looked at me and smiled and then grabbed a handful of French fries before he left to fill Kylie's order. Once he was gone Kylie smiled real big and chuckled. "I just love him! I could just squeeze him so tight those curls'd just pop right off his head."

"He's a sweetheart," added Whitney, finally free of her deadly French fry.

"He's not bad looking, either," chimed Carrie.

I gave her a look that told her *off-limits* and she reflected it with a smile.

"Don't you be all skank-eye'n my cutie-pie!" said Kylie with a point. "You best just drink that diet coke an' listen to that stomach a' yours growl all anorexic-like and keep your eyes on Mr. Muscle-head."

Just after Ian returned with Kylie's milk the second bell rang, which was our signal to get ready for our next class. Whitney, Carrie, and I said good-bye to Ian and Kylie and then made our way to our lockers. Just before we walked into the hall, the intercom screeched loudly and Mrs. Harrison cleared her throat.

"Homecoming is only a little over a month away! Anyone who wants to help out with the Homecoming decorations and the float must report to...umm...room three-fourteen by the end of this week. And don't forget, this Friday is Spirit day. Our Bucking-Broncos will be hosting the Lunsford Lumberjacks at six-o'clock. Any students available to work concessions please see Coach Irving before Friday."

Another screech ended the announcement.

"Wow, I can't believe it's already almost homecoming!" said Whitney.

"I know, I don't even have my dress," whined Carrie.

"Don't worry, I don't think anyone does," I said. For some reason the thought of going to homecoming didn't seem as appealing as it had my freshman year.

"We should all get together this weekend and go pick out dresses," offered Whitney.

"Yeah, we could stay over at my place on Friday night after the game and then..."

"Can't," interjected Carrie, "Date with Joe, remember?"

"Oh, yeah," both Whitney and I replied. The comment dampened Whitney's spirits before I reminded her that two people can have just as much fun as three.

"I'll ask my mom tonight and make sure it's alright," I said.

"Just you and Whitney?" asked Mom after dinner.

"Yeah," I replied.

"What about Carrie and Kylie?"

"I haven't asked Kylie yet, but Carrie's got a date,"

"A date?" echoed my mom, apparently surprised that such things occurred.

"Yeah, you know mom, a date...with a guy..." I said with a smile.

Ian finished his dinner and then walked over to Max's bowl and scraped his scraps off into it and then washed it off. Mom watched Ian as he walked across the room and then looked to me quizzically.

"So who's the lucky guy?" she asked, saddened by the news.

"Joe Gregory..."

Ian walked from the kitchen and climbed the stairs toward the call of geometry homework.

"What happened to her and Ian?"

"Mom, they never went out!"

"Yeah, but they were a thing though, right?"

"In Ian's mind, but not really, no!"

"Well..." she stammered, "What about homecoming? Who's he gonna go with? Has he asked anybody?"

I shrugged. "It's just a date, who knows?" I replied, "Besides, Ian's got school and football and..."

"Oh, come off it!" interrupted Mom, "He's no different

than any other high school boy... He needs someone just like you do, and Carrie, and everyone else. It's only normal to date in high school. Don't go placing him in a category all to his own because he's your brother."

I scoffed, "Mom, I don't think of Ian that way, it's just that...she's just...Ian said he really doesn't like her like that anymore."

"What do you mean?"

"I don't know, I think he's gay!"

"WHAT?" she howled.

I laughed, "Gotcha!"

"Erin *Elizabeth* Mitchell!"

I cringed. "No, Mom, honestly, she's just changed over the summer and I think maybe because he spent so much time around her he's actually starting to see her differently. It's not the same anymore, you know?"

Mom nodded and then started helping me with the dishes. "I guess childhood crushes *do* fade," she said, "She's just getting so beautiful, I thought..."

"I know," I said, though I really didn't. What did her being beautiful have to do with Ian?

"What about *you*? Do *you* have any plans for homecoming?"

"Uh, of course," I lied, "tons..."

"Other than Whitney," she asked, reading through the façade.

"I don't know..."

"Well, I'm not going to pay for a dress if you don't have a date!"

Chapter Three

August 28th - Tuesday

"Are you serious?" blurted Carrie. If there was ever a time when I wished I wasn't friends with the queen of drama, now was that time. She had managed to gawk, wave her arms hysterically, and finally blurt, loud enough to attract *everyone's* attention within a twenty foot radius. I'm sure there were guys across the way who either thought I was pregnant or had just heard the news that my mother was dying, or something else outrageous.

Kylie looked at Carrie as if to say something, but the words that everyone was depending on never came. She only shook her head and sighed. It was obvious that she was annoyed, she just probably couldn't decide what to start with. Whitney's eyes were wide.

"Wow, you only have a couple of days... We have to get started!"

The girls and I scoured the halls before first period. When I say *scoured* the halls, I mean we walked down them to see how many guys checked us out and then rushed into a dark corner to talk about them.

"Okay," whispered Whitney, "Jason Gardner was totally checking you out!"

"Really?" I said, "He's cute!"

Unintentionally, we looked in his direction and were spotted by his friends. Embarrassed, we turned and giggled. At least, most of us did. Carrie, however, refused to take her eyes off of them and continued to stare until they were the ones who felt embarrassed and turned away.

"Skank," mumbled Kylie. Whitney and I burst into laughter. I think it was Whitney who eventually snorted and all of us started laughing all over again just before the first bell rang.

Carrie and Whitney went to Art with Ms. Lipsius, while Kylie and I headed toward English and the ever-grumbling Mrs. Prichard.

Never the most pleasant woman, Mrs. Prichard covered her classroom with posters of Garfield and in the middle of her desk was a poster of the ugliest dog I think I've ever seen. For the first few weeks I didn't learn a thing! The dog distracted me with its fat rolls and wrinkles. But then, Joey Sullivan was moved in front of me and I haven't been able to see a thing since.

Apparently, the Nathaniel Hawthorne damage had been done and we were moving on to Drama and some guy named Tennessee. What a name! I'd hate to be named Colorado, but I guess there are cooler names like Virginia or Dakota. As a class we read through a play called the Glass Mena..gary... Mendagery... something like that. Anyway, afterwards Mrs. Prichard had us vote as a class on who should act out which part. I'm playing the sister, Laura. I think it'll be fun, but I'm not too excited about acting in front of people. I'm sure everyone will be horrible though, so maybe I'll look like a superstar or something.

The bell rang and everyone quickly shoved their literature books in their bags and funneled for the door. I hate English! I don't think it's the work that I hate so much as the reading. I mean, why read something if there's a movie about it? I don't care who you are, the guy in your imagination is not going to be any hotter than the guy they put in the movie! And plus, it takes up so much time to read. A movie is three hours, *tops*!

The shoving was nearing its end and I could see Kylie waiting against the opposite wall for me.

"Oh, Ms. Mitchell, I need to see you one moment before you leave."

I swallowed my gum as I walked over to her. She was a short and mean looking woman who reminded me of the poster she kept on her desk.

"The reason I'm keeping you behind is because I want to discuss something about your character. I am a fan of drama, and regardless of the age, I like it to be done properly; therefore, I am warning you that there are going to be some scenes where you are going to have to be close to a boy. With that in mind, I have a release form for you to take home to your parents and get permission first, but make sure and tell them that if they need to call me for whatever reason, my number's at the bottom."

I nodded, folded the slip of paper up, and then slid it into my pocket with a nod.

By the time I got into the hall Kylie was gone. I only had a couple of minutes to make it to Geometry and... "Crap!" I blurted. I left my homework in my locker.

"You alright?" a voice asked from behind me.

My jaw dropped when I saw who it was. I'm sure my lip quivered...and I might've even peed a little. It was Jake Cunningham, easily the hottest guy in the world.

"Yeah," I replied.

He continued to walk with me toward the end of the hall. I felt awkward with nothing to say. My mind screamed at me, *Erin! Don't say anything!*

"Who do you have next?" I asked.

"Tanner...government," he replied.

I couldn't think of anything else to say... I panicked. "I hear he's racist!"

Jake's expression contorted for a second and then he smirked.

"I've never heard of a black man who was racist before..."

I felt like a complete idiot. I could feel my face reddening every second.

Thankfully, the hallway was at its end.

"Well, see you later," I said quickly. Once I turned I scoffed at myself and debated on ramming my head into the nearest locker. *Stupid! Stupid! Stupid!* I walked calmly to my locker until he turned the corner toward

Mr. Tanner's government class and then I yanked my homework out, slammed my locker, and sprinted full speed to Mrs. Clark's classroom. The tardy bell rang only seconds before I got to the door.

"I'm sorry, Ms. Mitchell, a tardy is a tardy," said Mrs. Clark after class.

Her tone told me she wasn't going to waver on it and that I would probably have a better chance convincing her that desks were trees. Slowly, my worst nightmare came into focus. Now, regardless of my grade in the class, I would have to take the nine weeks test.

"That's stupid!" commented Kylie at lunch. "So Mrs. Prichard be keep'n you after class an' make'n you all tardy an' you s'posed to just..." she stopped her rant and made a noise that sounded like, "Oh no you didn't," but in hum form.

"So you can't do *anything*?" Whitney added.

"Nope! I even read the handbook and it says one absence, one tardy, or any grade less than a ninety has to take the nine weeks test."

"Can't you go to Mrs. Prichard and see if she'll give a note to Mrs. Clark?" asked Whitney. I could tell by the look on her face that she really cared for my situation. Tests suck!

"I heard from Kristy Carter that Mrs. Clark is having an affair with Coach Johnson," inserted Carrie, "Maybe you could just mention Coach Johnson and see if she gets all tense and then play it off, you know, like they do in the movies when they want to pressure someone into doing something they don't want to..."

We all looked at Carrie for a second as if to ask where she comes up with this stuff, but then Ian came and sat down next to me.

"I heard about the tardy. Have you tried talking to Mrs. Prichard about it?"

Whitney beamed.

"No, not yet," I replied. I looked at Whitney but then I noticed something odd. She was looking at Ian with a sort of glazed over look in her eye, like the way some of the nerdy boys stare at Carrie when she walks by. I thought to kick her under the table, but before I did, she turned it off and started playing with her food. It was mystery meat and noodles today. We called these days "diet days" and just bought a couple extra milks and ate the cookie.

"Well you should," Ian continued. "I'd do anything to get out of taking a nine weeks test, *especially* in Geometry."

"Yeah, I guess I should..."

"Oh!" he said, abruptly, looking at Kylie, "Guess what I found out?"

"That you fine and you want to take me to homecoming so I can show you how a girl's s'posed to work it on the dance floor?"

Everyone laughed. Ian started to blush. Why did Whitney looking at him bother me, but Kylie's comments were always funny? Maybe it was because Kylie and I rarely hung out after school and Whitney and I had been best friends for as long as I could remember. It probably didn't help that I was already cursed with keeping Ian's crush on Carrie a secret…if you'd even call it a *crush*. I mean, what guy is confused about wanting a girl like Carrie?

"So is that it?" asked Kylie, "Did I steal what you was gonna tell me?" she smiled, taking another drink of her milk.

"Um…yeah and no," he replied, a hint of redness in his cheeks.

"What'd you find out?" I asked.

"I took a shot at the waste basket yesterday in Mr. Tanner's class and missed. It rolled back behind his desk and he told me to get over there and pick it up, so I walked around his desk and guess what I saw?"

"A black man shining his shoes…" stabbed Kylie.

"A picture of his *black* wife…"

"So!"

"So, he can't be racist against his own people."

Kylie looked lost for words. "Hmm," she sounded.

Whitney looked at me and we both smiled.

"Yeah, but gay people marry girls all the time!" blurted Carrie.

Once again, she was so loud that I'm sure half the school now questioned my brother's sexuality. Whitney's eyes were wide, mine rolled back in my head, and this time Kylie didn't let us down.

"You about the mouth-n-ist white girl I ever seen,

you know that? Dang girl, eat somethin' so you keep that thang full or something!"

"It's true though," she tried to argue. "Gay guys marry girls just so people won't think they're gay!"

"Hell, erybody know that! You just gotta turn down that volume girl..." replied Kylie, smiling. She looked to Ian and me and shook her head, "She gotta built-in microphone or something..."

Ian smiled.

"What're you smilin' about?" Kylee prodded. "You need to be thinkin' bout where you're takin' me after homecoming! I ain't cheap!"

Ian's smile faded and the redness started to reappear.

"And don't you even think about takin' somebody else!" she said, standing, "Your fine butt's mine, cutie-pie! Don't you go cheat-n on me! Black girls be crazy you go cheat-n on em'!"

She winked at me and then smiled real big before she left.

"You don't think she really wants me to take her to homecoming, do you?" asked Ian once Kylee was out of earshot.

"No," I answered, "She's just playing..."

Ian's sighed. "Good, cause I don't think I could tell her no."

"At least not if you wanted to still *live* afterwards..." I added as the bell rang.

Chapter Four

August 29th - Wednesday

The breakfast table was set when I walked downstairs the next morning. From the smell of things I could tell that dad was making waffles, Ian's favorite. This could only mean one thing...

"I can't make it to the game on Friday, son," he said. The look in his eyes was enough to convince anyone. Dad was in line for sergeant and Mom said that eventually every policeman was made to roam around the make-out spots on game night and, well, Dad's number had been chosen.

"It's alright," shrugged Ian, "I don't think I'll play too much anyhow."

"Why not?" interjected Mom. It was obvious that her tone meant that someone was going to die if her son, who happened to be the best football player on earth, didn't get to play.

"I think coach is starting Jeremy Hale instead of me..."

"But that boy's a lousy blocker!" roared Dad, "You'd

think Cliff would know better than to have a lousy blocker in high school football. Almost all the teams do is run anyway!"

"Not this year," said Ian, "They're actually thinking about doing a lot more passing down between the forty-five and the twenty. He calls it his downhill game or something like that…"

"Yeah, it'll be downhill alright," replied Dad, shaking his head.

"Well, I guess it's better for me to get these make-out routes out of the way while you're not playing then, so I can be there for all the times that you are," he said with a smile.

Mom took another bite before she looked at me, "How's scouting going?" she asked in code with a wink. I didn't think it was funny that she asked in code, but that Dad talking about make-out spots is what made her think about it.

Dad looked at me with an expression that showed how confused he was. *Scouting?*

"Homecoming stuff," I replied. I felt it necessary to roll my eyes and shake my head as if it didn't matter, and that seemed to smooth things over pretty well. Dad wouldn't take too well to Mom enforcing her Must Have Date Policy, but then on the flip-side, Dad was often the cooler one about things like that, so…

"Speaking of homecoming…" he said, sitting up in his chair a little higher, "How much is this going to cost me this year?"

Ah, the truth finally came out! Mom looked from me to Ian, and then shrugged.

"No more than last time, I'm sure," she replied.

"Why can't you and your girlfriends just get together and swap dresses every year or something?" he asked, almost in desperation for the hundreds of dollars that would vanish before the weekend was over.

I couldn't help myself. I grabbed my boobs and said, "Because last year, I didn't have these and next year they might be bigger!"

"Aw, come on Erin," begged Ian, "I'm eating!"

"She *is* in that stage where she's…filling out," said Mom, confirming the obvious.

"Yeah, I've tried not to notice," mumbled Dad.

With another look that showed his lack of enthusiasm, Dad stood and walked to the sink to rinse his plate off. I guess his new grill set would have to wait until Father's Day.

It rained all morning, so everyone's shoes were squeaky, which was more than a little aggravating. As the day got closer, Carrie spent more and more time talking about her date with Joe Gregory. Whitney mentioned that she thought Carrie was just nervous, but it still didn't stop Carrie from annoying everyone with the detail none of us wanted to hear. On more than one occasion I noticed Whitney blushing, especially whenever Ian was around. I couldn't help but still be bothered, but I guess with it being homecoming and all, I'm sure Whitney is hoping Ian will ask her. I hate being in the middle of all the drama, but if I wasn't, I wouldn't have a life.

"So how's boy hunting going?" Carrie asked bluntly. "Any hopefuls?"

Not nearly as many as you, I wanted to say. It seemed like every day her skirt got a little higher and her shirt a little lower.

"I guess I'm just not worried about it," I said.

"That sure you'll find somebody, huh?" she asked, completely misunderstanding.

"No, I mean if I don't find a date it's no big deal! I can just go by myself."

"Oh," sounded Carrie, "but why would you want to do that?"

I shrugged. I wasn't sure what I wanted anymore. Everything seemed to be so weird lately. Everyone was changing. Carrie was on her way to becoming the skank Kylie always teased her about, Whitney was practically catatonic whenever Ian was around, and Ian was just… well Ian.

Carrie was seductively adding lip gloss in her locker mirror while I tried to manage the mess of papers in the aftermath of one of those freak locker tornados. Eventually, I gave up, dropped my whole foot in there and yanked them all out onto the floor and then piled them up and shoved them in my history book. I hardly use it anyway.

Carrie lost her breath suddenly and started twitching, almost convulsing.

"Jay...Jay...Jake Cunningham. Oh-my-God..."

She acted like she wasn't sure if she should jump into her locker, shut it, or continue putting on her makeup. I lost my breath. I'd seen him all last year, of course he never noticed *me*, but then again I was short and all of the other hundreds of girls swarming around him were much taller than me. Whitney seemed to be the only one of us who wasn't going to pass out, but even *she* was smiling. When I looked at Carrie again she had an expression on her face that reminded me of the girl-vampire in movies. You know the one who looked at everyone like they're potential food.

My heart skipped a beat, my stomach rose into my chest, and then for no reason at all breathing was as complicated as remembering the date of the Battle of Hastings. I could only stare straight ahead into my messy locker. I could see him through the mirror hanging on my door. Not only could I see him, but I could also see the mustard stain on my collar from hotdogs at lunch and how ratty my hair looked. I felt so insignificant, so small.

Jake Cunningham was a senior. He was *the* star athlete. He played on the football team, ran track, *and* he was the starting pitcher for the baseball team. According to all the rumors, he had been receiving letters from every college in the state, and it didn't hurt that he was really, really hot!

I tried to take a deep breath, but I kept seeing myself in the mirror and it only made me more nervous. My body temperature was soaring. I could feel my armpits leaking. Gross, I know! As the seconds ticked by a couple of things began to dawn on me. One, if I could see him in the mirror, he could probably see me… So I quickly shut my locker and reached for my bag. Secondly, by the height of Carrie's miniskirt today, chances were he was probably coming over to talk to…

"Hi, Erin," he said in that honeyed voice. I could listen to him talk all day.

"Hi," I replied. I hoped I wouldn't have to do much more than nod or say "Hi" again because I would probably stutter.

"I'm sorry," he started, then stopped. He kinda laughed in that really hot guy sort of way and then looked to the floor. Was he embarrassed? I thought being embarrassed stopped once you became a senior? Maybe he was embarrassed because he was talking to me? Maybe he's laughing because he noticed my mustard stain? What if I have something in my teeth? I didn't even think to check my teeth!

"I'm really bad at these sorts of things," he said and I wondered what *these* sorts of things were, because if it was being hot, he was failing at failing. I think he wanted me to say something comforting, but all I could manage was a half-smile and a nod.

"Would you…like to…go out on Friday night?"

"I can't!" I said it so quickly that I brought my hand to my mouth and Carrie swallowed her gum and started choking. I turned around to see if she was alright, but she only waved me away and continued struggling for her life.

"You can't?" he asked.

"No, you see my brother's game is Friday night..." Suddenly it dawned on me that he played too and I felt like an idiot.

"Oh," he reiterated, smiling, "No, I meant *after* the game...like dinner or something?"

"Umm, sure..." I replied.

"So, what do you like to eat?" he asked.

He stepped a little closer and I dropped one of my books. Embarrassed, I bent over to get it and realized that my head almost hit his crotch and then quickly stood back up, blushing.

"Anything really," I said hurriedly, hoping he didn't notice how nervous I was.

The bell rang and I breathed a sigh. At least now I had an escape route in case this turned any worse. Maybe I could move to somewhere remote after I finished completely embarrassing myself. I hear Montana's nice. He smiled, bent down and grabbed the book for me, and then slid it back on top. He was so close now that I could smell his cologne. Whatever it was fit him perfectly because it smelled a lot like what I imagined heaven would smell like.

"So you'll be at the game Friday night then?"

"Yep,"

"Well, I'll see you then," he said.

Before he turned to walk away he handed me a folded

piece of paper. As I watched him walk away in slow motion a thought popped into my head.

"What time?" I yelled, a little louder than I wanted to.

"What?" he asked, turning. His hair did the swoosh thing in slow motion.

"Umm," I fought to remember what I was going to say, Oh, yeah! "What time?"

"That's up to you."

"So where are we going?"

"I was thinking Giorgio's, but it's up to you..." he replied with a shrug.

Giorgio's! I tried not to gasp. My mom and dad don't even eat there... How can he afford it? *He's a hot guy*, I reminded myself...they come equipped with money.

"But that's really expensive."

"It's worth it!" he replied with a smile.

I lost all feeling in my legs. Instead of falling I just simply sank back against the lockers and sighed as he walked away. For a second I wondered if the girls would believe me, but then I remembered that by the start of first period tomorrow Carrie would have already taken care of that. I'd probably get a call from the president before lunch...or Oprah.

As I thought of Carrie, I looked over and saw her flush, waving a hand in front of her face. Her eyes were larger than I've ever seen them, her mouth was moving but no words were coming out. I think she was in shock...

I flipped the folded piece of paper over in my hands. "Look at the note!" Carrie pleaded.

Andrea,

I kept Ms. Mitchell after class yesterday discussing a literature assignment. I apologize for interfering with your class. Please excuse her from being tardy.

Thank you,
Margaret

I'm sure my jaw must've been at my knees. He got my tardy fixed? I stared at the paper for a minute and then watched the back of his head as he walked down the hall. Why would he do that?

Chapter Five ~
August 31st - Friday

I can't remember another evening that was so hectic. School went by in a blur, homework and notes galore. The past two days were the best days of my life. Jake introduced me to his friends and their girlfriends. All the girls in my class, including Carrie, were awestruck by my luck. I claimed to have stumbled upon a magical lamp and used one of my three wishes, but that rumor didn't stick the way that I wanted it to.

Whitney wasn't too excited that I was going out on a night that we had planned to have a sleepover, but she got over it and seemed just as excited for me as the others. Even Kylie was optimistic. Once Carrie and Whitney explained the importance of this date to my mom she had a hard time telling me no.

"A senior!" she asked, shocked. It was obvious she was nervous, but why?

"Is there something wrong with that?"

"No, I just... Well, I guess I thought you'd look for someone your own age."

"He's only a little over a year older, Mom."

"I know, I just…it's just a date, right?" she said with a shrug that reminded me of me.

Just a date? It's official! The largest understatement of the year had just been spoken aloud in my house. After that little comment, everything went haywire. Ian couldn't find one of his cleats, and Kylie called and wanted to know if we could give her a ride to the game. On top of it all, I had to get ready, not only for the game, but for my date.

"I thought she'd at least come to the game first," said Whitney, shaking her head.

We handed our tickets to the teacher sitting at the front gate while my Mom parked the truck.

"I told ya'll she was a skank," Kylee said.

"I just hope I don't freak out tonight," I added. "I think I have more than enough antiperspirant. I sniffed my armpits and Whitney nearly fell over laughing.

We walked up the bleachers and sat where we normally sat. The boys were out practicing on the far side of the field. The Lunsford Lumberjacks were lining up alongside their visiting bench, strapping on their pads.

"What number is Ian this year?" asked Whitney. I thought about the question for a second and wondered if I should ask her why she'd been acting weird, but I decided not to.

"Eighty, I think."

Whitney looked around. "I don't see an eighty."

"No, he's number Eighty-six," Mom corrected, taking her seat. "That's him, right there!"

Ian ran a route and caught the football and Whitney's eyes seemed to burst with excitement. In a way I felt kind of relieved. Just think. My best friend and my brother...that could be cool!

"Oh," Kylie cheered suddenly, scaring us all half to death. "There's my man! There he is!"

"Who?" Whitney asked. Even I sat up at the excitement in Kylie's voice.

"Number twenty-nine, Dyson Edwards," she explained and both Whitney and I sat back, suddenly not interested anymore. It was always the same thing with Kylie. She always talked about him as if they were a thing, but when we asked her to ask him out she used the excuse, "I'm just being patient" instead of "I'm terrified!" But who could blame her? Dyson Edwards was probably the hottest black guy in our school. He played basketball, football, and ran track. What was it with hot guys and tons of sports?

"Is that...yeah, that's Jake, isn't it?" pointed Whitney. He was the tallest on the team and man did he look great in those tights. Number thirty-seven.

Jake, Dyson, and one of Jake's friends, Mike, walked to the center of the field, and after the coin fell to the ground, they kicked the ball away, putting the Broncos on defense first. There was a mixture of emotions between the three of us. Kylie wanted offense so she could see Dyson run the ball, I wanted defense to watch Jake, and Whitney was the happiest because Ian was in on everything else. We all clapped for the poor kid who ran straight ahead into the wall of blockers and miraculously made the guy trip somehow. It was cool to watch, but I can't help but cringe every time they hit.

On the third play of the game, the Lumberjacks tried a pass across the middle and Jake nailed the guy. He hit him harder than I've ever seen anyone get hit on the football field. His feet went flying out in one direction and the ball shot away in the opposite direction. It was the most horrifying thing ever! All the girls gasped and the men stood up and cheered. The bench of the Broncos was electrified! Everyone jumped around shouting, "Ohhhh!" For some reason it made Jake *so* much hotter!

Some little guy came running out and kicked the ball high in the air on the next play, giving the Bronco's the ball. Kylie sat up straight and started washing her hands nervously. If someone were watching her they would truly think she was Dyson's girlfriend. Maybe she was in love? I spent most of my time watching how Kylie reacted to the game and thinking about love before Whitney and Mom both burst into excitement.

"Oh, it's Ian! Ian's on the field!"

"It's third down and four yards to go," said the announcer guy from the box.

"Broncos are in a single-back set, tight-end right, twins left. Here's the snap, Casey fakes the hand-off to Edwards, drops back, he's got a receiver open in the middle of the field, but wait, he trips and falls down. Oh no, Hale goes down! But wait...Casey scrambles away from the blitz...puts the ball in the air...someone's streaking down the sideline...he's got the defender beat...eighty-six dives for the ball...Touchdown!"

Everyone was on their feet. We all screamed and jumped around like we were on the Family Feud...not that I watch that show!

"Who's *this* kid?" said the announcer-guy, and we all laughed.

Suddenly, my dad was right beside us.

"Did you see that catch, honey?" asked my mom excitedly.

Dad tried to wave her away. He looked serious, but my Mom was so excited I don't think she even saw the look on his face.

"Honey, did you see Ian's catch?"

"Yeah!" he answered. His face was grim. He was looking right at me.

"What's the matter, Dad?" I asked.

Mom, Kylie, and I rushed out to the parking lot with my dad while Whitney held our seats. We got to my dad's police car and saw Carrie in the front seat crying. Before we could say anything we noticed Joe Gregory in the backseat. When she saw us she put her head in her hands and started crying harder.

"What's the matter?" I asked.

"What happened?" asked Mom.

"What'd he do?" asked Kylie. She didn't even bother to look at Carrie. She glared at Joe in the backseat. It wasn't a surprise who Carrie chose to answer.

"We were having a good time and then he reached his hand up my skirt, and I said no, and then he tried to touch my chest, and I said no, and he stopped for a while, but then he started trying harder and harder and I couldn't get him off of me."

My dad looked between me and mom. "I heard her saying 'stop' just as I walked up to the car. I'm glad I did too, because... Hey! Kylie!"

None of us saw Kylie walk around the car and open the back door. She took her shoe off and started beating Joe with it. "What you done did, boy? Huh? Who you think you playin' with? Don't you ever...ever...ever..."

I brought my hand to my face as Kylie continued to hit him with her shoe saying "ever" each time. He sounded a low grunt after each hit of her shoe. He scrambled to the other side of the car as she wailed on him and fought to open the car door from the inside, but his hands were cuffed behind his back.

Dad grabbed Kylie by the back pockets of her blue jeans and yanked her out of the car. She stopped immediately and slowly fixed her hair while she took a few deep breaths, and then leaned over and put her shoe back on.

"You can't do that, Kylie!"

"All he gonna get is a slap on the wrist anyhow, Mr. Mitchell! You ask me, I think he ought-a get a baseball bat taken to his car, too!" she said, shaking her head and leaning past my dad yelling it so that Joe could hear her through the now closed door.

Dad tried to keep a straight face and then shook his head.

"What's gonna happen, Dad?"

"Are you gonna call her mother?" Mom asked.

Carrie's eyes widened, "Oh, please don't, Mr. Mitchell," she begged, "Please, just let me stay the night over at your house tonight instead! I promise this isn't serious enough to tell my parents! Nothing happened! Please don't, they'll put me on lockdown if they find out my first date went so bad! I'll never be allowed to date again... My life will be *ruined!*"

Dad scratched his head and looked at me and mom. "Does that mean you'll stay home tonight instead of going out on *your* date?"

My heart hit my shoes. It must've passed my stomach on the way because it rose up into my throat. My one shot... I sighed and then looked at Carrie. *She wasn't worth it!*

"Yeah, I'll stay home," I said.

"You girls call your mom's," Dad said to Kylie and Carrie.

I took a good look at Joe while Kylie and Carrie talked more about what happened and dad stood to the side, talking to mom. Why would he do a thing like that? I had known Joe his whole life and never would've thought of him to be that sort of guy. I heard last week that a girl from Yellow Brooke was running track with a couple of guys and they suddenly attacked her, pulled her under the bleachers, and raped her. They were her best friends... She'd known them her whole life! The thought gave me a shiver. I felt nasty all over and couldn't look at Joe any longer. If someone like Joe could do that...

Once my dad left to take Joe back to his car, we went into the girl's bathroom and cleaned Carrie's face up. Her mascara had ran from crying so much and her eyes were a little swollen, but the temperature was starting to drop and my mom said the wind would bring that down in a jiffy. Whatever *that* meant? Old people have such weird words!

To our surprise, they kept Ian in for the rest of the game and the announcer-guy kept referring to him as Wonder Boy every time he made a catch. By the end of the game the Broncos won 38-7. How was I going to tell Jake that I couldn't go out with him? This was my shot... My one shot and I was blowing it... Or was I? What if he was another Joe?

I would've probably thought about it all night if Jake wouldn't have parted the crowd to walk up to me. It felt like every eye was on me. How could I say it in front of all these people? What would it do to him to have a *nobody* like me leave him stranded on a Friday night? Who was I to have this opportunity and then throw it away? I mean, you never hear the newsman say, "And today's lotto winner,

Erin Mitchell…oh, this just in, she doesn't want the three million dollars!" What if someone else takes my place? What if it's like football and if you aren't ready to play, the next person's right there saying, "Put me in coach!"

"Hey," he said, "Did you see your brother's catch?"

"Uh…yeah!"

My heart was pumping through my chest. How could I say no to those beautiful green eyes. Carrie didn't really *need* me, did she?

"So are you ready to go? I can just take a shower here if you want. I've got my clothes in the truck," he said with a thumb toward the locker rooms.

I took a deep breath.

"Actually, I can't go after all…"

I wanted to cry. My heart was racing. My life was flashing before my eyes. I suddenly saw myself as an eighty year old woman with a cane complaining because I was all alone.

Jake smiled that hot guy smile and said, "Hey, what's wrong?"

"I just…I feel *really* bad…"

"Don't! It's no big deal. We can go out some other night, can't we?"

I smiled. The world slowly came back into view. My armpits started to close the sweat valves. I wanted to say, 'Really?' but then I heard myself say it in my head and decided not to.

"How about Sunday night?" he asked. "Or do you have church or something?"

"I...uh...sure! I mean, no we don't have church or anything, and *sure* I'd love to."

"Giorgio's still sound good?"

"Sounds great! What time?"

"What time is good for you?"

"Uh..."

"Six?" he asked, smirking.

"Sure!"

"Alright! Six o'clock."

I smiled and nodded. I think I couldn't open my mouth because I would've probably squealed like one of those girls who stands outside the red ropes and tries to touch some celebrity. Jake walked off just as Ian walked up. Whitney and Mom gave Ian pats on the shoulders and listened to his stories of the game like they hadn't just watched it. I gave myself my own pat on the back and walked behind them smiling from ear to ear. I hope Sunday is better for me than tonight was for Carrie.

Chapter Six

September 1st - Saturday

Carrie seemed different all day Saturday. When I say different, I mean, the way she was last year. She didn't try to go out of her way to impress the guys around her, especially at the mall, which is the spot most girls thrived.

It was a little cooler today than normal, meaning *colder*. The winds picked up and the mountains in the distance had fresh caps of snow. Dad said we might have snow before November again. We got to the mall around eleven-thirty. We went to the cheaper places first, just to give Dad's new grill set a chance, but apparently all of the band geeks had already raided the clearance racks. Whitney was not enthused by that comment, but having come from Kylie she let it go. Ian went off with my dad and the two of them walked around the sport's stores. Ian was sooo excited about being able to play last night. I think dad said he was going to buy him some catching gloves, as if he needed them after the diving touchdown, but what do I know,

I'm a girl! Mom went off by herself to get a watch fixed and her jewelry cleaned and some other stuff.

Last night was short and fun; lots of talk and ice cream. The movies were a bust! Apparently, nothing scary looked any good and everything else was corny, so...

We saw my mom and then speed-walked past her store, giggling, and dove into *Halter*.

"I hate this store," Whitney complained.

"Who could hate this store?" replied Carrie, as if it were against some law.

"It's just so expensive...I mean look at these shoes! I wouldn't pay eighty-five bucks for *these*..."

"Yeah," I agreed.

I had to agree with Whitney. Not that I had to, but I found that I usually did because she and I were the closest out of the group. I think over the years our tastes have kind of melded into one and we're more like sisters than we are friends...sometimes conjoined twins. You know, the babies who are stuck together at birth. I really should pay less attention in Biology II, I'm starting to feel like a nerd. Maybe that's why it's so weird that she's all warm and fuzzy when Ian's around? Not because I'm a nerd, but because she and I are like sisters and he's my brother and that's just so...Kentucky.

Last night *was* comical though. I can't count how many times Whitney tried to be semi-sexy just so Ian would pay attention to her, but Ian was oblivious. Most guys are! If you stare at them and blush or even blow them a kiss, they'll think "Man, I think she likes me!" *Think?* It's like trying to teach a person with no rhythm how to clap. Frustrating! He did spend most of the night just being Ian though, which I guess translates into sweet and cute according to the Carrie, Whitney, and Kylie. Of course, it's also hard to try and act sexy around a girl like Carrie who can do it so much better without even trying. There's something about naturally being gorgeous that just helps.

"I don't like this store either, girl!" announced Kylie.

For some reason she had taken on the loudness that Carrie normally had and decided to broadcast her opinions to nearly every store we had been in over the past hour, which were only two.

"All this stuff must be made for white girls or somethin' cause ain't no bootylicious gonna fit in this here!" She held up a pair of jeans that clearly fit her waist, but not her butt.

We all met in the food court and had lunch. After that we separated again and this time Ian came with us. It was obvious that Ian liked Carrie, but he was too nervous to say anything. Carrie was still traumatized by her event from the night before. And poor Whitney was heartbroken that Ian didn't even notice her while Carrie was around. But then again, Ian didn't notice me, either... It all boiled down to that *sister* thing! But how could I explain it to Whitney without it being weird? There's no doubt in my mind that Kylie noticed every bit of this as well, but she took a different approach to things...

"So you two gonna make out or what? Cause I know you heard what I said about cheatin' on me cutie-pie! Now get your fine self on over here and help me pick out a dress! You gonna be the one starin' at it all night anyhow..."

Ian gave me this mortified look as if to ask once again, "Are you sure she doesn't think I'm going to homecoming with her?"

I only smirked.

Whitney walked into the dressing room to try on some jeans and Carrie walked over to me.

"Hey, Erin?" she asked, holding a shirt up to her. "What do you think?"

"I don't like that color," I replied, "But it *does* look good on you," I had to admit. Everything looked good on Carrie. Don't you just hate girls like that? You know, the ones that can wear pajamas to school and never do their hair and still get asked for their phone number more than all the other girls combined. Carrie suddenly got really serious and stepped a little closer to me.

"Do you think Ian likes me? I mean, do you think he'd go to homecoming with me? I mean, would it be wrong if..."

I thought to say something like "God no! You're repulsive!" but then it dawned on me... Oh no, how do I answer this? On one hand I've got Ian who I know absolutely adores Carrie, but then on the other I have Whitney who is head over heels for Ian. How can I choose something like this? I can't put up with all of this *and* worry about my date with Jake! What about me? Why does Carrie have to be in the spotlight all the time? Why does Ian have to be the star football player and I'm the one trying to keep everyone held by the collars like I'm a dog sitter or something? Who asks them to confide in me with all their dirty little secrets? By the look on Carrie's face it was obvious that I had been waiting too long to reply. I could see the light of excitement leaving her eyes. Ian *had* been really sweet to her last night – not that he isn't normally – but having someone treat you great after someone treats you horrible is a little more than refreshing.

"I'm sure he'd love to, but you might want to talk to him about it."

"Talk to who about what?" Whitney asked, suddenly right beside us.

Oh no, what've I done? I got so scared a little pee almost dripped out. How could I do something like that to Whitney? But then something odd happened. As I looked at Carrie I could see that she was nervous too. Did she know that Whitney liked Ian? I glanced at Whitney expecting to see a look of betrayal on her face, but she seemed normal, pulling another shirt from the rack to go try on. Carrie looked to me with that, *"Don't say anything!"* sort of look and we went our separate ways. I lingered around Whitney while Carrie started slowly making her way toward Kylie and Ian, her personal cart.

By five o'clock, Kylie and I were the only ones who had decided on a dress and Ian was happy with his nice button-up shirt and new pair of catching gloves. Before we left the mall, Carrie was warming up to him nicely. She was being just flirtatious enough to make my mom smile with excitement, Ian grin from ear to ear, and at the same time cause Whitney stare out the window wishing it were her not Carrie who was getting all the attention.

I thought of whispering my dilemma to Kylie, but we were both about to be sick just from hearing how stupid Carrie could sound when she really wanted to. Why do guys always fall for the "I'm an idiot" routine? Let's say the girl isn't even as gorgeous as Carrie... All she has to do is play dumb, do something cute, like put on Ian's catching gloves or his hat, and then say, "How do I look?" Suddenly, the guy thinks "Wow," and the girl thinks, "Gotcha!"

Guys are so simple! *Too* simple maybe... But then, is it really simple to do something like that? I mean, why has it been so hard for Whitney? Sure, she's not as hot as Carrie, but she's way smarter and more mature if you consider how Carrie's been acting this year. And I'm sure Whitney's tried the same things on Ian in her own little way... Or has she? Does that make Carrie smarter than Whitney because she can use these little tricks?

Suddenly, it reminded me of that play we're doing in Mrs. Prichard's English class. There's a line where Laura is talking to her mom about why she has to look so good when this guy comes over to their house. The mom really wants Laura to impress this guy and finally Laura asks something like, "But aren't we setting a trap for him?" Then the mom says back, "All girls are a trap, a pretty trap, and men expect them to be!"

I spent most of the ride home thinking about the pretty trap in the seat in front of me.

We dropped Kylie and Carrie off on the way home and once the annoyance was out of the air, Whitney started to come out of her hibernation. She sat in the back with me and started asking me exciting questions about what I thought Sunday night was going to be like with Jake. After another minute or two she asked, "If this date goes well do you think he'll ask you to homecoming?"

My heart skipped a beat. I hadn't even thought about going to homecoming with Jake Cunningham. "It's still a whole month away though," I said, "I'm sure he'll come to his senses and take a hot girl by then."

Whitney laughed and my mom gasped. "Erin Mitchell! You shouldn't say something like that, you're a beautiful young lady!"

"Yeah Erin," added Ian, "there's nothing wrong with you, except your face!"

It wasn't too often that Ian said something like that, but when someone gave him the opportunity he jumped on it. Through the rear view mirror I could see dad smiling. He was proud that the silent one had finally risen up to challenge the queen of the low blow. Mom got quiet. Dad looked expectantly through the rear view mirror. They were waiting on my comeback, but with surprising speed Whitney beat me to it.

"We'll see who's laughing when she gives Jake those big brown puppy-dog eyes and he starts hitting you in practice like he was hitting those guys last night!"

Ian smiled. The sight made Whitney smile, too. For a second I thought I saw something; I thought I saw a spark of something, but it passed before I could really see it.

Chapter Seven ~
September 2nd - Sunday

Time ticked by in slow motion now that I was finally ready. It's been five-fifty-two for the past ten minutes, I swear! Ian's stomach was upset this morning and he had loitered in and out of the bathroom all day. Because of him, it was on me to wash dishes *and* do most of the chores, which included having my room clean *before* I went out. I didn't mind doing the chores because I know that Ian is good for doing his share when I'm sick, but still *today*?

At four-forty-five I was finally able to get all of *my* things done. Shower, appropriate plucking, hair, make-up, and the list goes on and on. I promised my mom that my room would be 'clean', but we have an agreement about these sorts of things. Room 'clean' means *tidy*. Tidy is my friend. The mound of clothes and hangers on my bed that I had to go through to pick out what to wear is at least all in a semi-stack and can be easily placed back in the closet. Tidy. My makeup, while out and scattered across my vanity, is at least *on* my vanity. Tidy.

Time to check the clock...five-fifty-four...*Come on!* The doorbell rang.

I stood up from the bottom stair of the stairs and washed my hands nervously. My mom came out of the living room a second later and looked at me like I was crazy.

"What are you doing?" she whispered. She had that look on her face like she was embarrassed that I was even her daughter and then walked toward the front door. She turned the corner and I heard the front door open.

"Hi," Mom said.

"Hi, Mrs. Mitchell," said the voice of the most gorgeous man alive.

"Come on in, Erin will be down in a minute," she said. Wide-eyed, I ducked around the corner and into the kitchen. I don't know why. What's wrong with me? A moment later my mom peeked into the kitchen, scoffed, and then nodded for me to come out. I took a deep breath. It's just dinner! I've eaten plenty of meals before! Why was this one so hard? I checked my hair in the microwave window and made sure it was still where it should be...perfection. I took a deep breath and walked from the kitchen. Jake was dressed in his usual stylish, hot-guy attire: dark jeans and a long-sleeved polo...so hot! He smiled wide when I walked around the corner. I think my body temperature rose about ten degrees just from seeing him. I suddenly wondered if two cami's was one too many, but then I remembered how cold it was and was looking forward to the walk to the truck to cool off the sweat.

"You look nice," he said.

I'm sure I blushed. My mom shot me a look and I quickly said, "Not so bad yourself..."

Jake chuckled and then told my mom 'thank you' and that he would keep me safe.

My mom simply smiled and waved us on. As we walked toward the door, I looked back and she gave me a thumb's up and smiled really big. I could only cover my mouth and try to breathe so I wouldn't blush any worse. Jake's truck sat parked on the corner; a silver four-wheel drive that, by the looks of it, he had just washed. It wasn't as flashy as you'd expect for a guy like Jake, but then again Jake was flashy enough by himself.

I got inside and he quickly handed me his CD case and told me to put in whatever I wanted. As I turned the pages, he took a few of the back roads to the old square. Giorgio's Fine Dining was just off what everyone called God's Square. There was a large statue to some guy named St. Christopher in the middle with white Christmas lights draped out like a big canopy to the surrounding trees and fountains. I guess he must've done something cool because three churches were built on the square and almost all of the shops were Christian ones; music, coffee, books, and all. The restaurant was old, but supposedly people came from other states just to eat there. I couldn't wait!

"So are you having a hard time deciding which college to go to?" I asked.

He laughed and nodded. "Yeah, it's going to be a pretty tough choice, but the years' far from over, so we'll see..."

"What about you? Giving it any thoughts?" he asked.

"I'm thinking about state right now," I said, "but I don't know."

"Well, my dad wants me to go an Ivy League school, but I don't think they have the best sport's there and I really like sports..."

Wow, I knew he was smart, but I didn't know his grades were *that* good! It's just like a guy to pick sports over school anyway. After another ten minutes of small talk we pulled into the parking lot behind the old square and walked around to the front. Instantly, I could see why the place was so famous and expensive. There were pictures of almost every celebrity I knew, and many more I didn't, on the walls in the waiting area. All of them were signed and dated. The waiters were all dressed up and fancy. One of them pulled the chair out for me and sat a napkin on my lap. It was *really* nice.

"How can you afford this?" I asked. Immediately I wished I hadn't because that sort of question *is* kind of personal, but I couldn't help myself.

Jake smirked. "I work during the summer and most weekends with my family at the family business. It's a lot of work so we have kind of a deal about things," he explained.

"What kind of a deal?" I asked, digging myself in deeper.

"I work for them whenever they need me to and they pay me whenever I need them to."

"So I'd say after tonight you might need a few more weeks of work to pay them back."

He laughed. "Hey, stop worrying about it! Just do me a favor and don't look at the prices, okay. I really want you to have a great time and I'd like to get to know you a little better..."

Better? I don't know how he even knows my name, or that I even exist! A sudden urge trickled its way up from somewhere inside and I couldn't resist myself. All of my panic, all of my anxiety just sort of poured out.

I sat my napkin on the table so quickly he almost jumped.

"Why?" I asked, "Why do you want to have anything to do with me? I'm only a sophomore for one, for two, I don't even know how to act around a guy like you, and for three...well...there might not be a three, but I know there's more things that make this seem so weird. I feel like any second now you're going to just laugh and walk away or come out of your trance and say you were hypnotized or..."

I wanted to continue rambling on, but he looked at me, reached across the table, and took one of my hands. "Hey! Stop being so crazy... There's nothing special about me! Just like there's nothing *weird* about you!"

"Yeah, but I'm not beautiful like Jacqueline Seymour

or smart like Lindsey Hampton... I'm barely noticeable... Why me?"

"Well, you're not stuck up like Jacqueline Seymour or confined to your school books like Lindsey Hampton, either! But what you *are* is Erin Mitchell... Probably, the sweetest girl I've ever met. That's what makes this all worthwhile. I'm tired of dating the hot girl that every guy wants..."

"Oh thanks," I said.

His expression changed to one of fear, "No, that's not what I meant."

I laughed. "I know!"

Something about the way he panicked made me think he really cared about me.

"I'm just tired of all the expectations and the way everyone sort of makes things out to be larger than they really are, you know? High school is such a joke about things like that. Why can't people just date who they're attracted to? Why can't they just find someone they really like and treat them special?"

I'm sure I blushed. I'm almost positive that I could hear Whitney somewhere in my head say, "Awww, sooo sweeeeet!"

"Well at least now I know that you're not asking me out because of my looks or my brains," I said.

"You're *almost* right!" he replied, "I'm not asking you out because you're beautiful, or because you're smart, I'm asking you out because I like you and I really think that something like this can be *real*."

My heart melted. Oh, Cunningham *would* sound like such a sophisticated last name. What were the girls gonna think when I told them that Jake Cunningham poured his heart out to me? How long had he been thinking about me?

"How long have you thinking about me?" *Wow, that just came right out!*

"I saw you last year when I was dating Shannon Rogers. I saw the way she treated you that day when you accidentally bumped into her in the hall and how you reacted and I don't know...I kind of started noticing you more and more and how you act. You're not like the other girls, Erin."

If it were possible for me to get a deeper shade of red, I did.

"What do you mean 'I'm not like all the other girls'?"

"Okay, this is so weird! I didn't think I'd be talking with you about all this stuff on the first date, but..."

"Well you don't have to if..."

"No, it's not that...I just don't know how much I should say or how much you want me to say..."

Everything! My mind screamed. *Spill your beans!*

"I just...I've always had these relationships that didn't matter. They were dumb and childish and the girls only wanted to be with me so they could hang all over me in front of their friends or wear my jerseys or so I could drive them around... They never wanted to have anything to do with my friends, or care about what I thought, or..."

"*Really?* I like your friends," I said. I felt that I had to earn some sort of points where the others had failed. At least, if I wanted to make it through dinner... How could Shannon and all the others not have liked T.J. and Michael? They seemed real cool when I met them...

"I know," he added with a smile, "and that's another reason why I think you're so awesome. You're just...so... *perfect.*"

I think Carrie was speaking somewhere in my head now because my thoughts weren't very good. Something about the thought of Jake Cunningham feeling this way about me when he had dated the hottest girls in the school just made me feel tingly all over. I felt every beat of my heart. I looked down and wondered if I could see it through my shirt. Goosebumps rose on my arms and legs. Even the back of my neck tingled and made me sort of shiver in my seat. Thank God he wasn't looking!

I wonder if my expression changed, because after that point something triggered inside me; something told me that it was real and not just some Hollywood story or fairy tale come true. For a week now I had been afraid of being so close to Jake and he had been so excited about it. I had been nervous and so had he! He had wanted nothing more than to share all this heartfelt stuff with me that he had kept inside for almost a year and it was like him getting it all off of his chest got all of my worries off of mine too.

The time flew by like it always does when things are going awesome and you don't want them to stop.

By eight-thirty we were turning the corner at the four-way near my house. Our conversation was a lot better after all that was off our chests. I'm so glad I listened to myself...I'm so proud of me! Every other girl would have kept it all bottled up inside and just worried about it for no reason, but not me, not little Miss Blurts-a-lot!

The whole ride home I wondered about one thing: Would he kiss me? It *was* only the first date, but I couldn't help but wonder what his lips were like. Part of me wanted the best of both worlds, soft, but manly at the same time. But what about me? What if I wasn't what he expected? How could I hold a candle to the full lips of Heather Crawford? What would he think of me if I willingly let him kiss me on the first date? I wouldn't want him to think that I would just give it up to him... but would I? What would *I* do if *he* were upstairs right now naked? I felt tingly all over again and had to shake the Carrie-like thoughts from my mind.

What would Kylie, Carrie, Whitney, and I talk about once I got inside and called them? Would they believe me? Should I even tell them all the things he told me? Carrie would have his whole story told on CNN by noon. The president would probably call to congratulate me. Whitney would probably get all depressed because of her lack of her existence to Ian, and in a way, I couldn't blame her! Then I'd feel like crap for almost rubbing it in her face. And then there was Kylie and that's just a whole other story! I couldn't tell my mom things like this either, she wouldn't understand! What would Ian think? Na, he'd just blab it all to Carrie if she asked.

The truck came to a slow stop just down the street from my house. I could tell that he was thinking about leaning toward me, but he wasn't sure how I'd take to it. He looked nervous. His hands kept rubbing the steering wheel.

"Are you okay?" I said. I couldn't help myself. I wanted to hear him say something else that he didn't want to; something that would force him to tell me that he liked me just a little bit more.

"Yeah, I'm just...I don't know..."

"Nervous?" I asked. I felt like that girl in the movies who has been carefully planning this moment for years and now that I've trapped him, I'm taking my time torturing his mind. The lines of that play came back to mind. *All women are a trap, a pretty trap, and men expect them to be!* He started to say something and just smiled a sexy smile that only he could smile. Did I just call it a *sexy* smile? I *am* turning into Carrie!

"I just want us to take our time, but at the same time I don't! It's weird! I hope I don't sound crazy, but I don't want this to be too fast for you even though I know you're so different than all the..."

That's all I let him say. My lips stole the rest.

After a few of the best lip-locking minutes of my life, I smiled and told him, "See you tomorrow," and then slid out of the truck. I didn't want to, but then something about Carrie's first date came to mind and it rushed me...stupid Joe Gregory! But Jake wasn't that way at all. He didn't try to touch me or anything. He was exactly like I thought he'd be, gentle and real! I couldn't hide my smile as I walked down the street, and I did my best to hold it in check all the way to my bedroom, but once my door was shut I put my back against the wall and let out a large sigh. It had been the best night of my life!

Chapter Eight

September 3rd - Monday

When the next morning came around everything was back to normal, well...almost! Ian and I got ready, constantly revolving around one another like always. We ate breakfast and said a quick "love you" and "see you later" to mom and dad and then rushed out the door. We usually walked the railroad tracks to Davis-Buckley, but this morning a silver truck waited just down the street. Sitting on the tailgate was a gorgeous man almost exactly as I had left him the night before.

Ian took a double take and then looked at me with a smile.

"Did you know..." he started.

I shook my head no and smiled.

Jake slid off of the tailgate and then walked to the passenger side and opened it for me. My heart melted. Ian jumped in the backseat behind me. It was warm and smelled just like him. I started to get all tingly all over again. *Breathe Erin! Just breathe!*

The ride to school was awkward with Ian behind

us. Jake and I kept smiling back and forth to one another and I was sure that Ian probably thought the worst. Or maybe he didn't? We had been close for as long as I could remember and I wasn't sure if he'd mind the secrecy or not... The thought suddenly made me paranoid. Would Ian be upset that I didn't share all this valuable information with him? How could it effect his reputation with the football players if I was dating the star of them all, Jake Cunningham? And then there *was* Dyson Edwards too... I could really put in a good word for Kylie now that I'm on the inside.

"So how you feeling, *Wonder Boy*?" Jake asked Ian.

"Oh...," Ian sort of blushed, "I'm a little sore from that dive, but I'm feeling a lot better."

"Good, cause I'm sure coach will have us training extra hard this week for our game at Tisdale on Friday. Oh, which reminds me, one of my friends, T.J., said you guys can come out to his dad's cabin on Saturday night and hang out if you want? We normally just have a radio and make a bonfire and do whatever..."

I turned around and looked to Ian. His face was a mixture of excitement and skepticism.

"We'll talk to our mom about it and all, but I'm sure it'll be fine," I said. The look on Ian's face told me he agreed with my answer, at least, for now.

"They invited you to the cabin?" wailed Carrie.

Luckily the halls were scarce or else everyone would have known our business as usual. Ian leaned back against the locker with Carrie standing next to him. She looked between him and her locker mirror with an evil smirk on her face. Was she seducing him? Of course it would work, but she could easily do it with *less* work! It was obvious to me that Carrie had no clue how much Ian liked her. If she would've said, "You...me...now" I'm pretty sure Ian would have a hard time refusing.

"I don't know," chimed Whitney, "I've heard of a lot of things that happened out at that cabin..."

"Oh, come on!" argued Carrie, "It's *our* Erin we're talking about here," she said with a snicker. I felt trampled on, and she even laughed about it. What's that supposed to mean?

"What's that supposed to mean?" *Man! I've got to stop doing that!*

Carrie stopped putting on her makeup. "Look, no offense, but you're a *very* good girl! From what I hear most of the girls who've dated Jake were...well...*not*! As a matter of fact, they were very *bad* girls...the kind you watch in movies if you know what I mean? So most of the rumors you hear about the cabin are about *those* girls and the wild nights they had."

I sort of shivered, but this time it wasn't in a good way. How many times had he...you know...and how had I not heard of this before, but Carrie had? I guess she *is* the gossip queen of the world. They probably all have a website or something... Girls in Tokyo know what's going on with the sex lives of everyone in Davis-Buckley Colorado right now thanks to Carrie...

"Sounds like a bunch'a skanks to me!" said Kylie. She had been oddly quiet all morning.

"Are you feeling alright?" I asked.

Kylie looked at me and smiled really quick and then looked back down the hall with a glare. I followed her eyes to Joe Gregory rushing to put his things in his locker. He looked back and forth to Kylie several times before he hurried off and around the corner. Once she was done intimidating the much larger boy, she seemed more interested in the conversation.

"So, is my man gonna be there?" she asked.

"I'm sure he is," I replied, "they're pretty good friends."

"I ain't talking 'bout Dyson, I'm talking about my cutie-pie!"

Ian smiled and looked to the floor before he nodded.

"So who's your date gonna be cutie-pie?" She walked over to Ian and started dancing all sexy. "What you say you and me roast some marshmallows or something?"

I don't think I've ever seen someone try to force themselves into a locker through the tiny slits. Ian backed away embarrassed while the rest of us laughed.

"Come on, you gotta put your hand on my hip right here," she said, grabbing Ian's hand.

"Miss Hayes!" came a sudden growl.

Everyone's eyes widened and Kylie turned with a jump to see Mrs. Prichard. The old woman extended her hand slowly toward Kylie and signaled her for her come with her.

Ian blew a sigh of relief. We all tried not to watch, but Mrs. Prichard was about as quiet as Kylie and Carrie combined. It was impossible not to be embarrassed for her.

"Who *are* you going to the cabin with Ian?" asked Carrie once Mrs. Prichard and Kylie had disappeared into her room. Her voice was the same flirtatious, annoying one that we all had to deal with on the ride back from the mall. Whitney quickly turned from smiling at Ian to looking at me with a serious expression.

"So are you sure you want to do this?" Whitney asked. "I mean, how did the date go?"

I could see in her eyes that she wanted me to spill, but I could also see that she wanted Carrie's locker to grow a tongue and suck her into it, so Ian wouldn't look so excited.

I shrugged, "You know, it was a date."

The first bell saved my life and Kylie's too. A few minutes later we were all off and starting another boring day at school.

Chapter Nine ~
September 8th - Saturday

Saturday morning went as it usually did. My dad
left for work and my mom went on errands. Whitney
and I spent most of the day talking about clothes and
our favorite music, while listening to it. Not only had
this past week been a great week, but next week was
the big 1-6. Whitney asked me what I wanted for the
big day, but the past few weeks had been so crazy that
I really hadn't thought about it. I used to be worried
about having a car, but then again, I don't really need
one now that Jake picks me up every morning for
school.

By four o'clock Whitney and I were walking along
the railroad tracks to her house. We talked a little about
homecoming, but nothing too specific. She didn't out-
right say, "I wish Ian would ask me," but she might as
well have spilled. I hate the feeling of knowing things,
but then it's like no one tells you, so you don't want to
seem like you know...you know? I guess that's just one of
the prices you pay for being so smart.

With perfect timing, I arrived back at my house just as Carrie arrived. Sometimes I wonder if cheating on your friends is a real thing. I've been feeling that way a lot lately. She had on jeans and a really cute hooded shirt that said "My face is up here" with an arrow toward her face. She carried a black bag in her hands and I wondered if I had accidentally told her she could stay the night without asking my mom.

"What's the bag all about?" I asked.

"Oh, these are clothes to wear tonight," she said.

"What's wrong with what you have on?"

"I don't want to wear this for..." and then suddenly she remembered that she was talking to her date's sister. I heard Kylie's voice in my ears say, "Skank" and once again the phrase, "A pretty trap" came back to mind.

Carrie looked at me with an almost astonished expression. "Are you worried?" she asked.

"For Ian!" I replied.

"Why?"

"Because I don't want you to hurt him and I don't want us to have any problems as friends," I said. Something gave me an attitude and I know Carrie was confused by it. Even my hands were on my hips. I felt just like Kylie. How did she manage to sound like this all the time, it was killing me.

To my surprise, Carrie looked to the floor, sort of stammered, and then said, "Well, I would never mean to hurt Ian...you know that right?"

"Yeah, but what do you think happened with Joe? I mean, I'm sure you dressed the same way for your date with him, right?"

Suddenly, I lost whatever advantage I had in the argument and Carrie instantly angered.

"I told him to stop!" she growled.

"But that doesn't mean that your short skirt and barely-a-shirt said it, too! What do you expect him to do to you with everything all hanging out? It's like sticking a bloody leg in the ocean and not expecting a shark to chomp it off!"

She scoffed, pouted, and then finally replied, "So you think Ian's like Joe?"

"No," I replied instantly, "but we've known Joe our whole lives and I never would've thought he'd be like that, did you?" Carrie wanted to argue, but couldn't. Joe Gregory had been just like Ian two years ago, quiet and all, barely noticeable.

"It's something about high school that changes people, Carrie! I mean, look at you... Last year you were all into sports and now you're talking about guys every second of the day..."

Carrie scoffed again, "Well, I..."

We could both hear Ian shut his bedroom door and start downstairs.

"I'm not going to hurt Ian, Erin! I just want to repay him for being so good to me...that's all."

"So do you even like him?" I asked, "Or is he just kissing practice?"

"Of course I like him!" she whispered angrily as the footsteps neared.

"And what exactly does *repay him* mean?" I asked.

Carrie blushed, "Nothing more than you and Jake will be doing, I'm sure..."

Now it was my turn to blush and I shoved her in the shoulder.

"Look, let's just have a good time tonight, okay?" pleaded Carrie, more calm than before, almost smiling. There was a flash of excitement in her eye, one that told me she meant a *good time* to be just that. She held herself like a girl who was going to be in control of everything. And after her encounter with Joe, I imagined Carrie knew exactly what she wanted from Ian and she was more than prepared to take it.

I started toward the kitchen, but Carrie whispered something else that stopped me.

"What happens at the cabin stays at the cabin, okay?"

I thought to ask her what that meant exactly, but then it dawned on me how much freedom that little phrase allowed. With Carrie there it was almost certain every secret would be unleashed, but since she was the one making the promises... Did that mean that she was willing to let things be and not gossip? Could she?

Ian rounded the corner as she and I both smiled knowingly at one another. The look in her eyes told me that she was ready to agree to her end of the bargain if I was willing to give her just a little bit of space. I thought about Ian and his hopes as well. How could her mischievousness possibly *hurt* Ian? He would love every second of it! It would almost be like an early birthday present...just like I had promised.

I looked at my brother...my poor, sweet brother. He had no clue what Carrie was about to put him through, even I could only imagine. I wish I had her ambition! I smiled as I thought of taking a page from her book to use on Jake.

"Are you guys about ready?" he asked.

"Almost," I said, "but I think Carrie still has to change..."

Within thirty minutes Jake arrived, followed by T.J. in his jeep and Michael. Carrie, Ian, and I hopped into Jake's truck and we all set out for the cabin. T.J led the way through the back roads by Old Washing Machine road where all the dumped trash lay in the ditches and then onto the first dirt road past all of the make-out spots. The dirt road was fun at first, but after a while it was annoying. Bump after bump with no relief was starting to make me feel nauseous, but I just kept looking at Jake and before too long we were there. It would've been impossible to make it in a car, which is why they usually spent their time back here where the cops hardly traveled. The cabin looked old, but the guys had everything. There was a rack of chopped firewood, coolers, "...everything a growing boy needs," commented T.J.

"Hey, your Pop doesn't know anything about this place, right?" asked Michael once we'd all arrived.

Everyone looked to Ian and I and we both shook our heads no.

Before we left the house Dad started asking a few questions about where it was, but Ian and I didn't budge. If dad found out about this place, then all the cops would know, and that would only lead to punishment for the next two years for me and Ian.

A bean shaped pond stretched out behind the cabin until only woods surrounded it. Jake made a comment that there was really good fishing back there, but I hardly cared. I don't think I've fished since I was like eight. The grass looked recently mowed. Off to the side was a large mound of sticks and leaves for the fire. Right beside it was a charred black area where the fire had been the last time. The guys carried a few bags of ice and some snacks from the trucks, walked through the back door, and into the house. I waited until Dyson and Michael pulled out a small milk crate of lanterns and lighters before I walked in behind Jake. The kitchen was small and simple. Four coolers were lying on the floor.

"What are the coolers for?" I asked.

"Keeping things cold, duh!" T.J. replied with a laugh.

Jake snickered. "Summer time."

"So you guys come out here all year round?"

"Yeah, but when it gets really cold we bring the fire inside to the fireplace. T.J.'s grandparents don't really use the place anymore, so we keep it up...kinda."

I looked around the room, and except for some spider webs up near the ceiling, the cabin was nice and clean. I expected something from an old scary movie with rotting floors and rats and God knows what else, but it wasn't bad at all. There were two closets in the hall, and two bedrooms connected by a bathroom. The living room took up half of the cabin. The fireplace was just inside the front door, and it was easily the largest fireplace I've ever seen. Old deer heads and stuffed squirrels decorated the walls and some dust covered pictures on the mantle were impossible to see even after I blew on them four or five times. A large rug lay on the floor in front of the fireplace.

Jake turned and gave me a kiss. I beamed.

"I'll be right back," he said.

I watched him walk all the way down the hall and turn into the last door. It was the only one left and I'm pretty sure it was the bathroom.

"Want something to drink before I take these out?" T.J. asked.

I thought to say no, but something triggered inside me that made me want to fit in...

"Whatcha got?"

T.J. smiled, "Just about everything! Coke, Pepsi, Beer..."

At that moment Dyson walked around the corner with a couple of beers in his hand and handed one to Ian, who apparently hadn't expected the gift. Carrie glanced to Ian with an expression of excitement at his sudden toughness and then looked at me. My poor, poor brother. I had a bad feeling the vampire was going to feast tonight.

"I'll have a Coke for now," I said.

T.J. smiled and handed it to me.

When I walked back outside the girls were dragging chairs closer to the fire that Michael had lit. Ashley and Brittany were still laughing and Brittany was still talking excitedly with her hands. T.J. set the drinks down and both girls reached for a Coke. *Thank God!* I didn't want to be the only girl without a beer in my hand. Surprisingly, Ian had opened his beer and already taken a couple of swigs. His face changed when the other guys weren't looking, but that was understandable. I had taken a drink of one once on accident and it was disgusting!

Jake walked out and quickly took up a Pepsi. The guys started teasing him immediately.

"Aw, do you need a nipple for that Jakey-poo?"

"Man, I thought we only brought four girls not five,"

"What's wrong man, leave the boys in the dresser or something?"

Jake only laughed, "Yeah, well, some of us like to remember the night," he said.

"Maybe we don't want them to remember what we do to them out here," mumbled Ashley. Her smile was a lot like Carrie's often was. Brittany nodded along and both looked to their men. I heard Kylie say "Skank" in my head, but Michael inched his way over to her and picked her up. The two looked at one another the same.

"Are you gonna get me all drunk and rape me or something?" he asked.

"If you're lucky," Brittany replied, "but I don't think you can rape someone if they want you to!"

"Ohhh," the guys sounded in unison.

"What makes you think I like what you've got?" he asked.

"Oh, I know you do..." she said just before they kissed.

I looked to Carrie who seemed to be feeding off of this as if it were a children's show on the Disney channel. Both Brittany and Ashley were dressed similar to Carrie and Ian's eyes kept straying from Carrie's face when she wasn't looking.

Jake only smiled at them and then looked at me. I met his stare for a second and felt my body heat up all over again. What was it about those eyes–that look– that made me want to be bold like Brittany?

By the time it got dark, the bonfire was nice and warm. Dyson and Michael made a few hotdogs, Ashley started making Smores, and T.J. was going back for what I thought was around his sixth beer, but it was hard to say. Both Carrie and Ian occupied one chair with Carrie running her hands through his hair. They sat really close for a while just talking. I started to panic a little, but Brittany kept me talking about friends, parties, this and that. The thought of Ian's dreams coming true and Whitney's vanishing were pushed to the back of my mind when I let it slip that Kylie likes Dyson.

"So she really likes him, huh?" she asked. I nodded. *Stupid! Stupid! Stupid! Kylie will kill me!*

"Every weekend it's the same," she said. "Sure, he spends all week at school with girls all around him, but every weekend he's here by himself. I don't think he's ever had a girlfriend longer than a week."

"Really?"

"Really!"

Maybe she *wouldn't* kill me... "Well, do you think I could invite her next Saturday?"

Brittany smiled, "Like a trap? Yeah! Dyson will never see it coming!"

The comment made me laugh, but only because of the play going on in my mind, but there was something about the excitement in her voice to spring the *'trap'* on Dyson.

"Hey, Ash, come here!" Brittany yelled.

Ashley walked from the fire and Brittany whispered into her ear what we had talked about. Ashley's eyes lit up and she nodded excitedly.

"I'd like to see him have some fun," she said, "I mean, he's got to be dying not being able to...you know..." Both girls nodded, almost sadly and then looked to me.

I *didn't* know, but I didn't let them know that I didn't know, you know? Instead, I nodded along and smiled like they were. It felt so awesome to fit in with such pretty and popular girls. I never imagined myself hanging out with such a crowd. I felt cool. It was kind of how you imagine the new people in Hollywood feel when they get to walk down the red carpet next a *real* celebrity.

As the night continued, the bonfire was piled with more wood to keep it going and slowly Brit and Michael, and Ash and T.J. disappeared into the cabin. The thought made me nervous. I mean, who knows what's going on? I looked at Jake, but he was making another Smore and listening to the music. I wonder what he expected *me* to do… I mean, all the other couples had been all over one another all night, kissing and touching one another, but we hadn't done anything since the first kiss when we arrived. And where had Ian and Carrie wandered off to? How far would Carrie go? A scary thought erupted in my mind and I got angry. She better not go *too* far!

Dyson came and sat down next to me and smiled.

"So, where's your little bro at?"

"I'm not sure," I said, looking around again.

"Don't worry," he said, "He's inside with his girl on the couch. I'm sure he'll be a good boy though," he laughed.

"He better be!" I said, hardly able to restrain myself.

"Oh," he laughed, "and you a tough one, huh? I bet you be whoopin' some girls off your little bro, huh?"

Listening to Dyson I couldn't help but think of Kylie. They'd be perfect for each other!

"Hey Jake," he called, "Your girl's all crazy man! She's all talkin' bout whoopin' on some girls if they all up on *Wonder Boy* man," he laughed.

Jake smiled and stood from his kneel. He leaned

forward and blew out his flaming marshmallow and then placed it on his graham cracker.

"Well, that's one reason I like her so much," he replied. "She's not afraid to fight for what she wants and she doesn't take any crap!"

"So I'm your girl now, huh?" I asked. It almost felt weird to say it that way, but when Jake smiled in return I knew something felt right about it.

Dyson smirked, "Yeah, you his girl alright! This fool won't stop talking about you and how your birthday all coming up and..."

Jake cleared his throat and Dyson stopped. "Uh-oh, the white boy bout to lay it down if I don't close it off," he cackled.

"Yeah," agreed Jake, "and you're in my seat, too!"

He and Dyson exchanged a cool guy handshake and then Jake took his seat beside me and handed me the Smore he made.

"I'm allergic to chocolate," I said.

His eyes got big. "What about flowers?"

"Them too..."

"*Really?*"

"No," I laughed, "but wouldn't that suck for you! Then all you've have left to get me was jewelry."

"Or I could get you one of these," he said. From his black gym bag beside his chair he pulled a soft teddy bear and handed it to me. My heart melted. It had been doing that a lot lately.

"Aw," I sounded. I wondered how ridiculous I

sounded doing it for my own gift, but I didn't care. He leaned in and kissed me. I felt the warmth of his lips pass across my whole body. It was so soft and gentle. I closed my eyes and savored it.

I thought this was going to be the start of something that led inside the cabin like the others, but as soon as I felt the warmth of his lips they were gone. When I opened my eyes, his eyes were right there in front of mine.

"You're so beautiful," he said. The warm feeling shot through my body again like electricity. I couldn't help but smile. He looked so serious, but yet he wasn't pushy or anything.

"I hope you're having a good time," he said.

"Are you?" I asked, almost doubtful.

He smiled, "One of the best I've had this year," he replied.

"But..." I started to argue, motioning toward the cabin.

"Oh, you mean *that*?" he asked. He shrugged and then took a final sip of his Coke, "*That's* something that's worth waiting for. I think when you're ready it'll come. I don't want to rush you..."

He's being so sweet and patient with me. It's like he knows how scared I am and he's willing to do what Joe never would with Carrie. How many girls were forced to go further than they wanted to just because their boyfriends were in a hurry to have it all?

All at once, all that warmth and excitement inside

me burst. I felt my legs lift me out of the chair and toward him, but I hardly knew what I was doing. It was happening so fast I couldn't think. Suddenly, I was on top of him, kissing him. It was amazing! I was being so sexy, but yet not skanky like I'm sure Carrie and all the other girls were being. He ran his hands along my hips and then up by back to my head. He touched my cheeks so gently and then ran his hands through my hair. He didn't even try to touch my butt or bring them around to my chest.

My hands moved his hands down. *What am I doing?* I wanted to slow down, but I couldn't. The thing that shocked me was that it wasn't him, but me. He was being so patient and letting me choose everything, but I couldn't control myself. Everything was happening so fast. It was like his patience fueled me. I brought my hands to his face and then ran them along his chest. Something about the way he caressed showed me that he really meant the things he said at Giorgio's and the things he said just before I attacked him. *Oh my God, I'm attacking him!* I'm attacking Jake Cunningham!

He was slow and gentle. It seemed like we were in slow motion, but to me, inside my head, it was all rushing by so fast. I lifted up my shirt and slid his hand beneath it. I wanted to show him that I was ready for this, maybe not *everything*, but definitely for this. His hands touched me and I felt his love. It wasn't rough and scary like it had been for Carrie with Joe, but sweet and real. I couldn't help but feel how real it was; it was the touch you see in movies, the ones that show you when a couple is in love, all slow and romantic.

He gently ran his fingers across my body and kissed me until we could hear the sounds of laughter coming from inside the cabin. The others were getting ready to go. My night, the best night of my life, was finally coming to an end. It hadn't been nearly as action packed as I thought it would be, but I could've never imagined it being better.

Carrie and Ian stepped outside. Ian's eyes grew to the size of baseballs at the sight of me on top of Jake, but once he realized that all of my clothes were on he simply smirked. I wonder what he would have thought if they hadn't been?

I probably would have seen him blush if it wouldn't have been so dark out. It was that feeling you got when you knew something had been going on, but no one said anything. Carrie didn't need to, she was beaming. The look on her face told me how proud of herself she was. It was obvious that she had been in complete control of the situation this time and she was more than happy with the outcome.

I'm no expert at how parties go, but I was sure the others had done *much* more than we had. Don't ask me how I knew, but I did. The ride back was better than the ride there. Carrie and Ian continued making out in the back seat while I leaned close to Jake and occasionally kissed him while he drove. It felt so good to be able to show him how I felt. It was like a way of communicating without saying a word. No stuttering, no stammering, no thinking, just kissing. Everything seemed to fall into line once we reached the blacktop and a few minutes later I kissed Jake good-bye for the night. Ten-fifty-two...eight minutes before curfew. Could this night have been any better?

Chapter Ten

September 14th - Friday

The next week was amazing! Brittany and Ashley came over on Sunday and met my mom, she loves them. They're so cool! We sat around most of the afternoon doing each other's nails and talking about the night before, while Ian and Dad watched football. I had *no* idea what went on behind closed doors, but now I have a *really* good imagination. It was so refreshing to have someone who knew what they were talking about just open up like that. I suddenly felt like I had options when it came to friends now. Not that Kylie and Whitney aren't good friends, but when it comes to things like this they don't really know what's going on, you know? It's just a relief to finally talk to some people who *did* know what I was going through; girls who had done much, much more.

Whitney was sort of disconnected all week. She's taking Ian and Carrie's relationship pretty hard. I guess she didn't think Ian was good looking enough for Carrie or something? I don't think she even said three words all week, and that includes "hi" and "bye".

I feel bad for saying this, but I'm actually kind of glad that she hasn't been coming around lately. I've come to the conclusion that she just needs time to cool off. The more she's away from Ian the more she has a chance of getting over him, and once she does that, then there won't be all this moping around like her dog just died or something. It's such a downer when I'm on cloud nine and she's in the Grand Canyon.

There *is* one thing that's bothering me lately though, and I'm not sure what's going on. Carrie has been acting a little strange, almost fishy. You know, like the one character in the movies who you think is the bad guy, but then they just turn out to be this weirdo...that's how Carrie's been acting! She hangs out by the lockers as usual, but then she's just occasionally not there, almost like she's mastered the art of disappearing.

She came over to the house on Tuesday night. We went to my room first, but then she snuck across the hall into Ian's room while I finished my Geometry homework. I'm sure Ian was excited about that!

Jake called on Wednesday right after school and said he needed to see me. I told him that my mom wouldn't allow me out on a school night, but he insisted that it was important, so I snuck out the window and ran down the street to meet him. We sat in his truck and talked for a minute before he handed me a rose and a sweet note. He told me that I should hurry and get back inside before my parents caught me, but he should've known better than to think I was going to let him rush away. Lucky for him, I wasn't even wearing a bra this time.

When I came back inside I could still feel him touching me. I was hot all over. I'm beginning to understand the meaning of cold showers. What was odd was that I had this urge inside of me to blurt it out to the world. I *had* to tell someone or I would explode. I thought about calling Carrie first, but she was acting so weird lately that I decided not to. Of course, Whitney and Ian weren't options either, so I called Brittany.

"They love it when you do things like that," she said. "If I want attention, I do things like that and Michael can't keep his hands off of me! When we were first dating I *accidentally* touched him. You should've seen his eyes light up... Oh, and there's another trick too..."

On the way home from school yesterday, Jake and I stopped at the gas station and I got a drink while he pumped. When he got in the truck I slid the bottle between his legs when I leaned over to kiss him, just like Brittany suggested, and then on the way home I reached over to grab it and *accidentally* missed. Our eyes met for a second but I didn't take the drink. Instead, I scooted closer and kissed on him while he drove. I never did get a drink...

That night Jake begged me to sneak out of the window, just like Brittany said he would, but I gave him an excuse, like she said. I felt so bad for him, but Brittany said I performed perfectly.

"Good girl!" she said, "That's how you do it! If you give them what they want when they want it, then they have no use for you...you're like a puppet. But *you're* the one who is the puppet master, not them! Do you see how easily he yanked toward you when you did that simple little thing? That's how you keep them interested, you tease them!"

"It's that easy, huh?" I asked, surprised.

"Well you don't want to keep them out there forever though," she said, "Sometimes you have to let them think they win too."

"What do you mean, *let them think they win*?"

"You know, you've just got to let them have what they want,"

I gulped, "*Everything* they want?"

"Yeah," she laughed, "What, do you think you're the only girl in line for Jake? This *is* high school, Erin! If you don't give him what he wants, he'll find it somewhere else!"

That scared me a little, but then she assured me that as long as I kept doing what I was doing, there would be nothing to be afraid of. And with both my birthday and homecoming right around the corner, it seemed like one of them was going to be a monumental night...

School went by really fast today. It's like one second Jake and I are driving to school and then the next we're coming back. Things are so much better when you're in love. He let me wear his jersey at school today. Brittany and Ashley told me in the bathroom that T.J. and Michael love it when they wear their jerseys just before sex. I could tell that Jake might be thinking that when I was walking down the hall toward him after school. His eyes were all glossed over and he looked entranced. I've never had a guy look at me like that, especially one like Jake. I could see it in his eyes that his mind wasn't where it was supposed to be, or was it? I liked the thought of his mind being where *I* wanted it to be, instead of where it could be. After all, I wanted his eyes wandering on me, *not* some other girl!

Whitney called before the game and said she wasn't going to be able to come. She said her mom had some things for her to do, but I'm sure that wasn't entirely the truth. Whitney had never missed one of Ian's games before. I'm sure it had nothing to do with the hot girl that would be sitting by her cheering for the guy *she* liked. She asked if I wanted to get together tomorrow and hang out, but I told her that I was going back out to the cabin again with Jake. She asked if Ian was going this time, but I tried to avoid the answer. I really wish she would just get over him already so it wouldn't be so hard to be friends. I mean, I can't make my brother's choices for him!

Brittany and Ashley put our little plan into action and just happened to bump into Kylie today on the way down the hall. They asked Kylie if she would want to come hang out for a while on Saturday and then I just happened to walk up and overhear them and said, "Yeah, you should come!" It was brilliant! Kylie said yes and now I was well on my way to handing her the man of her dreams on a silver platter. Could this week be any better?

The football game started at six o'clock and the Deadwood Daggers were not an easy team. Some of the old men in the stands said this game would be better than the playoffs. "The Daggers," they said, "are the only team that has it all. Not only can they run the ball just as good as any team, but they can pass it too." I'm not sure how scary that's supposed to be. I mean, aren't all football teams supposed to be able to do that? All I knew was that the old men said that Jake was in for a tough night.

On the opening kickoff, the Daggers ran the ball all the way down the field for a touchdown and then on our first play the quarterback fumbled the ball and the Daggers defense recovered it. A few minutes later the Daggers drove the field and kicked the ball between the posts, ten to nothing. We got the ball back and Dyson shredded the defense apart all the way down to the thirty-five. Ian caught the ball, spun around a tackle, and got down to the twenty, but then our quarterback threw an interception and the guy ran all the way back to the ten yard line. Let's just say it wasn't a pretty first half! By halftime we were down seventeen to nothing and nobody looked happy on the Bronco sidelines.

The second half of the game was almost a different game. The Broncos came out ready to play. On the second or third play, Dyson ran the ball all the way down the sideline for a touchdown. Kylie was cheering so much mom said she thought she should have pompoms.

When the Daggers got the ball back, the coach sent Jake on this thingy where he runs after the quarterback instead of guarding the receiver... Dad called it a "Blitz" or something like that, but anyway, whatever it was worked because Jake knocked the guy off his feet and he fumbled the ball. One of our linemen got the ball back and it gave the Broncos the ball with only thirty yards to go for the touchdown. On the first play, Dyson got a pitch around the side toward Ian's man. Ian hit the guy so hard it knocked his helmet off and Dyson got all the way to the seven yard line before he was knocked out of bounds. Dad was so proud of Ian that I thought he might even cry. All the old men around him were patting him on the shoulder as if dad groomed him to block from birth.

It was the most action packed game I had ever seen. My eyes were glued to the field. Well, except when Carrie came back from the concessions with Nachos, but even then my eyes were mostly on the game. Dyson ended up scoring that touchdown making it twenty-one to twenty with only a minute left on the clock. Our defense held the Daggers to a fourth down play on the fifty with four seconds left. The quarterback dropped back for the pass and launched the ball deep, but Jake knocked it down in the end zone and the game was over. The Broncos won twenty-one to twenty.

It wasn't until after the game that my mom brought something to my attention.

"Where was Carrie for half the game? Has she been feeling alright?" she asked me once Ian went upstairs to shower. I thought to answer or to make up some kind of excuse, but then I couldn't manage one. I really wasn't sure... I thought she had been beside me for most of the game, but now that I think about it she had been gone quite often. She came back a few times with food from the concessions, but the lines weren't that long, were they?

Ian didn't seem to notice anything weird when I asked him about it before bed. I told him that Jake and the guys had invited us out to the cabin again, but he said that he was going to pass this weekend, something about studying for a test on Monday. I got furious! Why was it that girls had to do everything to keep the guy entertained, but the girls were forgotten about when the guys had football or something more important on their minds?

"What about Carrie? Are you just gonna leave her out with nothing to do on a Saturday night?" I asked. "You know, for as long as you've waited on this chance I would've thought you'd be more willing to spend more time with Carrie. What about what *she* wants?"

Ian looked at me like I'd stabbed him. "Look, she's the one who said she couldn't do anything this weekend.

She said her mom was keeping her in because she had been over here and out all last weekend. She said she had chores or something?"

"Oh," I said. Part of me wanted to apologize for being so mean, but then the other part saw the look on his face and it made me not want to.

"Why are you so mad?" he asked, "Did Carrie tell you I wasn't spending enough time with her or something?" The look in his eyes told me he was scared.

"I'm not mad, I just thought you were blowing Carrie off!"

"No way, are you kidding me? I've practically been begging her to hang out lately. She seems *weird*, like she's mad at me, but then she'll come over to visit and sneak into my room and then it's like nothing's wrong." He shrugged, almost sad.

"I've noticed her acting a little weird too," I said. Unfortunately, my words weren't as comforting as he was hoping for.

"I think she's gonna break up with me," he replied, even sadder than before.

"He's smothering me!" griped Carrie when I called her a few minutes later.

"What do you mean, *smothering you*?" I replied. I mean, really, could she see how she flirted with him? Did she know who *she* was? I wouldn't be surprised if *smother* was one of her middle names right beside *drama, gossip,* and *loud*.

"He always calls, always wants to hold my hand at school, writes me love letters all the time, asks me to come over every day...it's annoying!" she said.

"Carrie you *always* call me, you walk right beside me at school talking about all your latest gossip, and you came over *every* day during the summer!" I said.

"Yeah, but this is different!"

"Yeah, but it wasn't when Ian was drooling all over you all last year and all summer! He's been in love with you for years now! He's finally got the girl of his dreams and now she doesn't want anything to do with him. Can't you see how this is important for him?"

"Why do you always take his side just because he's your brother?"

"I don't take his side just because he's my brother!" I snapped, "I'm just taking his side now because he's right when he says that you're acting weird...cause you are!"

"Well, I'm weird because he's smothering me. I just need some space!"

"Okay, I'll tell him that you need space since all you want to do is lie to him and tell him that you have chores, but while he's giving you your *space* you'd better think about how you're going to start treating him because he's my little brother and he loves you!"

Carrie was quiet for a second and then she said, "Well, I've gotta go. See you Monday."

I thought to give her another threat before she hung up; maybe mention how Kylie would rip her apart for hurting her cutie-pie, but I didn't think Carrie was really listening. She's funny about things like that. Sometimes she really cares, but other times she could look a murderer in the face and say "I'm hungry" without blinking an eye.

Chapter Eleven

September 15th - Saturday

Like always, boys never understand girls. If there was a list of top five excuses that girls give boys, one of them would be "I need some space." And if there was a list of top five reasons why girls gave boys that excuse, guys would always pick, "She's gonna break up with me."

I called Whitney and told her that Carrie was acting weird and I gave her the dirt. She tried to sound worried, but deep down I know that I personally answered her prayers. I thought I should get her involved in things again by asking her to go over to Carrie's and hang out for a while just to see what was *really* going on. I'm almost sure that if she's up to something she won't share it with me or Kylie. Brittany and Ashley are closer to me than they are her, so Whitney would be her only shoulder to cry on. And since she and I haven't been around one another much over the past couple weeks, it seemed like a perfect idea. Now that I think about it, I'm getting really good at this. I should be a special agent when I grow up.

I even ended the conversation by telling Whitney that Ian was going to be home all day if she wanted to call him or stop by and tell him what she found out. I thought that'd be good too because it would give Whitney some one on one time with Ian while Carrie was acting stupid. This way, if Carrie did break up with Ian, Whitney would get first dibs. First, Kylie and Dyson and now this...I'm a genius!

Brittany and Ashley stopped by around noon and picked me up. We went to the mall and walked around a while talking about our *strategy* for the night.

"I've been kinda tough on Michael lately, I think I'm gonna let him win tonight," admitted Ashley. Brittany gasped and slapped her girlishly on the shoulder.

"I can't believe you! That's like what, three times this week?"

"Twice!" corrected Ashley, "besides, last time it was *a lot* better."

"Yeah, but you parked on Wednesday didn't you?"

"Yeah, but that one was just a little lip action..."

"What about you?" she asked, looking at me, "Are you finally gonna drop those panties or what?" she teased.

We all giggled and I took a page from Brittany's book and slapped her girlishly on the shoulder. "I'm not sure, maybe?" I lied. I wasn't sure when it was going to happen, but I knew for sure whatever it was, *wasn't* happening tonight.

"*Maybe*? Girl, you've got to show him what he's missing or he'll turn up missing!" she teased. I could tell by her voice that she wasn't entirely joking.

"She knows Ash...," defended Brit, "We've been talking a lot on the phone and she's really keeping Jake on his toes. He even begged her to sneak out last week and she brought him to his knees." Ash smiled.

"I'm glad you're learning the game," she said, "cause it *is* all one big game, you know?"

I nodded along.

"She even did the accidental touch..."

"Really?" smiled Ash. Her eyes flashed. I could tell she loved the thought of being a puppet master. "Okay, but just remember, Jake's played this game for years now! If you want to stay on top of things, you've got to stay *under* him...

It's amazing how much you don't know about the real world until it all starts happening to you. I mean, how else is a girl supposed to compete with all the hot girls out there? Especially, the skanky ones! I'm so glad I met Brittany and Ashley. Without them I would've surely lost Jake to some hotter girl.

"Look, if you want to know how crazy he is about you, just act like he's no big deal. Ride in the car on the way to the cabin and do something with your nails or talk with us...yeah, that's better, talk with us the whole way there and keep him in his own little world."

"Once you have total control, *you* determine what happens and when," added Brit.

"And nothing is hotter to a guy than a girl who's in control!" added Ash.

"What's wrong with your shirt?" asked Brit, almost worried.

I looked down. I couldn't see anything wrong with it. "What do you mean? Is there something on it?"

"Oh, no," gasped Ashley, "There's something definitely wrong with it!"

"Where? What?" I asked. The boys were going to be here any minute and I didn't want to look bad before another big night.

"Oh, maybe this is it?" said Brit as she pulled a silky halter out of her purse. They giggled.

"Try this on and see what you think about it?"

"You guys got this for me?"

"No," Ash replied, "We got it for Jake!"

"But my bra's in the way..."

"Who needs one?" Brit commented. She lifted her shirt and flashed me and Ash nearly died laughing. I took off my bra with the both of them standing there. It felt kind of weird changing right in front of them. They didn't even turn around or anything. It was like changing in front of a guy, but then again I've never had friends like them before. All of my friends were *good* girls. They didn't know what it was like to be in love and have to learn this whole new game to keep up with the other girls; the ones who would take the man of your dreams right out of your arms if you let them.

It felt so weird sitting next to Jake after I had spent the past day talking about sex and the games we're supposed to play. I couldn't keep my mind from wandering. I thought to start messing with him while he was driving, but Ashley, Brittany and I had a game plan, and I didn't want to let them down. We laughed about a few of the things that had happened over the past week. Jason McAllister got caught grabbing Danielle Adams' butt in the hall and he was expelled for three days.

"If they only knew what me and T.J. have done in the chemistry closet during lunch, they'd let Jason off with a warning," laughed Ash.

When we got to Kylie's house I ran up to the porch and knocked. Kylie's mom answered the door and I suddenly remembered that I was wearing the halter the girl's gave me. After a quick disapproving glare from her mother, Kylie and I were stepping off the porch and Brit and Ash moved back to ride with Michael.

"What you wearin' girl? I thought you was Carrie for a second!"

At first I thought the comment was a compliment because Carrie's gorgeous, but I knew Kylie too well to think that. "It's for Jake," I said. Kylie tilted her head and scanned me over.

"Uh-huh," she sounded, "It better be to look at too, cause ain't nothing else for sale!"

"What do you mean?" I asked.

"What I said girl! That's what I mean!" she countered,

"You better keep them panties where they ought to be! I done beat one boy this month, I ain't scared to beat another one! And I got my heavy ones on too, so say I won't! I done told Carrie an' I'm a' tell you too, I ain't have'n no skanky friends with their boobs all hang-n out like they need to air dry-n or something..."

"Well, we'll see what you say once you see the surprise I got you," I said with confidence.

Brittany, Ashley, and I all stood next to Kylie when T.J. pulled up in his jeep and we watched the expression on her face when Dyson stepped out of the passenger side. She looked to the three of us and then shook her head with a smirk. She couldn't hide the fact that she was excited, but she still shook her head.

"So..." I asked.

"So what?" she replied.

"So what do you think?" asked Ash.

"I think I'm a' beat the crazy out some white girls if they don't stop giggling at me with my man all lookin' fine bout to walk right up here. Get on! Go put on some makeup or something! Don't be all stare-n at me like I'm bout to sing or something!"

Brit and Ash ran for the cabin. Jake walked up beside me and wrapped his arms around me. He kissed me on the neck as I reached up and held his hands.

"I thought about you all night last night," he whispered.

"Good," I said. I was so proud of how confident I

sounded. I'm sure it was driving him crazy like the girls said it would. It had to be! They had been right about everything else so far.

Jake snickered. "You seem different. Is everything okay?"

"Yeah, why?"

He shrugged, "I don't know, you just seem worried or something..." Did I? Oh no, maybe I wasn't as confident as I thought. I thought that after a whole day around Brit and Ash I would have the upper hand, but maybe I wasn't doing something right. *Face him, let him see the goods,* I heard an inside voice say, so I went with it. His eyes darted down for a second and then back into my eyes. *Gotcha!*

"I'm not worried," I said in my sexy voice. I leaned forward and kissed him real gently and then wrapped my arms around his neck. "Why?" I asked. "Should I be? Is tonight important or something?"

I could tell the light in his eyes meant that he wanted it to be, but then he shook his head and said, "No, not unless *you* want it to be..." Suddenly, a couple of things came to mind and I was confused. I thought the point of being the puppet master was to be in control but he wasn't supposed to know I was in control? Kind of like letting him think he ran the show, when he didn't. But how could I do that if Jake was admitting that it was my decision? Maybe I missed a step somewhere?

It was then that I realized how close we were and how quiet we were getting. The fire was roaring behind us and the sun had finally set. With a quick glance, I noticed that Ash and Michael were gone. Kylie and Dyson were sitting by the fire. T.J. and Brit were walking around the side of the cabin toward T.J.'s jeep…it was just me and Jake all to ourselves.

"I want to be honest with you," I said.

"I hope you always are," he said with a laugh.

"I am," I replied with a smile, "but there's just something I want to tell you…"

He looked into my eyes, concerned. "What is it?"

Instantly, it felt so surreal all over again. How was *I* with a guy like Jake Cunningham? How had *my* body – these little b-cups – kept Jake so entertained, so excited?

"Don't tell the girls," I said.

"Why would I…"

"We just have this plan and I don't want them to be mad at me."

"I don't think they'll…"

"Just promise me you won't say anything to anyone, okay?"

He nodded and held me tight. "What is it?" he asked.

"I…I don't want to let you down, but…"

"Hey," he said, stopping me, "Look at me… Erin, look at me… I'll wait as long as you need."

Something warmed inside of me. How could he be so patient, but the girls talk as if he would leave me any second now if I didn't drop my pants? Then he answered my question for me.

"I told you…I'm not that way anymore. Remember

our first date! I told you that I wanted something real...
You are that something. I'll wait as long as you need,
baby."

He caressed my face and ran his hand through my
hair.

"Are you sure? I mean, I know there are a lot of other girls who wouldn't make you wait..."

"But I don't want them! I want you! And since I've
been with you I've noticed a lot of guys that think of you
the same way, so I could say the same, you know..."

"Yeah right! Guys have never lined up to take their
clothes off for me," I said with a laugh.

"Any guy would love to have what I have and if they
don't they're blind!" he said, scanning me over one more
time.

I felt my body warm to his touch all over again.
I could see the fire in his eyes. He didn't need what
Michael or T.J. needed, only what I was ready to give
him. That's what made what we had love and what they
had a fling. He pressed himself close to me as we started to kiss. I moved his hands where he wouldn't and
then I moved mine where he didn't expect me to. After
a couple of minutes outside, he took me by the hand and
led me inside to the rug on the floor in the living room.
We were both so close and so quiet that we could hear
each other breathe. His hands felt how honey tastes,
sweet and perfect. Before the end of the night his lips
had covered *almost* every inch of my body.

Once the others started coming out of the rooms,

we walked outside to see Kylie and Dyson in the same position Jake and I were in on our first night. It was good to see her smiling ear to ear and to know that she was feeling the same things I had felt. Now I was the one in position to share with her the things Brit and Ash shared with me. It was like I told Ian in the kitchen, "Sex is like a rite of passage" and though I wasn't over the hill yet, I had certainly climbed a few steps higher tonight.

After we dropped Kylie off at her house, Jake drove me home. When we passed the house we saw my mom sitting on the front porch swing. He pulled along the curb and we thought it smarter for me to hurry out of the truck so she didn't ask any questions. I gave him a gentle kiss on the cheek and walked happily toward the house.

"He could've stayed for a bit, you know?" she said as his truck passed by and we waved.

I only shrugged in reply. I tried not to appear overly excited, but I'm sure I failed miserably. I had been doing that a lot lately. Jake was amazing!

"So how was your night?" she asked.

I thought she might like a fib better than the truth, but I didn't want to lie to her, so I settled for a "Great, as always!" instead, which was a little of both.

She took a second to eye me over and then asked, "When did you get *that* shirt?"

Of course, I am far too much of a genius to have

left it as it was… On the way home, with little objection from Jake, I took the halter off and put my bra back on and then pulled the back down and tucked it into the back of my jeans. This kept what little cleavage I had from showing and looked like nothing more than a cool fashion trend. Besides, what did my parents know about what was cool anyway?

"Oh, the girls got it for me…Do you like it?" I knew what her answer would be, but I tried to play dumb. I don't think it worked.

"The girls, huh?"

"Yeah, it was a surprise. We went to the mall and they must've got it for me when I wasn't looking."

"Hmm," she sounded, nodding.

"Did Whitney stop by?" I asked, hoping for the best.

"No, she called though, why?"

"No reason, she just said she might…"

"I got a call from Kylie's mom too," she added quickly.

"Really, why, did Kylie want to stay the night?"

"No, she called a few hours ago…she sounded concerned."

"*Concerned*? About what?"

It was starting to dawn on me that theatre might be a good option next semester.

"She said that when you came to pick up Kylie your shirt was pretty low. She said she could've sworn that you *weren't* wearing a bra…"

Her eyebrows rose in that motherly sort of way and

I knew this was my signal. It reminded me of those intense scenes in movies where the guy has to decide which wire to cut, the red or the blue. If he cuts one, the bomb will blow up the building, but if he cuts the other, he saves his life. This was that moment! And I only had seconds before she exploded...

Should I go for the red wire and tell all...or the blue and try to laugh it off...

"Well, you know, she is a tall woman," I replied, nodding along as if I were convinced with my own answer, though I noticed my mom wasn't. Dang it, blue never works!

But the explosion didn't come as I thought it might. I took in a steadying breath. Was it one of those delayed explosions that came in the form of a surprising "you're grounded for the rest of eternity" moment, or a subtle "we're not going to mention this to your father" moment? I waited, but still, neither came.

Mom only smirked and then slowly scooted over on the swing and patted the warm seat, which only meant one thing: it was time for *a talk*. I knew this look because I had seen it twice before. Once, was the highly dreaded and equally embarrassing puberty talk and the second was the very lame sex talk. It wasn't very lame then, more like disgusting, but now that I know what I know now...

"There's a couple things I want to say, but I don't want you to say a word, just listen, okay?"

I nodded.

"I just want you to remember that your father and I were in high school once too. And I know it seems like an eternity to you, but it was only a blink to us. Not too much has changed since then. We had parties and did a lot of things we probably shouldn't have, but just remember that we were there once too, so there's no fooling us, Erin," she looked to her lap and I watched as her smirk melted off of her face and she looked at me more serious than I could ever remember seeing her.

"I think if I've ever told you anything that you should listen to, it should be this. Don't let me or your dad catch you! Because if I can catch you, then chances are you're being reckless, and if you're being reckless, then you deserve to be caught, and if you're caught, then you deserve to be punished!"

I could only look at the porch. I know it showed how guilty I was, but I didn't care.

"I know there are certain things that usually happen in high school and I don't expect you to do anything less than I did. I would love it if you did none of the things I did, but I think that would be foolish of me to expect. Just remember what I said, Erin...Don't let me catch you!"

I leaned my head on her shoulder for a second and thought of all the things I had been doing over the past weeks. The only thing that came to mind was what I said next.

"I really do think I love him, Mom."

"I know you do, honey," she said a moment later,

"but I've come to learn that what I *think* and what I *know* are sometimes two different things."

After a moment of silence she asked something that I know was pretty hard for a mom to ask. "Do I still have my little girl or are you past that point?"

I froze. How do I answer this? I know my delay said a lot, but once again something inside me kept me from worrying. "Yeah, Mom. I'm still your little girl." *For now,* I thought.

Chapter Twelve ~
September 21st - Friday

Today is the day! The one I've been waiting for all year...the big 1-6. Most families have celebrations on the weekend near the birthday, but my family has always stayed true to the exact day, whether it's on a Wednesday or a Monday... I'm so excited! This morning started off so great. Dad made pancakes, mom and Ian did the dishes...so far so good. When I got in the truck this morning Jake gave me a kiss and asked me how I slept, just like always. He totally didn't say a word about my birthday until I started quizzing him.

"Do you know what today is?"

"Game day!" he replied. I scowled. Ian laughed from the backseat.

Jake smiled and pulled a small box from the side of his seat. I'm sure my scowl disappeared faster than it appeared.

"Happy birthday!" he said.

I wanted to attack him, but stopped myself. I opened the box and my breath left my chest. It was a silver locket with the word *Love* engraved on the outside.

"It's beautiful," I said. It was one of those girly moments where my eyes started to tear up. I think it's just something that women do sometimes? I opened it, but there was nothing on the inside.

"I don't have any small pictures, we'll have to get some..." he apologized.

He got kissed anyway.

Whitney, Carrie, and Kylie all said "Happy Birthday" when I got to school. Brittany, Ashley, and the boys all said it as well. With this Friday being my birthday and next Friday being Homecoming, it seemed like the past few amazing weeks would keep their streak going a little longer.

In Mrs. Prichard's English class we practiced our lines with our partners while the others worked on corny little props for the apartment scene. Mrs. Clark didn't give us geometry homework for once. In history class we had a substitute who let us divide our class in half and have a paper ball fight. He said it was to simulate how battle works, but we know it was just something to keep us busy. It was awesome!

At lunch Carrie wasn't *overly* loud. She and Ian had slowly drifted apart over the past week despite the fact that he was doing every single little thing she wanted him to. I hate it when girls say what they want, but then don't mean it. It's so sad to see a guy like Ian is right now, all down and depressed. Whitney has come to the rescue though...she's been over almost every night this week right after school. She says it's to get help on homework, but I'm sure we both know the *real* reason. On the flip side, Kylie and Dyson are officially girlfriend and boyfriend now, and as of yesterday he asked her to homecoming.

My mom checked us out of school early today. She dropped Ian off at home and then we went to the mall. It was so fun just walking around and talking about this and that. It was almost as if our little talk the week before had brought us closer. We walked into all the usual stores, my mom stopped and picked up her jewelry that she sent off to get fixed last month. We were getting ready to leave when we heard a "Hey!"

When we turned two security guards were walking straight for us.

"Yes," replied my mom.

"We need you two to come with us for a moment if you don't mind," the man spoke, annoyed.

"Why?"

"We'll talk about that once we're somewhere more private."

My mom glanced at me, and then to the men, and nodded. The security guards led us around the corner and down to one of those random doors that you always see but never think anything of. My mom and I sat down in the coldest, most uncomfortable chairs known to all mankind.

"Do you know why you're here?" one of the men asked.

"No," my mom replied. She looked at me. I nodded that I had no idea, either.

"Would you mind opening your bags for me, please?"

"What? Are you accusing us of stealing?" Mom blurted.

"We're not accusing you of anything *yet*," the man replied. "We just want to check your things if you don't mind..." My mom handed the men her bags and her receipts.

"You don't have to pour them out, but would you also mind opening your purses for us as well?"

My mom shot the man a disgusted look and opened her purse wide and sat it on the table. I did the same. "What are you looking for?" she asked, obviously flustered.

After a few seconds, the men checked everything off the list and closed our purses and handed them back.

"We're terribly sorry to have bothered you, but we felt like we had good reason..."

"And what reason is that?" Mom asked.

One of the security guards turned and pushed a button on the machine just above one of the televisions. Both my mom and I had to squint to make out the people on the camera, but almost instantly I noticed who they were. It was Brittany, Ashley, and me! It was last Saturday! I held the halter up to my chest, handed it to Brittany, turned around and she shoved it into her purse. I gasped. *Oh my God! That's how she got it!* My hand shot to my mouth and covered it. I looked at my mom.

"I...I didn't..."

My mom's scowl was so strong it cut me. By the look in her eyes I could tell she thought I was guilty even though I honestly had no clue. "Mom, I didn't know..." I pleaded.

She looked from me to the security guards, "What's going to happen?"

Both men looked to one another and then one stepped forward and sat down in the chair in front of me.

"You had no clue?" he asked, doubtfully.

"No," I said, shaking my head.

"And did you ever see the shirt afterwards?"

"Yes," I admitted. My heart fell to my feet. My stomach rose to my throat.

"How did you not know it was stolen?" he asked.

"I don't know. I just thought they had bought it when I wasn't paying attention," I tried to explain, but I know how it sounded. It sounded like a lie. The truth was that I was having so much fun, my mind so intent on Jake and sex and high school, that I wasn't paying attention to anything. It didn't even dawn on me that they would do something like that.

The security guards glanced to one another as if to say, "Yeah right", but I was on my feet.

"I know how this sounds! I know it doesn't make sense, but you have to believe me! I didn't know it was stolen!"

"How long have you known these girls?"

"A month?" I guessed.

"A month?" the guy replied, just as doubtful as before.

Finally my mom intervened, "She *has* only recently started hanging out with these girls!"

Suddenly, because an adult spoke the words, it was considered the truth. Apparently, the words of a sixteen year old meant nothing.

"I'm going to ask you one more time," my mom started. It was obvious her patience was gone. "Either you're going to give me a straight answer or we're going to walk out of here. What's going to happen?"

One of the security guards shrugged. "She'll be banned from the mall for six months and I'll need the names and numbers of these other two ladies here," he said.

The urge to go down swinging came into my mind. Nobody likes a snitch! My mom looked at me with her eyebrows raised. It was time to choose again, red or blue?

The car ride home was long and mostly quiet. The radio was off, but I didn't dare reach for it to turn it on. How had this day turned out so horrible after it started out so amazing? The tension was so thick I could have probably grabbed some out of the air and stuck it in my back pocket. It was a scene from a movie, no one particular movie, but nearly every drama had a scene in it like this one. It was the moment where the person is wrongfully accused of something, but she doesn't have the evidence to prove her innocence. Except in the movie I would've miraculously escaped the security room, slid down the elevator cord thingy, climbed out of the ventilation shaft, snuck to my secret safety deposit box, got a gun, some fake I.D.s, and a few thousand dollars, and then began my mission of redemption. And even though the cops were on my trail, I would find a way to outsmart them time and time again. By the end of the movie I would win and be looked at with these new eyes from everyone that said "Innocent" in them. But mom's eyes were far from saying that. They were still revolving around the big red flashing sign that read, *Guilty!* Maybe I watch too much T.V.?

As it usually turns out, we were quiet all the way until about a block from the house.

"How could you let something like this happen, Erin?"

I would be lying if I said I felt as guilty as my mom thought I was, but I would look like an idiot if I didn't take at least some of the blame on myself, but why should I? The cameras showed that I wasn't even looking when they did it, and I honestly had no clue! How much more innocent do you have to be? O.J. was there, bloody glove, ran from the cops, and he still got off, but not me! Why don't we call Carrie over and have her take all the key notes for the media while we were at it… Something bold swelled inside my chest. I wanted to be able to defend myself, but for some reason my mind jumbled all that up and my mouth did what it does best.

"How could *I* let this happen? *Right!* Now I'm supposed to be able to read people's minds and stop them from doing things that I don't know they're doing."

"Don't you take that tone with me!" she interrupted.

"Oh, I'm sorry, I just thought since you were going to put me in handcuffs that I should at least go down swinging!"

"Keep talking and you'll just dig your hole deeper!"

"I'm sure you've already dug it, thrown me in it, and filled it back up for me, Mom!"

"And what's *that* supposed to mean?"

I decided to take a page from Kylie's book.

"Exactly what I said! I'm innocent! I didn't do anything wrong and you're ready to...to..."

"I'm not ready to do anything. I just expected more out of you, that's all!"

"More than being innocent! How much more do you want? I didn't even know!"

"Well, you're not hanging out with them anymore, do you understand?"

"Pssh," I sounded. I even rolled my eyes, threw my arms across my chest, and looked out the window.

"*Do what?* Don't you *Pssh* me! What's gotten into you?"

"How about being treated like I'm a criminal when I haven't done anything!"

"I'm not treating you like..."

"You already thought I was guilty before the tape stopped, Mom!"

She tried to argue, but I interrupted her.

"Why don't you just cancel the party, ground me, lock me in my room, and do whatever else it is you want to do because it's not going to matter! I know the truth! You can say all you want, I don't care!"

We pulled up the house just as I finished. Perfect timing! I opened the car door and slammed it shut. Mom tried to yell, but I was already through the front door. It slammed shut too! Ian rushed around the corner from the kitchen, his eyes wide, "What's wrong?"

"Nothing! I'm just running for my life!" I said sarcastically.

I could tell he didn't appreciate the attitude, but I didn't care. Before the sun went down I'm sure everyone would be thinking of how they could punish me for my terrible crime.

I could hear mom and dad talking downstairs. I think I heard Ian try to argue for me too, but I knew it wouldn't matter. It was the same as always! Parents are right, children are wrong. If a teenager ever tries to prove anything to their mom or dad it always results in, "Oh, I forgot, you're a teenager, you know everything!" I think if I hear one of them say that I might throw something through my window! Or maybe I shouldn't... Maybe I should sit in my desk chair and play the role of the evil villain who's the mastermind behind it all... yeah, I'm sure that'd really piss them off!

A minute or two later my door burst open like I

knew it would. I guess knocking's not a big deal when you're a mad parent. I thought about being naked when they came in just to make it harder for them, but I didn't care that much. It's amazing how weird my mind works when I'm mad!

"You had better explain yourself, Erin," my dad said right away.

"Like that's gonna matter," I scoffed, rolling my eyes, "I'm already guilty, right *Mom*?"

"One more attitude from you young lady and..." she started.

I shook my head, threw my arms out wide, and said, "and what? I'll be punished because you're too *stupid* to listen? Maybe if I say it slower you'll understand! I...didn't...do...anything!"

My dad only stood, perplexed, while my mom and I argued.

"Can't you see how you're acting? Can't you see that your new little girlfriends are responsible for this and you're acting like its okay?"

"*What*? Are you nuts? I'm acting this way because you're accusing me of something I *didn't* do!"

"Look! No one's saying you did..." my dad tried to calm down the situation.

"No! Mom is! And now she's too mad to admit it!"

I threw myself down on my bed and crossed my arms over my chest again.

"You heard what I said Erin, you're not hanging out with them anymore!"

"Yeah, and you heard what I said too…"

"ERIN!" My dad's voice made me jump. Ian shoved his way into the room and pushed his sleeves over his elbows.

"That's enough!" he yelled. My mom and dad turned around, their eyes wide that Ian would ever raise his voice to them. "If she says she didn't do anything, she didn't! I can believe her, why can't you?"

"Ian, stay out of this!" my mom growled, "Get downstairs and…"

"She didn't do anything! She's not a thief! I know Erin and so do you!"

"We're not saying she's thief! We're saying she's an accomplice, which is just as guilty, Ian! What you do is just as bad as who you hang out with! You both have to start understanding that… Look!" he continued, pointing to both of us, "I'm only going to say this one time. I don't know what kind of disrespectful water you've been drinking, but this stops NOW!" he slammed his fist down on my vanity and makeup rained from it. My mom and I both jumped. Ian did too but he masked his with a grimace.

"I don't believe you stole anything, Erin, and neither does your mom…"

I tried to speak up, but dad growled and I stopped.

"But those girls *did*! Now I want you…" he paused and pointed to Ian, "*both of you* to start looking really hard at these new kids you're hanging out with! You had better start cutting yourselves away from the bad ones now or else next time you'll find yourselves in Juvenile hall! Got it?"

Ian nodded, but I only stared at my mom and dad. "Got it?" he asked again, but I only looked away. I wanted to be far away from the both of them right now, but now I had nowhere to go even if I could. Carrie was acting weird, Kylie's mom was already looking at me differently because of that stupid halter, and Whitney was too busy gawking over Ian. And now Brit and Ash were thieves! When it all boiled down to it, Ian was the golden child. I couldn't depend on him to stick by me forever. There was only Jake.

My dad took a couple of forceful steps toward me, but I stood up instead of cowering. What was he gonna do, hit me? A police officer hit his daughter? Can you say "Bye-bye badge!"

"I said..." he started.

"I *heard* what you said! So ground me or whatever, but don't think that I'm talking to you! You've never picked my friends and you're not starting now! Don't think we're going to be all buddy-buddy anymore... daddy's little princess and mommy's little...whatever..."

My dad swelled with rage, my mom took a hesitant step forward.

"I'm serious!" I said, despite the fact that I was sure a hard slap was about to come. "Leave me alone! I've never done anything wrong and now I get this..."

I shook my head and sat back down on my bed. "Just leave me alone... Just get out of my room and leave me alone..." *Some birthday...*

Chapter Thirteen ~
September 24th - Monday

My brother called Jake, Whitney, and unfortunately Carrie, and gave them the dirt on what was going on over the weekend. So it was no surprise when I walked outside this morning and Jake's truck wasn't parked alongside the street. My mom and dad knew better than to try and talk to me. I didn't do the dishes before I left, either. Maybe that'd give them some time to think about how they were treating me when I wasn't even doing anything wrong.

Ian was mad too, but I think it was a mixture of things for him. He was probably upset he had decided to stay in that day instead of spend it with me. Even though he was younger he still had this big brother attitude whenever something happened to me. It was cute most of the time, but now it was almost annoying. Everything was annoying... A few blocks away we turned and started along the railroad tracks like we used to and then I saw it, a silver truck parked at the next railroad crossing. I smiled from ear to ear.

"Erin, we shouldn't! You know how mad..."

"Yeah, I do!" I replied with a glare. But maybe if I kept mom and dad scared they'd see how much they missed the *good* me, the one that would never steal a halter...maybe they'd start trusting me; after all, I *am* sixteen. I ran into Jake's arms and almost started crying. It felt so good to be so close to him after a whole weekend away. He smelled so good. I almost forgot the smell. He was so cute.

"I'm sorry babe," he said.

"It's not your fault my parents are stupid!" I replied.

"Hey Jake," Ian said.

"Hey *Wonder Boy*."

"Hey man, I don't think you should..." Ian started, but Jake interjected.

"Look, it's nothing man...don't worry about it. If anyone asks I punched you and made you two get in the truck," he said with a smirk. Ian couldn't help but crack a smile.

"Come on..."

As soon as we got in, Jake turned down the radio and shook his head. "I can't believe Brit and Ash would do that," he said. "That's so wild, man..."

"I just hope they're not mad at me..." I replied.

"Why, you didn't nark, did you?"

"No, I think that's what made mom so mad!"

The more I thought about it, the less it made sense... I mean, why would I take up for them if they stole something, especially when *I'm* the one getting in trouble?

"Good, because..." he started.

"*Good?*" I blurted, "*I* didn't say anything...that doesn't mean that my stupid mom didn't!"

At school I was surrounded by hateful looks. Brit and Ash stood by Michael and T.J., all of them glared at us like we were the scum of the earth.

"What's your problem?" Jake asked.

"I got no beef with you, man... it's your girl's mouth."

"What about it?" he said, stepping up to T.J.

"I smell a rat," teased Michael.

"She didn't say anything..." interrupted Ian. "It was our mom!"

"Sure," nodded Ash. She glared at me. Brit rolled her eyes and turned around to look in her locker mirror.

"Well maybe your mommy needs to shut her mouth too, Mitchell!" said Michael.

"Maybe I'll shut yours!" growled Ian. He dropped his book bag and everything in the hall came to a halt. There was complete silence.

"You better tell your boy to shut his mouth!" T.J. said, glancing between Ian and Jake.

"The both of you need to shut yours, first, and listen to what I'm saying. They didn't say anything!"

"Yeah, whatever, it's just like you to take the side of your *trophy*, ain't it?"

Jake shoved Michael back against the locker and pinned his arms against his sides.

"You better go take a cold shower or something pee-wee, unless you want practice to be painful..."

"Screw you, Jake!" he yelled.

"We'll leave that up to his little whore," chimed Ash.

The halted crowd sounded, "Ohh!"

My face blushed. I couldn't think of anything else to do...so I smacked her!

Ian yanked me away from her just as Brit dropped her bag and reached for me.

T.J. punched Ian when he leapt forward to pull me off of Ash. I guess he thought Ian was reaching for one of the girls. Jake let go of Michael and grabbed T.J. and then slammed him into the locker. Michael grabbed his chemistry book and hit Jake in the back of the head.

Mrs. Prichard tried to intervene, but Dyson cut her off.

"I got it Mrs. P!"

Jake fell to the floor after another hit. Michael and T.J. both separated when Dyson stood over top of Jake and shoved them away. He growled and stepped toward the huddle that was Brit, Ash, Ian, and I, but Ian shuffled away from Dyson so quickly that we both fell backwards and Brit and Ash cowered by the locker. I've never seen anything so scary in my life. His eyes were huge!

"Thank you, Mr. Edwards! All of you on your feet! Now!"

"So you're all suspended tomorrow?" Whitney asked at lunch.

"No, just the ones who threw punches. Michael, T.J., Brit, and Me..."

"And Michael and T.J. aren't allowed to play in Friday's homecoming game, either," Ian said with a sort of chuckle.

"I don't see how *that's* funny," inserted Carrie. "I mean, you should all get in trouble and your mom should be..."

"Girl, shut yo mouth an' drink the rest o' your skinny white-girl juice or whatever it is you be drinkin' that makes you talk so stupid!"

Carrie mumbled the rest to herself. Ian looked mad at Carrie. It was a sight I thought I'd never see. "So you're taking their side?" I asked.

"I can't believe you would think that the most popular girls in school would steal a shirt," she replied.

"I wouldn't *think* that, but I saw it on tape! They did it right behind my back!"

Carrie rolled her eyes.

"Oh, so now I'm a liar, too?"

"Whatever," said Carrie, standing from her seat, "the only thing we know is what *you've* told us and that's that your mom is the one who gave the security guards their names..."

"So you're trying to say that she's a snitch?" asked Whitney.

"Oh, and of course *you're* so quick to defend *her*," commented Carrie, rolling her eyes.

"Yeah, and so should you!" countered Whitney, "Isn't she your friend?"

"I'm not friends with snitches!"

The comment hurt, but the expression on Ian's face hurt worse. She said *snitches*. Carrie had just dumped him because of me, and with only four days until homecoming."

"Enough a' that stupid skank!" said Kylie with a wave, "Did ya'll see the way my man laid the beat down? He ripped through you fools like a tornado...like a... *fine*, black tornado!"

"Suspended!" howled Mom.

"Erin, I thought we had an understanding?" added Dad.

I refused to answer.

"First, you storm out of here this morning without doing the dishes and now you get suspended?" added Mom.

"She didn't..." Ian started.

"*ERIN*, NOT *IAN!*" growled my dad, "If I want your input I'll ask for it!"

"I don't care what you *want!*" growled Ian. He slammed his fist on the table, "I'm telling you the *truth*! And I'll say it when *I* want to!" He looked a lot like my father right now, only about a hundred pounds lighter. He was mad, madder than I've ever seen him. It was obvious that losing Carrie was starting to weigh on him and he only had one way to get it all out.

"Boy," my Dad said, as he started around the table.

"The girls started it! Erin was defending *you* for snitching!" finished Ian, pointing to Mom.

"Oh," sounded my Mom. She touched her chest and

made a face like she was shocked. "Well, how wonderful, I guess I need my own A-team to go around beating people up for me!"

Ian and I looked to each other, confused. *A-team?*

"*Snitching?*" scoffed my Dad, "What's gotten into the two of you? Don't you think that turning in a couple of thieves is important?"

"Not when it makes your life a living hell!" I said, "Can't you see what you two are doing to us? You're turning our friends against us." When that didn't seem to phase him, I added. "Those girls, they're two of the most popular girls at school! Jake almost got his head bashed in with a chemistry book because of *you*, Mom!"

If my mom was at all bothered by this, she didn't show it. Her face was hard and cold, just like my dad's.

"I *will not* tolerate these attitudes in my house! Do you understand me?" said my dad. I could tell that he was trying his hardest to calm down, but it was my turn not to care.

"Look Dad," started Ian.

"Look *NOTHING,* damn it! If *you* want to play football and *you* want to date Mr. High school stud, then you'll both stop acting like you ate bowls of stupid for breakfast and get your heads out of your butts! This little rebellion ends now! I work too hard to put up with *this* nonsense when I come home. I deal with idiots all day and then I have to come home to my own kids getting in trouble over the same stupid stuff! Popularity and little high school he said, she said crap...none of it matters the second you graduate and I don't know why you two are so deep in this! I thought your mother and I raised you better than this..."

"This is our life you're saying isn't important. You realize that, don't you?" asked Ian.

"No one's saying...," started my mom.

"No!" he interrupted, "Listen to yourselves... You're saying that Jake shouldn't be important to her and the football shouldn't be a big deal and that popularity isn't anything and that being picked on is no big deal...but it is! You just don't remember what it was like!"

"I'm done with this conversation," said my Dad, "Remember what I said! If you two want to keep this up, then homecoming and football and everything for the next couple of years depends on your attitudes. I'll not put up with this! I won't! Don't test me!"

Ian and I took that as our "you're dismissed" and gathered our things and walked up stairs. For some reason that's beyond me, my mom had a snotty look in her eye like she proved something, so I couldn't resist the urge to snatch it away. I wanted to *make* her feel bad that this was all her fault. I wanted her to see that she started all of this by not trusting me and now that we stood up for her, she was the one being childish by taking none of the blame.

"Happy?" I said. I almost wanted them to try and tell me I couldn't date Jake; I wanted them to say I couldn't go to homecoming, but they didn't. My mom only raised her eyebrows and continued to look at me as I walked past. When did my parents become *so* stupid?

Chapter Fourteen

September 28th - Friday

The week went quickly, just like the others. Tuesday I stayed home on suspension. My mom tried to give me extra chores, but I just looked at her like she was stupid and only did my usual chores. I'm not her slave! I refuse to be punished when I didn't do anything wrong. Have Brittany and Ashley come over and dust the living room, not me!

Kylie told me that her mom doesn't want her hanging out with me until all this is cleared up. I guess she's afraid my *rebellious* nature might rub off on Kylie. I should just call her and tell her that as long as she trusts her daughter she won't have to worry about things like this. Kylie said she told her mom to keep dreaming, that she'd never abandon me, but I could tell in her eyes that she was saying and doing two different things.

Carrie hasn't said a word to anyone since the argument in the lunchroom on Monday. Rumor has it that she's going to homecoming with Joe Gregory. I think Ian almost cried when he heard. If I get the chance to hit anyone else, I think it'll be her.

Whitney has been my only shoulder next to Jake, and I think that even she has her motives. It's obvious that she's sweeping in for the rebound on Ian, but I'm not sure he's picking up on her hints. She keeps waiting on him to ask her to homecoming, but I still don't think he sees her that way. He's been in love with Carrie for over a year now and I'm sure it'll take some time for him to get over her before he even thinks of another girl. But so far, now that Carrie's at least out of the way, Whitney seems more patient, and as determined as ever. If she unbuttons her shirt a couple more buttons and gets a little more aggressive, I'm sure he'll notice her in no time. Maybe I could give her some hints.

My mom allows Whitney to come over one afternoon a week to study, and once she thinks we're done, she makes Whitney go home. I feel like one of those prisoners in movies who is allowed a visitor once a week. Maybe I can trade a pack of cigarettes and get a phone call? We're learning about Hitler in history and the similarities between him and my parents are amazing. I keep waiting on a train to stop on the tracks down the street so my parents to load me up.

Ian and I walk down the tracks every morning to the first crossing and get a ride to school from Jake. He's so great! What other boyfriend would risk so much for the girl he loves? I wish the situation was better so that we wouldn't have to put up with my stupid parents coming between us. It's almost like Romeo and Juliet in a way, except I haven't even met his parents, but I'm sure they're five times cooler than mine. It was like every-thing was going so great between us, but now there's all this confusion and drama. I can't wait until my stupid parents get their heads right and things can get back to normal.

On Wednesday he asked me to sneak out with him tonight after the homecoming game, but I don't think that sneaking out on the weekend is such a good idea. Parents are always watching on those days, if you ask me. At least, I would if I were a parent, and that seems to be when the kids at school get caught the most. So I said, "Why wait two days for what you can have to-night?" By the look in his eyes I could tell that he thought it was sexy and boy did Wednesday night go well. He wants me, and bad! It's such a cool feeling to have him so ready, but yet at the same time know he's so patient. I wish I could bottle how he makes me feel and sell it...I'd be rich!

My mom and dad came to the game as always, but I refused to sit beside them. I wasn't going to let them ruin what little fun I got to have these days. My mom said she only let me come to support Ian, but I don't care. I would've come anyway! Like a locked door and a "Oh, no you won't young lady" keeps me from going where I want to go... I keep waiting for the final blow or another threat so I can show them how serious I am. They sound like a skipping CD, saying "grow up" but they don't realize that I'm just playing this game the same way they are; the only difference is I have one thing on my side that they don't...I'm right. It makes it so much easier to do things when you know you're right.

Whitney and Kylie say that my mom and dad won't tell me I can't go to homecoming because they've already spent the money for a dress, but I know better. They'll do anything to prove a point, and apparently it doesn't matter if they're right or wrong. Anything to remind me that "I live under their roof" or any of those other millions of corny lines parents have used since the world began. As long as I'm a *good little girl*, I can go outside and play...*whatever*, I'm not a kid anymore!

Our homecoming game is against our rivals the Yellow Brooke Bobcats. Michael and T.J. are being punished by Coach Irving and have to bring water out to the players with the freshmen. It's so degrading, I love it! Brittany and Ashley were here earlier, but they're probably too embarrassed to show their faces around here. I mean, after all, their boyfriends went from being the starting fullback and tight-end to benchwarmers and water-boys. Jake wasn't as happy about the punishment as I thought he'd be.

"I wish they could at least play!" he said. "Sure, what they did was wrong, but we're going to be hurting without them..."

After the game, Whitney and I walked out onto the field and congratulated our boys. Mom and Dad were giving me the Nazi stare so we had to leave soon after. When we got to the car there was wet toilet paper all over it and in the middle of the windshield, in bright red lipstick, was the word "*Snitch!*"

My mom and dad were furious. They looked at me, but only one thing came to mind.

"What?" I said, as if I didn't see it, "Oh, that? Oh, but *that's* no big deal, right?"

I got a thorough butt chewing for that one, but I enjoyed it. I think I proved my point. Maybe they'd learn what it was like for me to walk down the halls every day? After all, for high school to not be such a big deal they were really getting all bent out of shape about it.

Chapter Fifteen

September 29th - Saturday (Homecoming)

The morning went by almost painlessly. Around noon, mom and dad started ranting about chores and making promises that Homecoming would be missed if Ian and I didn't finish them in time. Yeah right! I'd like to see my mom and dad stop me from going. Who wastes hundreds of dollars on a dress and *then* decides to make rules?

Ian didn't seem to care though. He spent most of the morning skulking around mumbling things under his breath. He seemed completely miserable and who could blame him? I mean, what Carrie did was hideous. How could she choose popularity over her friends? And so close to homecoming?

Whitney called at two-thirty wondering how everything was going and if I needed her help getting ready. I thought about it for a moment and told her to come on over. At best, we could all travel together and they would at least look like they had one another. I asked Mrs. Hitler if Whitney could come over and she told me it was okay as long as Mr. Hitler didn't care. I'm sure they kept a close eye over us hoodlums though. I mean, you know how teenagers can be with makeup these days, especially if it's stolen makeup. Whitney didn't think it was all that funny, but I got a good laugh. She wouldn't understand! After all, she wouldn't know what it's like to have parents that don't trust you and punish you for things you had no control over. I spent most of the day wondering if I was going to get punished for the car being decorated last night, but surprisingly nothing came of it. I guess I had an alibi this time? But technically, since I go to the same high school as the kids who did it, according to my dad I could be an accomplice. Parents are so dumb!

Ian did lighten up a bit around Whitney. I was beginning to wonder if something was coming of this, but then I remembered I had more important things to worry about, like how I was going to keep my control over Jake. Was tonight going to be *the* night? After all, there were going to be a lot of hot girls at the dance, and there's no way I'm losing him to some chick at homecoming! That's how most couples' separate, at stupid little dances where others can interfere, especially with everything setup the way it is; the lights turned down all low and mysterious, the slow and rhythmic songs that almost promise passion, and then the next thing you know people are all rubbing on one another and it's like sex, but standing up and with clothes on.

Jake was there to pick us up like always. It felt like months since he and I had been together, at least with my parents *knowing* that we were together. I had been sneaking out a lot lately to meet him down the street. Longer and longer each time, it's been relieving to have him there for me. Ian's been *too* sidetracked with Carrie and Whitney's been *too* obsessed with Ian to worry about me. It's just nice to know that someone's there for me. Of course, it wasn't all about me once I got in the truck, but what's a puppet master to do?

Before we got in the truck, Jake gave me a tender kiss and leaned close to me.

"I've missed you," he said, "I even had a dream about you last night."

"Really?" I asked, "Was it a *good* one?"

I wondered if he would know what I meant by a *good one*, but by the look in his eye I could tell he did. He's dreaming about me now? Wow! I must be doing better than I thought. Something about that little comment made my night. In a way I wasn't really worried anymore. Jake has dreams about me. It's such an awesome feeling to know that someone cares about you so much that they dream about you.

The gymnasium was transformed into this basketball court of a dance hall, equipped with balloons and ribbons and whatever they could find to hang from the basketball goals. There were tables scattered across the court with folding chairs circled around them. People were everywhere. The boys who don't dance sat on the bleachers in the darkness just beyond the dance floor. *Losers!* If they would only get some courage they'd probably get a number or two before the night was over, or maybe more, well, if Carrie were here.

On one end of the gym was the stage for theatre. Two separate sets of stairs led up to it. In the middle of the stage a big sign read: *Homecoming.* Groups and couples waited in front of a black starlit wall to take pictures. Dyson and Kylie were already in line.

Mrs. Prichard scoured the room like a predator, or better yet, *the* predator. Some stupid couples thought they could just slip back into the darker areas and make-out, but they must've forgotten that Mrs. Prichard could simply turn on her heat seeking eye-balls and see them in the dark. Okay, seriously, I watch *too much* television!

Kylie and Dyson spotted us and Kylie waved us over.

"In line already, huh?" Jake asked Dyson. Dyson rolled his eyes and pointed his thumb toward Kylie.

"We're takin' pictures before we get all steamy," commented Kylie with a look to Dyson like she was undressing him with her eyes. "I won't see you complain'n on the dance floor in a couple a minutes!"

Ian stifled a chuckle.

"What you laugh'in at cutie pie, *you* my date, he's just my suga-daddy!"

Ian's chuckle turned into a snort.

"Huh-uh," countered Whitney, jokingly. She grabbed his arm, "He's here with me!"

Kylie glanced at me, her eyebrows high, but I was waiting to see what Ian's reaction would be. Surprisingly, he looked at Whitney and smiled. She nearly blushed. I hadn't seen her so happy in months.

"You just make'n your way around the group then, huh?" teased Kylie. Whitney's beam diminished a bit, but then Kylie quickly added, "I think this one's a lot better than the last."

"A'ight *Wonder Boy*, back off my woman then, so she don't get all excited," said Dyson.

"Huh-uh," waved Kylie, "Don't you be tryin' your black tornado on me and my cutie-pie."

After a few minutes they pointed out their table and we walked over to put our things down.

"I'm gonna go to the bathroom," announced Jake. I gave him the thumbs up, as if I was proud of him. He smirked and shook his head.

"Want anything to drink?" Ian asked Whitney and me. "Yes."

Ian went to get the drinks and I sat down beside her. "Ian, huh?" I asked as if I hadn't expected it.

"What?" she asked, innocently, "It's just…"

"A dream come true?" I inserted.

Her face went blank. She stammered for an explanation.

"It's okay," I said with a laugh.

It was adorable how sweet she seemed. Wait a minute! Why did she seem so sweet and innocent to me? We used to be mirror images of one another…

"What's the matter?" she asked.

Apparently, my little realization stole the expression from my face. I looked at her and it was obvious how worried she looked. She probably thought I had a problem with it.

"Oh, nothing," I said.

"No, Erin, please tell me...does it bother you?" she asked.

"No," I replied.

Why did she seem so sweet and cuddly like a little puppy right now? Did I still seem that way? How had everything changed so quickly? I know we hadn't *exactly* spent every waking moment together like we had before I was with Jake, but that didn't mean that...

Ian was back and handing us our drinks. He looked at me with that confused stare, but I ignored him and quickly took the drink and guzzled it. If I wasn't sweet and innocent anymore then what was I? I suddenly wished, and not for the first time, that I had someone to talk to about these sorts of things. The only person to talk to would be Kylie, but she wouldn't be interested in my drama. She'd probably say something like "Why all you white girls gotta be all *'Oh, no, what am I going to do'* all the time? It's just life!" And then there's a good chance that would only make things worse.

Jake came back from the bathroom just as a slow song started to play. He must've seen the expression on my face because he leaned really close to me.

"Would you like to dance?" he asked as he kissed me gently on the forehead.

I started to answer, but Mrs. Prichard materialized out of thin air behind him like the villains always do in the movies and quickly spat, "Mr. Cunningham, let's try to keep tonight's PDA to a minimum, shall we?"

"Yes, Mrs. Prichard," he replied almost methodically.

He held his hand out again and I took it. As we walked to the dance floor, Jake looked at me almost the same way Ian and Whitney had.

"What's the matter? I haven't seen you this scared since the first day I spoke to you."

I smiled. It seemed like so long ago now, but it'd only been a couple of months. A voice urged me to tell him how I felt. *It's Jake...you can trust him*, it said.

"Am I still sweet and..." suddenly the thought of me asking my boyfriend if I was innocent crossed my mind. Of course I wasn't innocent anymore...

"What's the matter?" he asked again, "Erin, you're acting so weird. Of course you're sweet! You're the girl you were when I met you," he said, "nothing's changed."

The weight lifted off of my shoulders. *Oh, thank God!*

I slid closer to him and laid my head on his chest. It's times like these when I wished he was shorter. It didn't matter though, because being close to him was what was comfortable. There was just something about his smell and the fact that he could wrap his arms around me that made me relax. It felt like I was being swallowed with love...and cologne.

Chapter Sixteen

October 31st - Wednesday (Halloween)

The whole month of October was a blur. School was getting a lot harder. My grades were going up and down for a while, but currently they're staying on the upside. I think I've managed all B's. The play was such a success in Mrs. Prichard's class that they've decided to show it to the whole school in December before Christmas break. I'm not too excited about it, but Mrs. Prichard's agreed to get the whole class involved and use it for a test grade instead of writing a term paper at the end of the class. Have I mentioned how much I *hate* writing?

Jake has somehow managed excellent grades, even though we spend almost every other night together. Of course, I'm still grounded, but that doesn't really stop anything. Whitney and Ian are *officially* a thing now. I've never seen either of them happier, which is just as annoying as it is exciting. There's just such a difference between puppy love and the real love that Jake and I have for each other. Tomorrow will be our two month anniversary. I can't wait to see what he has planned. I thought about talking to my mom about the important day, but she wouldn't understand. Her and dad both have turned into these machines, these *Nazi* machines, that don't listen to anything anymore unless it has to do with grades or something unimportant, football this or coupon that...

Whitney's over almost every other day now. She says it's for *studying* purposes, but I know better. Mom and dad sort of slacked off from Ian; mainly because he's their favorite anyway, and secondly, because he manages to play football and miraculously pull straight A's out of his butt, just like Jake. I thought girls were supposed to be smarter than boys? Why can't I make it look easy like Ian does? Maybe I could if I just cared more?

Earlier this month mom mentioned that she *might* remove our grounding if we continued doing well. I felt like the warden was promising me parole or something. I mean, does she think I forgot who *actually* stole the halter? I've been the innocent one on death row for the past month now and she's acting like she's going to do me a favor? I thought to continue to defy her, but the sound of freedom and weekends with Jake merely inches from my grasp outweighed my stubbornness. And besides, Jake told me to keep my cool.

"Just play the game," he said, "If you just play the game a little longer then we'll be able to play our games..."

As exciting as it sounded, I have been biting my tongue for the past few weeks in anticipation. Any day now and Ian and I are free. Well, I think he's about as free as he's ever been *now*, but as for me, I'll be back on the road again. Oh, and the best part of all is that *ungrounded* in Hitler-mom lingo also translates into *driving license*. German is a funny language, isn't it?

Dad got his promotion the fifteenth of this month. He's officially...uh...something? I think he just graduated from having to sneak around the make-out spots with a flashlight. What a job! Speaking of make-out spots, Carrie and Joe Gregory *were* dating for a week or so back around Homecoming, but then another few nights in the backseat of his car and Carrie dumped him for another guy. Talk about rejection! Apparently, she stayed with the next guy for a week or two, just long enough to get a few gifts and what she wanted from the backseat of his car, and then she moved on to her latest victim. She's turning into Davis-Buckley High's Tramp of the Year. At first, I thought Ian might care about how bad she's been lately, but I was wrong. It was like he never knew her. Whatever Whitney was doing was working because Ian's eyes were fixed on her.

Coach Irving made Jake start hanging out with T.J. and Michael again. It wasn't something he forced them to do, but he sat them next to one another on the benches and on the bus rides out to the football games. I guess over time they started getting along again. Yesterday they apologized to me for what they said and it seemed genuine enough. I told them that I didn't have any problem with them, but that I didn't want to hang out with their girlfriends anymore. Jake said that he finally got it into their heads that my mom was the culprit. I also said that whoever decorated my mom and dad's car is awesome. T.J. and Michael only smiled and nodded along, that told me enough.

My mom said she was going to hang around the house tonight with dad and pass out candy. Ian and Whitney are going over to her house to watch a scary movie marathon. Wee!

How much actual *watching* will be involved, no one knows...

As for me, Jake, and the rest of the *cool* world, Rochelle Winslow's dad is out of town for the week, so she volunteered to host the Halloween party. Her older brother Danny and his friends are coming up from the Big Green – Greenhorn University – to show us how to throw a *real* party. I can't wait! Everyone's supposed to be keeping quiet about it so the teachers can't warn anyone and the small town gossip doesn't spread like it always does, to the police. It's only supposed to be around fifty people, but you never know how these things turn out. The only catch is to find a way to tell my mom that I'm going out with Jake to a party, without saying I'm going out with Jake to a party.

"And Kylie's going to be there?" Mom asked for the seventh time.

"Her *and* Dyson, as far as I know," I replied. The *As far as I know clause* is just as handy as our mutual definition of *tidy*.

Mom looked at me skeptically. Its times like these I wish Ian was here to say that he'd be there too, but unfortunately he was getting to have his fun without being held beneath a microscope. It's so annoying to be so treated like such a child. It's not like I'm six and about to cross the street for the first time.

"What's the phone number?"

"Phone number?" I echoed stupidly.

"Yes, so I can reach you if I need to,"

"If you need to *what*...see if I've peed? You have my cell number, just let me take my cell with me and you'll have a number..."

"No," she snapped, "I need a number!"

"Want Jake's?"

"Now that you mention it, yes, and why don't you call him to see if he knows a number where I can reach you at tonight,"

"Mom, be serious! I don't know the number of the place. As a matter of fact, I don't even know where *it* is, he's the one who knows. There's going to be more than thirty people there, so there's plenty of protection..."

"Or harm!"

"Yeah, well, I'm sure the same can be said about high school mom, but let's face it, there's danger everywhere..."

She huffed. I was beginning to get the feeling I was winning. I needed to say something to seal the deal, something clever.

"Kylie will be there and she always knows this sort

of stuff. You can call her if you need me, and maybe even her mom will know? You'll have my number, Jake's, Kylie's, *and* I'll be home by curfew. I've never been late for curfew, nothing's changed, you know?"

"We'll see?"

I couldn't help myself, "What's *that* supposed to mean?"

"Well, you haven't necessarily proven yourself trustworthy since the incident."

"Well, I haven't had much of a chance boarded up in my room, have I?"

My mind screamed at me. *To much! Abort! Abort!*

"Mom...," I quickly added. I could see the stress lines across her forehead. I was beginning to strike a nerve...the *no* nerve. "I'm responsible, I'm trustworthy, and I'm comfortable with who I'm going with. Jake wouldn't let anything happen to me, and neither would Kylie, or Dyson. If you don't trust me, you can at least trust them."

The *no* nerve diminished with the stress lines.

"Okay, but remember curfew is eleven,"

"*Eleven?* But we don't have school tomorrow!"

My mom gave me the sideways look that said how dangerously close I was to seeing the *no* nerve resurface.

"*Eleven it is!*" I said, mocking enthusiasm.

By the looks of the cars parked alongside the driveway up to the house, there were a lot more than fifty people at the party. Music screamed out of the wide open front door. Bodies were everywhere, some conscious, some not. The second floor bedroom lights flashed on and then off and then on again. Jake pointed and laughed. By the looks of things, the Big Green showed up, and Rochelle and her brother got more than they had bargained for. To say "the house was trashed" would have been the understatement of the century. Plastic Dixie cups lay surrounded by little pools of what looked and smelled like urine. The whole house was a sauna even though it felt nice outside. Everyone stood inches away from one another practically shouting over the music. I didn't recognize half of the people. As soon as we walked through the kitchen into the living room, Rochelle rushed by with a large bowl and disappeared around the corner. We heard a guy retch and then a loud splatter sound that told us she didn't make it in time. I couldn't help but wince. I did my best not to try and look as we walked past. At least it was a hardwood floor and not carpet…

We found Kylie and Dyson by the pool in the back. The boys walked away to get some drinks.

"Has my mom called you?" I asked.

"No, why, am I your secretary now?" she said with a smirk.

"So, who all's here?"

"Now that you're here, every skank I know!" she teased.

"Aw now…" interjected Dyson, as he returned with a drink in his hand, "You just jealous *Wonder Boy* done stood you up for that quiet lil' sweet thang…"

Kylie rolled her head around to look at Dyson, "Don't you be talk'n bout my cutie-pie cheatin' on me!" she said, waving her finger, "I'll beat down some white girl she steal my cutie-pie from me, say I won't!"

Dyson saw another guy from the football team and walked away shaking his head, laughing. Kylie turned to me, looked over her shoulder, checking on Dyson, and then said, "You had better keep your eyes on Jake tonight, cause I know there's a lotta eye-candy out there keep'n their eyes on him."

I was shocked, hurt, and insulted all at once. "What do you mean? Do you think I shouldn't trust him?" I spat.

"I didn't say all that! I'm just sayin' that boys can get all distracted if you don't make em' hungry for what you got for em'. And Jake, well, he's always hungry, so I hear."

I wanted to smack her, but even in the heat of such a moment I knew better than to sign my death wish with Kylie. "Well, he hasn't been!" I replied. "He's been patient and sweet the whole two months. Maybe you're hearing wrong..."

"Yeah, but you gotta remember girl, he's gotten the goodies before," she said, with a hint of sadness in her eyes. "Now it's like a drug and he's gonna be addicted."

"What do you mean?" I wanted to laugh at how crazy she sounded. It was like some sort of vampire movie or something.

"Crack heads be gettin' their crack from wherever they can, girl," she explained.

So what if Jake always wanted to have sex with me, that *is* what people who're in love do, isn't it? Even though we hadn't yet, I wasn't going to tell Kylie. I couldn't hide my emotions.

"Maybe I like the fact that he's addicted to me," I said.

"Yeah," she smirked, "ain't nothing wrong wit that... I just hope you're the only dealer he has though."

She might've continued if something wouldn't have happened to distract her. From behind us, Carrie walked past in a miniskirt. Her shirt was so low that her cleavage was distractive, even for me, and I'm a girl. Most of the girls on the deck were staring at her with a love, hate glare. They would love to have her body, but they hated her because they didn't and their boyfriends' drooling over what they saw only reminded them of the fact. I decided to use that moment as a break to get away and go to the bathroom. Before I could even begin to grumble about the nerve Kylie had in warning me about something she didn't even understand, a girl rushed past me, followed by a guy on her heels.

"Come on..." he pleaded.

"No! I can't believe you were checking her out right in front of me!" the girl growled.

Uh-oh! It looked like Carrie was doing her usual damage and doing it well. Once I came back from the most disgusting bathroom ever, Jake was standing next to Kylie and Dyson beside the pool.

"This party's a bust..." Jake commented. "What'd

you think? Wanna head out and waste the night some-where else?"

Kylie eyed me and then Dyson smirked. "Course she does," Dyson teased, "look at them little pigtails ready to just spring to life." As he cackled and cowered from a shower of smacks from me and Kylie, Jake only laughed.

"Let me know if her mom calls, aight?" Jake said, shaking Dyson's hand.

My coat was shed as soon as Jake and I got in the truck. I could barely keep his hands off of me. Well, at least off of me enough to keep his eyes on the road. I could tell that our time apart had bothered him. This had been the first night in a long time that we had been able to spend together.

"You know," he said, eyeing me like clothed candy, "my parents are having dinner with some friends in Yellow Brooke tonight..." He raised his eyebrows excitedly. My heart skipped a beat. What should I do? I mean, I told my mom where I was going to be.

"I don't know," I replied, "My mom's all weirded-out and she might call the president or something."

His expression saddened a little. We came to a stop sign and he looked at me.

"Just you and me for an hour by ourselves," he offered. It did sound tempting, but what about my mom?

"If my mom calls Kylie and she finds out I'm not there..."

"Dyson's already covering for us..." Jake interrupted.

"But my dad's out on patrol tonight. If he sees your truck at your house, he'll know that..."

"It'll be in the garage. My mom and dad are gone, remember?"

I couldn't help but smile. "You've got this all planned out, don't you?"

With a smile, he pulled a rose from the same place he had kept my birthday present. My heart melted. When I looked up I could see the intensity in his eyes. He wanted me so bad. I couldn't refuse him now, could I? What kind of girlfriend would I be if I kept denying him? I mean, how long could I keep him if I didn't let him win at least once in a while? And what would happen if I didn't? Why was everything playing out just like Ashley and Brittany said it would? He caressed me for a minute and gently kissed me. I closed my eyes. I could smell the rose in my face. He traced it across my cheeks, over my lips, and then down my neck to the bend in my shirt. Goosebumps rose all over my body, and then a speeding car passed by and I remembered that we were parked at a stop sign. I felt warm all over my body. My chest was heaving in anticipation. This was it...this was the moment.

"We don't have to stay long," he offered, recognizing the moment for what it was. "I just want to hold you for a while."

I couldn't speak. My thoughts were scattered. All I knew was that I was ready. I was finally ready. After two months of games and kissing and touching at the cabin and in the car I was ready to move on to the next stage, the last stage. I couldn't speak, I only nodded. We didn't say a word the entire drive to his house. The thought of being in his arms was overwhelming and I could tell the thought was the same for him.

I wanted things to go so much slower than they did, but just like always everything happened before I could think. The truck came to a halt in the garage and I was out the door. He led the way to the door, but I couldn't let him waltz in, I had to make it dramatic like it was in the movies. I attacked him just before the door. We stumbled in the house. He dropped his keys on the counter and lifted me up. I wrapped my legs around him. Soon, we had climbed the stairs to his bedroom and the door was shut behind us. Before I could blink, my shirt was off and so was his. It was so real, so passionate. My heart was racing. I felt so warm all over. It was so quiet in the house. Our voices echoed in the room. I could hear the sound of his breath against the stillness of the rest of the house.

Chapter Seventeen ~
Noвember 15th - Thursday

Over the course of the next two weeks it seemed like all Jake and I did was have sex. I mean, it wasn't *every* night, but then again we couldn't see each other every night. He's had to work a lot lately, so we've been texting back and forth while he's at work. When I *do* get to see him though, I make sure I make it count.

My mom and dad finally returned to a semi-reality and I guess the Hitlers inside of them surrendered. I was allowed to go out on a school night as long as I was back by eight and my homework was done. Now that I can live again, I'm so happy. I've been talking to a few other girls lately, trying to make friends, but there just doesn't seem to be any true potential out there since Whitney's too busy revolving around Ian and Carrie's with her sixteenth or seventeenth guy now. Jake and I have a bet that she'll be pregnant before we graduate. I think I'll win, but he thinks I'll never know and that she'll have an abortion before the gossip gets out. I think he's right.

To add an odd twist to my life, as if I needed it,

Brittany and Ashley walked up to me on Monday and apologized for all the hateful things that happened. They said that they'd like to invite Jake and me out to the cabin Saturday night if we wanted to come. We had a short, but good conversation. They really seemed like they meant it. Jake wasn't so sure about them, but he did say that Michael and T.J. had been really cool, so...

"Saturday night then?" he shrugged.

"I guess,"

"If it blows, we'll just find somewhere else to go," he added, pulling me close. I tried hard not to smile when he kissed me and then grabbed my butt. Girls walked past and giggled, the guys admired him, but I smacked his shoulder. I pretended like I was mad, but I'm positive that it didn't work. The thought of other girls noticing me and wanting my boyfriend was awesome. Everyone knew we had been to that last stage, even though no one talked about it and I think that made the guys even crazier. I never thought I'd see the day where I'd catch guys checking me out in class, or as I walked down the hall. For a while I couldn't get used to it. It reminded me of the days I walked next to Carrie, but now I think the girls who walk next to me feel that way.

Classes were *still* boring. After all, school doesn't change much even when everything else in your life seems to be going great. At lunch we saw Mrs. Prichard walk by with Carrie on one side and number eighteen or nineteen, Joshua Davis, on the other. She was probably caught making out with him, or worse. It didn't matter what it was because Mrs. Prichard looked pissed! Kylie said something that sounded like her usual rant. I wasn't really paying attention. I was too busy listening to Ian and Whitney talk about Thanksgiving. Not that I was listening to that conversation either, but I was actually wondering if they'd had sex yet. I noticed intensity in Whitney's eyes when she looked at him, a flash of something familiar. It reminded me of the way I felt every time I thought of having sex with Jake. There was even once when I dropped my fork and when I bent down I saw her leg rubbing his under the table. It was so sexy that it surprised me that Whitney would even do something like that. When she saw that I saw she stopped immediately and almost blushed. The fact that she blushed made me wonder if they had gone that extra mile yet.

At five o'clock Jake called and said he couldn't come over and pick me up to hang out tonight. His parents wanted him to come to work for the afternoon. I'm not *overly* upset about it, even though it is like the fourth time this week he's had to work. I mean, one night away from him shouldn't kill me, and it doesn't, but still... He really does have an awesome deal with his parents though. He mentioned something about *maybe* having to work on Saturday and Sunday too, but he said that it's not for sure yet. So it looks like my weekend is going to be pretty boring. I'll probably get dragged into raking leaves or something stupid, but I guess it's no worse than anything else. I *could* make it out to sound like I ditched him this weekend because I needed to study for some important test if I wanted to, but I'm sure Ian would botch that up nicely if mom happened to ask him, so I'd better not.

Whitney came over about thirty minutes later and we hung out in the kitchen until Ian came down. It was actually kind of cool talking to her for a while, but then I remembered that things were different now. She wasn't there to spend time with me anymore; she was there for Ian's pleasure. I spent most of the night in my room, painting my nails and reading part of some really boring story for English. It had to do with some yellow wallpaper and this crazy lady, it was weird. I'm supposed to write a report about it, but I can't seem to get past the fact that she was a crazy lady and that the story was so weird. It would've been a cool movie to watch though.

Ian came home by curfew and about forty-five minutes later the phone rang. That close to nine was a big no-no and I kept my fingers crossed that it wasn't for me. I cracked my door and listened downstairs. Mom sounded like she was trying to calm someone down and by the sound of things it was another adult. A few minutes later she yelled up the stairs for me and Ian to come down.

By the look on Ian's face I could tell he had been listening in on her conversation too. We hurried down the stairs, glancing oddly at one another. I'm sure we both thought the same thing: Dad. It wasn't until we walked into the kitchen and got a good look at mom that our stomachs tightened. I quickly slid into a kitchen chair. She was pale and shaking. My legs started shaking. I felt weak. Her eyes were darting back and forth, like she was lost in her own kitchen.

"What's the matter?" Ian asked immediately, "Is it dad?"

"Mom, are you alright?" I asked. *Your father was shot! He's been in a car accident!* My mind screamed.

She shook her head at Ian's question. We both blew a sigh of relief.

"It's Nana," she said, "She's in the hospital...your aunt Beth doesn't think she's gonna pull through this time." My hand came to my mouth. I was lost for words. It was one of those moments where I needed that perfect thing to say and I didn't have it. Ian looked at the floor for a second.

"When are we leaving?" he asked.

Mom looked up at him. "Well, honey, there's nothing we can do... I wouldn't want you guys to have to sit around and..."

"Come on, Erin," he said, "Let's go pack our things."

My mom hesitated. She looked at me like she was seeking *my* approval. I nodded along with Ian. "I'll call dad if you want to start packing mom."

She just looked around the room blankly and nodded. I can't imagine what she must be thinking knowing that she could lose her mom. A hole punched itself into my gut just then and made me wonder what it would feel like to lose my mom. I'd rather take a lifetime of the Hitler regime as long as I knew that when I came home at the end of the day she was going to be there. Ian started packing and called Whitney to tell her about everything. I called Jake, but he didn't answer. He said he thought his cell might not get reception inside the warehouse, but a girl could hope, right? I left him a voicemail instead.

Dad was home fifteen minutes later. We were all packed and ready, and once he changed we were in the car and gone. It's amazing how a boring night can turn into something that brings everyone together in an instant. Sure, Ian and I both were still a little sensitive around our parents after the whole incident. Even *we* hadn't been as close once Jake and I started dating and he and Whitney starting doing their own thing, but all that disappeared when we noticed the expression on our mom's face. When our family was in trouble, everything, every hurtful word, every accusation, it all sort of fell away and brought us close again. Ian and I are a lot alike when it comes to dealing with things. If I'm worried, I'll try to cover it up with a good laugh of some kind. Between the two of us we spent the first hour of the drive telling stories and joking about the time Nan tried to teach Mom how to make meatloaf. I guess Mom didn't form it into a loaf and made a giant meat patty instead.

"I thought it would rise!" Mom replied in defense.

"Your Nana laughed so hard she cried," added Dad.

OVERCOME

His eyes in the rear view mirror seemed hopeful, but I could still see a trace of sadness in them. After a little while we stopped talking about her once mom started crying. I couldn't help but cry a little too.

Chapter Eighteen ~
N͟ovember 16th - Friday

Aunt Beth's house hadn't changed at all. She was a very cool woman. The kind of woman you see in movies where they stay at home and make neat little gardens and their houses always have these cool trinkets and decorations, that's her. At first sight you'd think the house belonged to some eighty year old woman. On the front porch sat two rocking chairs with an uncomfortable looking wood swing in between them. The porch was long and wrapped around both sides. When I was little, my cousin Sarah and I would run around the porch and play games. I think we must've buried about ten dolls in the yard.

As we pulled into the drive, Aunt Beth stepped out the door, a giant blanket huddled around her, her long hair pulled back into a ponytail. My mom took a couple of the smaller bags and rushed up to see her. She dropped them on the steps and hugged Aunt Beth. I saw their lips moving, but both of them were talking so low that I couldn't make out what they were saying. It didn't help that the wind was swooshing across the yard so fast that I might've stumbled if I wouldn't have been carrying two of the heavier bags.

I sat the luggage just inside the door and walked ahead into the living room. Ian and Dad poured in the door right behind me. A large glass case occupied an entire wall. It was like the awards and trophy case at our high school, but much nicer and more...*homey.* In it were all Aunt Beth's pictures. She had two kids, just like my mom did, but hers were older. Luke was the oldest. I think he's a junior in college, maybe twenty-one? Sarah is only two years older than me. Beside them, a picture of Uncle Jim wearing his army fatigues and a floppy hat was in the front of the case. Scattered around him were some family pictures of them all together. He died two summers ago in Iraq or somewhere over there. It was really sad. Mom came and stayed with Aunt Beth and Sarah for about two weeks.

The house was quiet. The sound of a crackling fire somewhere in the living room called us over there. Ian and I took our time to marvel at the sights we hadn't seen in over a year. The old wood floors creaked. It was so cool. Dad stepped back outside and shut the door behind him. The living room was small, but the fireplace was big.

"Wow," Ian breathed, "This isn't at all how I remembered it."

"Me either," I said. There was an old sofa where Aunt Beth had clearly been laying only moments before. Beside it, lying on the coffee table was a book with an envelope in it. People use the weirdest bookmarks sometimes. There were a couple of other chairs too, but something seemed to be missing.

"It's really quiet," said Ian.

I nodded. Boys *are* a little slower.

Suddenly, there was a jingle, followed by a slight crash, and then the unmistakable sound of claws on a hardwood floor. Ian and I turned to see Jojo run into the living room through the kitchen opening. He was a boxer, or at least something like a boxer mixed with another small dog. His hair was short like a boxer, but his face was longer almost like a pit bull. He stopped, his tongue hanging from his face, panting. He glared at us for a moment, cocked his head, sniffed the air, and then jumped and ran at us all excitedly. It was like watching a dog who'd been raised by rabbits. I laughed. Ian smiled and crouched down to pet him. Big mistake! Jojo hopped so close to Ian's face that instinctively, Ian tried to back away, but couldn't. Instead, he fell on his back and lost the battle of the tongue lashing before it began. Jojo was the craziest dog I've ever known. When he was a puppy he used to run around the room and attack people's ankles and wrestle with socks. He was hilarious to just watch. Another thing about him was the invisible springs in his legs. He could easily jump as tall as Ian and lick your face if he wanted to, and he did...often.

Mom, Dad, and Aunt Beth rushed in at the sound of something large slamming on the wood floor. They all got a good laugh as Ian tried to fight Jojo away without actually harming the crazy dog. I imagine it was a lot like fighting Muhammad Ali. He'd try to grab his neck to shove him away, but Jojo would just dodge him and throw in a quick lick before he was hopping and dodging again to find another opening to lick.

"I need a shower," Ian said once Aunt Beth calmed Jojo.

"It looks like you've already had one," Dad managed through fits of laughter.

Ian's hair was plastered in places and his face glistened in the firelight.

"Mmm," sounded Dad. "And just think, he's probably been in the garden eating the kitty yummies too!"

Everyone laughed, except Ian of course, who only looked at Aunt Beth with this horrified expression. It reminded me of how he looked when he thought Kylie was serious about homecoming. Homecoming, *wow*, it seemed like *so* long ago... Everything changes so fast in high school.

"Sarah will be excited to see you two," Aunt Beth said.

My thoughts were jumbled, my mind on homecoming and Davis-Buckley. "Uh...um...where is she?" I finally sputtered.

"At the hospital."

"I thought there were visiting hours?" asked Mom.

"There are for Mom," Aunt Beth replied, "But Sarah's visiting the others in the meantime."

"*...the others*?" echoed Ian. He looked at me, confused. "Who else is there?"

"No one from *our* family," replied Aunt Beth.

I know my face must've shown my confusion because Aunt Beth smiled and said, "She visits people there sometimes, just to give them some company. She reads to them and does a little thing with some of her friends on Fridays...you two should go tonight."

I shrugged and nodded. I was up for just about anything. Ian seemed like he was too, but we were both in dire need of a shower before we went anywhere.

"Wait a minute," Mom said, "Why isn't she in school?"

"Oh, I didn't tell you? She's home schooling now."

"*Home-schooling?*" Ian echoed, nodding approvingly. I nodded also.

"It's a lot harder than it sounds," Mom interjected.

"All it means is that you have to do your school work, reading, tests, *and* homework in the same places *all* the time," added Aunt Beth. "And *most* of the times you don't even have friends around to chat with, either."

"Sounds like it sucks!" I chimed. I couldn't help but retract my earlier nod. I don't know what I'd do if I couldn't walk from class to class. That's like the best break I get during the day. Well, that and lunch. But no friends, or stupid kids being disruptive, or goofy guys making me laugh? Just reading, work, and then tests... Man that *would* suck!

"What about dances and homecoming and things like that?" I asked.

Aunt Beth simply shook her head and shrugged.

"So Sarah doesn't get to do any of that?" I gasped.

"She *could*, but she doesn't want to..."

I nodded along, but I was almost sure that any girl would want to dress up all Cinderella like at least once. How did she meet guys? When did she have the chance? What about friends? Suddenly, I pictured Aunt Beth in my mom's Hitler outfit and wondered if she was secretly a sweatshop owner or something. She probably has a small room somewhere under her house where ten foreign kids are making soccer balls right now. I'm beginning to think I need serious therapy.

"I mean, how does she even have friends?" I asked Ian, once he and I were upstairs putting our luggage on the beds in one of the spare rooms.

"I'm sure she meets people just like you and I do. And plus, she went to school for a while before she started home schooling, so at least she *knows* people."

"Yeah, I guess..." I replied. But then another thought occurred to me. I would've never met Jake if I wouldn't have been in public schools. I would've never been able to go to the cabin, or sneak away to Jake's house. None of the past three months would've ever happened if I would've been home schooled. I would've been cooped up in a house all day, every day. How lame!

"Man that would suck!" I said for about the

hundredth time. I felt so bad for Sarah. It was like meeting a kid from Rwanda or somewhere remote where MTV and DVR didn't exist.

Ian shrugged, "I guess it'd be cooler if you just wanted to learn everything and then go to college," he tried to argue. My brother, ever the optimist...

"Yeah, but no football...or boyfriends...or cool teachers..."

"Or *boring* ones..." he countered.

I had to nod. Touché brother, touché...

"Why do you think she did it?" I asked a moment later. "I mean, if our dad died would you want to do all of your work in our house? I'd think that being at home would be one of the last places I'd want to be."

"Some people are different," he replied, "Besides, it seems like she gets out enough."

"Yeah, to visit sick people," I scoffed, "Some fun!"

"I think it's kinda cool that she does that sort of stuff though."

"You would," I replied. "So when do you think Whitney will find out that you're gay?"

"She already knows I'm not..."

I'm sure that if I'd said I was shocked, it wouldn't have given him nearly as much satisfaction as my expression did.

For lunch Aunt Beth pulled a few containers of leftovers out of the fridge and made my dad's day. Pot roast... His favorite! Aunt Beth's kitchen was much nicer than the rest of the house. At least, I thought so anyway. Her kitchen table was big and made of some kind of super wood that made it weigh about four thousand pounds. There were so many windows in the kitchen that it was perfectly lit without any lights on. There was a large one right beside the table that did a little bendy thing and had a cushioned seat on it. It was something that you'd see on some old movie. You know, the one where it's raining outside and the little girl's wearing a bonnet and sitting in the window seat gazing out over the fields of corn or something. Kind of Little House on the Prairie-ish, not that I've watched that or anything...

"So how's Luke doing?" asked Dad.

"Oh, he's fine. He's at the Big Green now."

"I thought he was at the community college," Mom asked.

"Nope, he doubled his course load and finished early over the summer so he could register for the Big Green and get in this fall. He said if he didn't get in this fall he'd have to wait almost another year before he could get into the program."

"What's he going for again?" asked Dad.

"Education"

"Ah, a teacher...that's a first for our family," replied Mom.

"Yep, he says he's really excited about it and that it's pretty demanding, so..."

The conversation fell off for a few minutes with everyone eating.

"So what about you, Miss Erin? Have you decided what you're going to do yet?"

I stammered for a second. In all honesty, I had no clue. I hadn't even thought of college.

"Uh...no, not really."

"Well, you'd better get a move on. I'm sure your mom and dad could tell you how fast High school passes by. If you don't have a plan you'll be stuck wishing you did."

"What's Sarah doing?" asked Mom. I breathed a sigh, thankful to have the attention off of me.

"She's going to start taking some college classes this summer. Did you know you can start taking them once you're seventeen?"

"No," my mom and dad echoed, astonished. I got the sneaky suspicion that all of this was going to bite me hard once we got back to Davis-Buckley. Oh, look at how prepared Sarah is... Oh, look at how smart she is... So have you given any thought to what you're going to do, Erin? Why don't you be more like Sarah, Erin? Maybe we could trade you for one of the foreign kids that your Aunt Beth is working to death in her basement...

"Yeah, she's going to start taking some basic classes this summer, only two or three and then maybe one during the fall and spring until she graduates. The best thing about it is that it's free! The program we're going through will sign us up for the grants and everything.

"Hmm," sounded Mom, nodding.

"If everything goes like she wants it to, she'll have almost a semester done when she graduates this May."

"Wow, that sounds like something you two should look into!" said Mom.

Great, I thought, *just great...here we go!*

"So does she know what she's going to do yet?" asked Dad.

Aunt Beth shook her head because her mouth was full of food. She finished chewing and then smiled that sweatshop owner smile. "No, that's why she's just getting some the basics out of the way for now. The best thing is that she's not too far behind Luke, so she even gets some of the books for free."

My parents spent a few more minutes praising Sarah and Aunt Beth's old fashioned raising and then starting talking about some more important things.

"So when are we going to see Mom?"

"Whenever you're ready?"

"Do we need to call Sarah or anything?" asked Mom.

"No, she'll probably be there when we get there."

I pulled out my cell. "What's her number? I can call her and..."

"Oh, she doesn't have a cell phone..."

I think my heart stopped. "Did she lose it?" My mom and dad both looked at me like I was stupid and Aunt Beth giggled.

"No, she doesn't *have* one...because she doesn't need one..."

I was still in shock...

"Now that I think about it I'm actually shocked that *your* mom let *you* have one."

Let me have one? Did she think it was the eighties or something? Everyone has a phone, it's called technology! I'd probably bounce my head off of a wall if I didn't have a phone. Better yet, my mom would probably bounce *her* head off of a wall if I didn't have a phone.

Mom smiled at Aunt Beth and shrugged, "You know how teens are..."

"I'm going to wash these dishes while you guys get ready," said Aunt Beth.

Dad waved her away and rolled up his sleeves.

"Ian and I'll take care of these, you just go freshen up or whatever you girls do. I'm sure it'll be an hour before we're even able to get in the shower anyway."

Aunt Beth smiled and it showed that she needed something like that. She and my mom left the kitchen. Once they were gone my dad looked at me and Ian and nodded seriously.

"Take a good look at how her kids have been raised guys. This is almost how you were raised if I wouldn't have gotten that job in Davis with the police department. I know there are a lot of things you guys have grown accustomed to like cell phones and new clothes whenever you want them – and stuff like that – but they're *privileges*..."

Blah, Blah, Blah! How many times were we going to hear the same stuff? You should feel lucky to have such things... Your mom and I work hard for... Haven't parents ever heard of divorcing your parents? There are just certain things that everyone needs to survive and they *happen* to sound a lot like Abercrombie, Starbucks, and cell phones! I wanted to argue and tell him how ridiculous it was that people thought it was okay to live in the past in a world where everything was centered on technology and fashion, but I decided not to. It was no use arguing with parents, especially mine. I'd hate for Ian to have to lie and tell Jake the story about how I was tragically lost in some freak snowstorm and that his new adopted sister Ye-Chang would have to do in my place.

Chapter Nineteen ~
November 16th - Friday Afternoon (Visiting Nana)

Between Aunt Beth's house and the city of Hammond Falls there were over five little mini-towns, called *townships*. She lived about forty-five minutes from the actual city, which was both boring and beautiful at the same time. Boring because she listened to some sort of Jesus music that was slow and sounded like really bad old country music. Every song was either about flying away to heaven or how they can't wait to die or something really weird.

The first community we came to was called Salem. It was small, almost like Davis, but the streets and shops were older. *Everything* was pumpkin-ed out! There were small ones on fence posts, large ones at the end of every driveway, and all sorts of scary stuffed clothes hanging with carved pumpkin heads. It was a mixture of cool and creepy at the same time.

"They don't know Halloween's over, do they?" mumbled Ian.

Aunt Beth made some sort of a noise and then

looked at my mom. "This place gives me the willies. They go a little too far for Halloween if you ask me. I can't wait til' they take it all down!"

"So is this where you said you..." Mom started to ask.

"Heaven's no!" replied Aunt Beth instantly. "No, I think I'd just walk home if my car stopped dead right here! I wouldn't even ask to use a phone here."

"I bet she'd wish she had a cell phone then," I mumbled.

Ian smirked. I could feel Dad's piercing gaze from beside me burning a hole in the side of my head. I decided to pretend like I was interested in the scenery instead of glancing to see if my guess was right.

"No, I do my shopping right up the road here, in a little place called Clarence. Wait til' you see it. I think you'll like it," she said, almost proudly, as if she had something to do with its construction or something. The road continued on through Salem and then winded along another mountainside before it led into the small community of Clarence.

"The address is called Hammond Falls, but this is where I'd love to live if I didn't have so many roots out at my place. Look...," she said with a point, "that's where we go to church. It's called Lakeview Assembly. Over there's the grocery store, and there's the little coffee shop I told you about right next to the bakery. Oh, they make the best rolls..."

As I looked around the old town I couldn't help but

think about how everything was so antique looking, like an old movie. I expected to come to an intersection with horses and carriages or lantern posts. Even some of the streets weren't paved. They had little reddish bricks in them. It sounded neat when the tires rolled across them. We had to weave around one part of the township because there were streets that weren't allowed to be driven on during the weekends and Friday was considered a part of the weekend. Ian pointed out a candy shop and had a look on his face that reminded me of one of those old television shows you watch on the TV Land channel. Not that I watch that sort of stuff, but it was like watching someone's eyes light up when they get what they want for Christmas. It was kind of cool. I haven't felt that way in a long time.

Once we left Clarence, the road started to wind downhill and we could see the whole valley for miles. All the communities were scattered in little patches and then boom, there was Hammond Falls. Off to the right, shimmering almost blindingly was Grover's Lake. We pulled off in a lookout spot and glanced around a bit. We would've looked longer, but it was even windier here than it was at Aunt Beth's house and much, much colder. Dad said it had something to do with all the trees or not enough trees or something, I wasn't really listening.

Ten minutes later we were through the other podunk communities and into civilization. I sat back and took a deep breath. All of my stress melted away. I guess

I had been waiting on someone to jump from the woods with a pitchfork and hijack my Aunt Beth's blazer or something, but not anymore. Starbucks, Malls, and fast food...thank God! Speaking of God, the only thing that seemed weird about the whole thing was that we were still listening to the old twangy Jesus music instead of something more modern, or at the very least, *new* country music. I'd rather hear about horses and tractors instead of some guys singing about the sweet by and by...whatever *that* is.

It'd only been a little over a year, but I'd forgotten how huge Hammond Falls really was. It was like twice as big as Davis-Buckley and with way cooler shops and stores. On the way downtown we passed two convention center looking places that mom said were actual theatres where people act on stage and a giant ballpark for a minor league baseball team they got just last year. Amazing! Ian was as hard-pressed against the window as I was, so at least I didn't look like a *total* idiot.

The hospital was five times larger than our little community hospital in Davis. Nana was on the third floor, room three-twenty-eight. Mom and Dad stopped to get flowers on our way in while Ian and I stood near the elevator with Aunt Beth.

"So is school going alright for you two?" she asked.

We nodded.

"Both of you have sprouted up so much since the last time I saw you, especially you Ian," she added, "I bet Sarah won't even recognize you two. And Erin, your hair looks darker than I remember it being, have you dyed it?"

"No, it just keeps getting darker," I replied.

"It's really helping her grades too," added Ian. I punched him in the shoulder and Aunt Beth laughed. Mom and dad came out of the gift shop with some enormous plant with gigantic leaves and a few small blooming flowers on it.

"I thought you were getting *flowers*," said Ian.

"Flowers...a small tree?" I added, joking.

Dad shrugged, as if to say his opinion hadn't been worth too much. Mom scoffed, obviously offended by our joke and did something that sort of looked like she was petting the plant.

"I think it's pretty," she said defensively.

Ian elbowed me. "Isn't that the same way she treats us?" I held back a laugh.

"Do you think it's a boy or a girl, Erin? I've always wanted a younger brother..."

It suddenly hit me what was happening. Everyone's personalities were starting to react to how they were going to feel when we saw Nana. Dad was quiet, Mom was clinging on to the ugliest plant in the world for dear life, Aunt Beth was talking about hair and little distractive stuff, and Ian was joking and being outgoing, two things he was never really any good at until he was nervous...

As the elevator climbed closer and closer to the third floor, my heart sank a little bit more. I glanced to Mom and Aunt Beth for support, but they too were looking gloomier with each step down the hallway. Dad and Mom were nearly inseparable once we walked into the door. Aunt Beth kept her long sweater jacket wrapped tightly around her with her arms crossed. I wanted to walk up and wrap my arms around her, but I wasn't sure how either of us would feel about that. I suddenly wished Whitney and Jake were here with me and Ian. I'm sure it would make Ian feel better to hold someone and I know I could sure use someone to sink into. The television was on AMC, some western with lousy acting. Nan always called them "shootem' ups." It was likely that if she was watching it, it had John Wayne in it. She had a whole collection of his videos before DVDs came out. It was always funny to hear a seventy-something year old woman call John Wayne her *man*.

"He gets my motor running," she'd say. I never really knew what that meant until now.

Beeps and clicks followed by the sound of air releasing echoed across the room. In the middle of the bed was a thin lump under a mass of sheets and blankets. Her neck and arms were bruised from all the times she'd been poked and prodded by the nurses. She had about three or four different tubes and hoses hanging from her, running to sacks with clear liquid in them that hung from a crazy coat-hanger looking thing next to the bed. The room smelled weird. Dad said it was a mixture of stuff, but mostly Iodine. He also said that's why her skin looked so bad, but I think it's just because old people bruise easier. She was asleep. She looked so different. Maybe it was because I wasn't used to seeing her asleep, but there were a few things that seemed out of place. For one, she wasn't wearing her fat, round glasses with coke bottle lenses or any of her old fashioned gold jewelry. The sight that shocked me the most was that her hair wasn't done up like it normally was when we came to visit. I tried to think of a time when I had seen her without her hair done, but I couldn't; it had always been prepared up all nice in a bun on the top of her head like all the old ladies her age.

We all stood in silence for a few minutes listening to the sounds of the machines. There was an old tray of food off to the side that looked like it hadn't been touched. If hospital food was anything like cafeteria food, I can understand why.

Aunt Beth leaned close and whispered, "We can come back later if you want..."

Mom nodded and wiped a few tears from her eyes before they fell. Dad pinned himself against her, set the small tree on the table next to the window, and we slowly made our way out of the room. I wish I could say that we resumed our nervous personalities once we reentered the elevator, but we didn't. It was oddly quiet all the way down to the first floor. It was that sort of sad silence that accidentally said what no one wanted to say. Nana already looked like she was dead.

Sarah was downstairs waiting on us when we stepped out of the elevator. She had grown to almost perfect supermodel height. Her face was chiseled and thin and beautiful. She kind of looked like Keira Knightley, but with boobs. Her hair was long and blond, rolled up in a nifty little hairdo behind her head, almost librarian-ish. Now that I think about it she kind of looked like a taller version of Carrie, but dressed like she was from the forties. She had a long blue jean skirt that was the exact opposite of the ones Carrie usually wore. Her shirt wasn't old-fashioned, but it didn't even try to cut any lower than a normal v-neck shirt.

By the way she dressed I thought she was one of those Amish girls that walked around neighborhoods handing out bibles. You know, the ones that wear bonnets and ride in carriages and make things out of wood and stuff, but then she ruined the whole oldies outfit by sporting a pair of new shoes. It seemed so weird to see someone dressed so…*weird*, but yet she was so confident and comfortable in public. It almost made no sense at all. I mean, there're all sorts of girls who wear clothes they shouldn't, but now I saw a gorgeous girl who doesn't wear what she *should* be wearing. I felt like I was sent to introduce her to fashion. After all, I don't make the rules, I just abide by them.

"Hey," she said.

She gave each of us a hug, smiling in that somber sort of way the entire time. It's almost like you're happy to see someone, but you don't want to be *too* happy.

"My goodness Sarah, you look beautiful," Dad said.

Sarah smiled, almost blushing.

"You look just like your mom did when she was your age," added Mom.

Ian and I exchanged doubtful glances. Aunt Beth was pretty, but to say she looked like Sarah...wow! As we walked toward the parking lot, I leaned close to Ian.

"Remember, this is Colorado not Kentucky, cousins are a no-go here."

He only scoffed and shook his head like he was repulsed by the comment, but I have a feeling he was trying his best not to look at her and to think about Whitney instead. After all, guys were creatures of habit, and aside from immediate family, hot was hot no matter who you were, at least, that's what the magazines say.

Chapter Twenty ~
November 16th - Friday Night
(The Party)

When we got back to Aunt Beth's house, Ian's cell phone rang. It was Whitney. I tried to call Jake, but there was no answer. Why didn't he answer his phone? I mean, here I was out in the middle of nowhere. I could've died in a tragic car accident and he'd never know. *I'm over exaggerating, he'll call! He's busy with track or basketball or something like that.*

Just when I thought my mind was going to explode with the endless options of why Jake wasn't calling me back, or why I hadn't received even the smallest text message, Sarah came out the door onto the porch and sat next to me.

"So little cuz, how have things been with you?"

She was oddly happy given the situation with Nana, especially since it was only going to be her and Aunt Beth once Nana passed away.

"Alright," I replied, "I mean, school's going okay and me and my boyfriend are doing well."

"Boyfriend?" she asked, almost intrigued. The look

on her face told me that the thought of having one might be against the restrictions of her outfit.

"Yeah, his name is Jake; he's a senior." I said.

She nodded along like she'd met him or something. "So what's he like? Are you two in *love*?" she joked, rubbing her elbow against me with a childlike smile.

"He's tall and gorgeous, like a Meet Joe Black sort of Brad Pitt hot, you know?"

"Ah," Sarah said, realizing the depth of Jake. "So school's all…," she made this expression with her hands that I guess had something to do with going well.

"Yeah, school's fine. Grades are good and all."

She nodded. After a quick moment of odd silence, she turned to me and had an expression on her face that made me wonder what she was thinking. I started to ask, but she blurted out her thoughts almost instantly.

"I know we haven't seen one another in over a year. We used to be sort of close. I mean, you'd come out every summer for about a month and we'd hang out and stuff…I…," she stammered, "I should've called or something…I'm sorry we didn't stay in touch."

I started to shake my head. I wanted to say something like, "No, don't worry about it," or, "Hey, it's no big deal," but she beat me to it again.

"It meant a lot to me how close we were. I still have all of our old stuff in a box upstairs in my closet. After the first couple of summers, I'd pack it away and wouldn't touch it until you came again. It was sort of our own little thing, you know?"

I chuckled a little. "Yeah..."

She smiled as the swing slowly rocked back and forth and a stiff breeze rushed around the house. "Anyway, I just wanted to tell you how sorry I am that I haven't called more or written, or emailed or anything. I'm sure there's a lot to catch up on. I think we're both past playing with dolls and having make-believe kitchens in the back yard..."

Boy, did she not know the half of it! Quick, think of something witty...

"Yeah, I can't stand the kitchen now," I replied.

She laughed and nodded. Something told me that she had more chores than I could ever dream of, but I didn't want to give that away.

"So do you think you and Ian would want to hang out with me and my friends tonight? We're sort of hosting this party thing down at the coffee shop and you guys are more than welcome to come if you want," she asked, almost shyly.

It was so amazing to see such a beautiful girl who seemed so real and excited about everything. I mean, shouldn't she at least be mad at her mom for giving her a life like a prisoner? I would loath my mom if she had me home-schooled. Shouldn't she be all sheltered away from the world because her father died? I would! I mean, especially if I didn't have a cell phone. Who can live like that? What kind of hot teenage girl wants to spend her days at the hospital with sick people instead of in the back seat of some guy like Jake's truck?

I thought about the party and then what Jake would think if I went to one without him, but then I remembered the fact that he hadn't even tried to text or call me since I'd been gone. So what if I went out with my cousin to a party. I'm sure Jake would be upset if he knew about it, but maybe he didn't *need* to know about it? Maybe that'd teach him to appreciate what he's been getting! Ian came out the door right as Sarah popped the question, rescuing me from my lack of response. I hate how I zone off and think all the time.

"What sort of party?" he asked.

I could tell by the look on his face that he was reluctant. Hot girls often migrated in flocks, or so the boys always said. And for Whitney's sake, I hoped that little comment wasn't true.

By five o'clock the three of us piled into Aunt Beth's blazer and headed toward the township of Clarence. Sarah's outfit struck me as a little odd. She wasn't wearing a skirt now, but a pair of blue jeans instead. Hmm... Was this a hint of rebellion against the forties I was detecting? Almost defeating her slightly more modern choice of fashion, she wore a long-sleeved buttoned-up dress shirt with a sleeveless sweater over the top of it. Yuk. I mean, the sweater was pretty and the whole outfit matched, but honestly!

I thought to ask some questions about why she was no longer a prisoner to the skirt, but Ian beat me to it.

"Why'd you change?" he asked.

She shrugged. "No reason, I just thought this'd be warmer, I guess," she replied. I could tell he felt like an idiot by the way she answered all nonchalantly, so I thought I'd try and cover for him a little.

"Aren't you...I mean, isn't it against your beliefs to..."

"I'm not Pentecostal, if that's what you mean?" she answered with a smirk.

"*Pente-costal?* Is that what they call the girls who always wear skirts and wear their hair up a certain way?" I asked.

"Geez, Erin," interjected Ian, "You didn't know that? I mean Maggie Tanner and Gina Dawes wear skirts all the time and they're Pentecostal."

"Yeah, but they also wear eyeliner and paint their nails black like the Goths too," I replied.

Sarah laughed.

"What?" I asked.

"That just kinda makes no sense," she replied, still laughing. "I mean, the whole reason Pentecostals dress that way is to preserve certain traditions they believe in, and to intermingle it with something like that is just... funny," she added.

I almost felt dumb listening to her talk about something so intellectually. I mean, she even used the word *intermingle*... That's like an SAT word or something...

"So if you're not Pentecostal, why were you dressed like one?" asked Ian.

"Do you have an NFL football jersey?" she asked.

"Yeah,"

"Do you wear it?"

"Yeah."

"Are you a professional football player?"

Ian and I both must've shown that we understood, because then she added, "I just like to wear a skirt sometimes."

"But you go to church though, right?" Ian asked.

"Yeah, me and my mom go every Sunday morning and night and then on Wednesdays too...and then I go on Mondays for prayer and then Thursdays for bible study and youth..."

"Wow, that's a lot, isn't it?" I asked. *Four days a week... Is she insane? I can barely stand going on Easter.*

"I guess it's more than most, but all my friends are there on Thursdays and Sundays and then prayer is important too, so..." she explained with a shrug.

As we passed through the township of Salem, I thought about what Sarah's life must be like being home-schooled. I guess I'd have to go to church every day of the week too if that was my only chance to see my friends. We passed the painted log that said *Clarence* in fancy carved lettering and then turned down the first brick street and looped around the block. Sarah told us that the brick looking stuff is called cobblestone and then she mentioned some story about horses and carriages and how the cobblestone was used for something...I really wasn't paying attention. She parked the blazer across the street from the cute little coffee shop and the bakery next door. The old buildings looked like rows of old houses with cool etched designs along the porch rails and upper windows above the businesses.

"Where're we going?" Ian asked.

Sarah walked around to the back of the blazer and opened the back hatch. She pulled out a book bag and a small cherry-colored wood case.

"The coffee shop," she said, "and the bakery too, if you want..."

Outside the doors and in the windows there were simple wooden signs that read very plainly Coffee and Bakery - Fresh Bread, but once we stepped inside the door of the coffee shop and the little bells attached to the door jingled, I could tell it was much more than it appeared from the outside. The place was a lot larger on the inside than it looked like on the outside. Whoever decorated the place was definitely into fashion. The tables were cozy and scattered out comfortably. It was almost like Starbucks, but better. I gasped. Was it possible to be better than Starbucks? The walls were painted in smooth colors, almost like something in a movie, how everything's more perfect than it should be. There was a long U-shaped bar that had three workers standing behind it, one of which was a *very* cute guy. To the left was an open seating area with larger tables and chairs for meetings and groups. In the back corner was a couch crammed full of kids our age. They all sort of waved simultaneously and jumped up; each of them had things similar to Sarah, a bag of some kind and a wooden or plastic case.

As they came closer, I noticed that Ian's night would be a little easier. The girls weren't nearly as gorgeous as Sarah. The guys weren't too much to gawk at either. Two of them were the blackest black people I've ever seen. The girl's face was so smooth and round, almost unreal, like a doll's face. She was as tall as Kylie, but her hair wasn't short; instead, it was long and done into round braids. Her eyes were large and...were they *gold*? Suddenly, she seemed so beautiful to me. I've never met a girl that seemed so alive. She smiled and it was like her whole face shaped into one large white grin. It was like I knew I could trust her just by being around her.

Beside the girl was a guy that by the looks of things seemed to be her brother. He was taller, with all of the same features. His hair was short and he wore a long-sleeved button-up shirt and a pair of khakis. The second guy wasn't nearly as hot as the guy behind the counter, but he was cute. He was wearing something stylish and had the hairdo to match, almost the look of a lead singer of a band or something. The girls were, to no surprise, dressed similar to Sarah. It was so weird. Everyone smiled the same, almost stupidly, like they were actors taught to be a certain way.

"Bou' time," chimed the black girl. *Wait a minute... did she have an accent?* Was she *actually* African?

"Well, we went to visit my Nana and my family came into town too, so..." Sarah said with a shrug. Everyone was still smiling oddly.

"These are my cousins, Erin and Ian from Davis-Buckley..." she introduced. "Guys, these are my friends, Lavender and Henry," she pointed to the African girl and her brother, "Savannah, Lisa, and Evan," she finished.

"It's grea' to me'ch you," said Henry, shaking Ian's hand.

How cool! I've never met someone from a different country before. I looked at Ian and he smiled. I could tell that he was thinking the same thing. These poor people were about to be bugged all night with questions.

All of the other girls and Evan sort of gave the usual wave and "Hi" that you give when you meet someone for the first time, but this time it was different. It was like they were *actually* excited to meet us, not just forcing themselves to go through the routine of pretending to care.

We stood around and listened to Sarah talk about her week with them for a few seconds. I was still admiring the room when I heard the hot guy from behind the counter say, "The room's ready, whenever you want it, Sarah."

"Thanks Nick," she said.

Nick... *Hmm.* Even his voice was hot. Watch out Jake! Don't answer the phone when I call and we'll see who has to work hard to keep who... Sarah smiled stupidly like everyone else as we walked by the bar to the stairs on the far side of the room. I did my best to stare just a little bit longer than everyone else just to see if he'd notice, and he did. I was sure he'd notice me over the other girls. Next to Sarah, I was easily the hottest and unlike the rest of them, I had a sense of fashion. I just hope he heard Sarah's intro and didn't think Ian was my boyfriend. I'm sure if Ian knew what I was thinking he'd reach down and grab my hand just to try and be a jerk, but thankfully he didn't notice.

We walked up the stairs and into another room nearly as large as the one below. It was filled with chairs and tables and in the back was a small wooden stage with curtains and lights. Henry and Lavender sat in two of the front seats and waved for us to join them while Sarah, Lisa, and Evan started opening their cases. Savannah walked to the back of the room to a small booth and stepped inside it. It was kind of like a DJ booth, but smaller, and it didn't look like it had much more than a small board with some knobs and bars on it.

The room was simply decorated. There were a couple of doors off to the side of the room that were open with extra chairs in them. Hanging from the ceiling was this ribbon stuff that reminded me of a canopy bed, only larger and more beautiful. The ribbons were gold and dark red and purple. Ian elbowed me and pointed above the stage. Carved into a piece of wood that was shaped like a shield was a lion's head, weaving behind the shield was another wooden strip that flowed to look like a ribbon that read, "The Lion's Den".

"Cool, huh?" Ian whispered.

I nodded and continued to glance around. There was something about this place that made me feel the way I feel when I'm in between waking up and dream-land. You know, like how everything around you *could* be real, but you're not quite sure. After a few minutes the curtains slid back and a dimly lit wooded stage emerged. There were microphones, a set of drums, and amplifiers. Evan stood front and center with a guitar strapped around his shoulder, strumming it softly. I knew he looked like the lead singer of a band! Behind him, Lisa lightly touched the golden cymbals on the drum set and adjusted her seat. From her cherry-wood case, Sarah pulled a beautiful violin and a bow. Each of them worked with their microphones for a second chiming something into them so Savannah could adjust the instruments on the panel to make sure it sound-ed decent. When she finished, she walked over to the door, shut it, and then took her place next to Sarah and grabbed a guitar of her own.

"How long have they been practicing?" Ian asked Henry.

"Oh, I don' know…maybe six or seven mon-s," he replied.

Suddenly, the thought of how cool this was came to mind. I'd only seen things like this in movies, not in real life. It was so neat. Sure football games and other high school stuff was cool, but this was different. I was excited…

"So, where're your instruments?" I asked Lavender.

"Here," she said, holding her hands out. "Dey're your-s too," she added, pointing to my own hands.

"We'll start off with a favorite and then take requests until the others show up…" said Evan into his microphone.

Why was that suddenly so hot? Ian was nervous with anticipation. This was soo cool. Whitney would love this, too. Evan looked at Savannah and nodded. Both started playing at the same time. Lisa got ready. Sarah sat her violin down and stepped up close to her microphone. Instead, she grabbed this half-moon looking thing with little cymbals attached to it. Before I could ask what it was, Evan starting singing.

"Hold me in your arms, never let me go, I want to spend eternity with you…"

Lisa rocked the drums. How cool was it that a chick could play the drums so well? It was so neat to see all these kids my age doing this… I'd never heard the song before, but maybe they'd made it up? I mean there're a lot of groups that do that, even amateur ones. Why couldn't I play an instrument?

Evan, Savannah, and Sarah leaned in close to the microphones. Henry and Lavender clapped in beat, and to my surprise, so did Ian. How did he know the song? Maybe he didn't…maybe he was just following their lead? Lavender glanced at me, her face wide with a bright smile. She nodded to me as if to signal me to use my instruments. I guess these puny things would have to do.

"I stand be-fore you Lord, and give You all my praise, Your grace is all I need, Jesus you're all I need. My life belongs to You, You gave Your life for me, Your grace is all I need, Jesus you're all I need. Hold me in Your arms, never let me go, I want to spend eternity with You... And now that You're near, every-thing is different, ev-erything's so different, Lord. Well I know, I'm not the same, my life You've changed. I want to be with You...I want to be with You."

Jesus...Hold me in your arms? I thought Jesus was dead? Wasn't it a big deal that somebody killed him and he was supposed to be God or the son of God or something?

I looked at Ian. He didn't seem to be having nearly the same problem that I was. He seemed to be enjoying himself fine, clapping right along with Henry and Lavender, who from time to time weren't even clapping at all, but raising their hands and singing. I guess the one thing that sounded cool was their accents shouting the words into the air. But why this? Why Jesus music? Was this some church thing or something? Why would Sarah spend four days a week at church to sing *this* on her free time with her friends? At least it wasn't the slow country crap her mom listens to. After a few minutes people started to trickle into the room in small groups and fill in the seats behind us. They were all our age, some a little older. By the time the song ended there were more than twenty people in the room, all clapping and saying different things. It was like church, but for kids and ran by kids...it was kind of cool.

Chapter Twenty-One ~
November 17th - Saturday

"It wasn't all that bad," Ian remarked with a shrug. He continued past the mound of empty cups to the glob of green gelatin, sliding his tray. I've recently come to the realization that hospital food *is* worse than school food, hands down. I walked behind Ian mostly growling back at the food that I thought might growl at me first. Aunt Beth, Sarah, Mom, and Dad were all upstairs talking with the doctors and nurses and checking in on Nana. I guess over night she took a turn for the worse and they think her kidneys are going into failure. I'm not sure exactly what happened, but whatever *did* happen made her look about three times worse when we walked in this morning.

The pressure was a little too much for Ian and me, so we decided to step down to the cafeteria and sample some food, a choice I wish I wouldn't have made after all.

"It was one boring song after another, but with a beat," I replied.

"They were cool though, I mean, you can't say that watching a group of kids our age rock out wasn't cool!"

He was right, that part *was* cool.

"So what if it's Jesus music, Erin, it's what they like. I mean, Kylie listens to rap and I can't stand that! You listen to R&B stuff, and I listen to older stuff like Dad. We're all different! They just happen to like Jesus stuff..."

He grabbed a handful of ketchup and mayonnaise packets to concoct what he called his "secret sauce" as the lady in front of him piled a heap of the springy looking french-fries onto a plate and passed it over the glass.

"So you're saying you had a good time?"

He shrugged. "It was fun. Besides, I've never been to anything like that, so yeah."

We made our way to a booth and Ian immediately began his chemistry composition of appropriate numbers of ketchup packets to the lesser amount of mayonnaise packets and then dribbled pepper and salt in such a way that I thought it might explode if he didn't do it correctly.

"Why does it bother you so much?" he asked.

I thought to answer immediately with something like, "Because it sucks," but then realized that I didn't have a *real* answer. There was just something about it that screamed at me to hate it, or to call it lame or phony.

"Doesn't have anything to do with the fact that Jake hasn't called, does it?" he asked. His face was saddened, like he was worried for me, but I covered it up.

"Pssh! No... He's busy working and with practices and stuff. Besides, I'm not holding my breath for a call or anything. I mean, I'm not all 'why haven't you called me' or anything like most girlfriends would be right now."

"Well," started Ian, rubbing his hands on his jeans to get the salt off of them, "I think it's a load of crap that he hasn't called you yet, and so does Whitney! You're all the way out here in the middle of nowhere watching your grandma in the hospital and he doesn't even call you to see how you're doing? Or tell you he's sorry or nothing? What kind of boyfriend does that?"

I don't know why, but Ian's words smacked me in the face. "The kind of boyfriend who's busy!" I replied. "Who... What makes you think you know so much? Jake's a great boyfriend, and he's always been there for me! Just because Whitney's obsessed with you and calls you more doesn't mean that your relationship better than ours!"

He tried to say something, but I jumped up from the table and stormed out into the lobby before he got the chance. I had to stand up for Jake! Sure, maybe he hasn't called, but I'm sure he'll have a good reason. I'm sure he'll tell me how sorry he is when he finally gets the chance. Unlike everyone else, Jake's never let me down. He's always been there when I've needed him. Like when mom and dad were all against me saying that I stole that halter, or when Ashley and Brittany tried to say I was a snitch. Jake was right there for me. We don't have to be attached at the hip or dress in matching colors to prove that we're in love.

Sarah came down to the lobby a few minutes later and told us that things weren't looking too well for Nana. "The nurse said that it's likely she'll pass before the day is over, but no one wants to give up hope yet," she relayed with a somber nod. It was one of those rare moments where a smile wasn't on her face.

"Have you guys eaten yet?" she asked.

"Kind of," I replied. The thought of the growling food made me snarl.

"Do you think you'd want to keep an eye on Nana while we go get something?"

I thought to say "no" but how horrible would that be? I mean, how could I say no to that? But at the same time, the smell of the room and the sight of Nana withered away to nothing were overbearing. Before I could reply, Ian agreed for the both of us and Sarah led us back to the elevator. The ride up was dreadfully silent. I could tell Ian felt bad, but he wasn't going to apologize any time soon. After Jake calls I'm sure he'll choke out some sort of a half-hearted apology just so he doesn't get annihilated at practice. We met mom and dad in the hallway and talked for a minute about what the nurses had said.

"She's in and out of consciousness," Mom explained. Their expressions alone told me why Sarah had asked us to watch over her. They needed time away. Dad had his arm around her, but even then her face was pale and she looked frail, like if I pushed her she wouldn't fall over... she'd shatter. If I didn't know her, I'd say we were here visiting *her*. Aunt Beth offered to stay once she came out of the room, but Sarah insisted that they go and get a bite down the street.

"If you need anything..." Mom started.

"We have our phones..." interrupted Ian. "It's alright Mom, just take a break and get something to eat."

Ian reminded me of someone responsible in the movies, you know, the person who comes the rescue when everyone else is caught in the chaos. I tried to remind myself that I was mad at him for attacking Jake, but the moment carried me away and I stepped beside him.

"We'll be here, Mom," I said. "And if anything changes or any nurses come, we'll call you."

The smell of the room seemed worse than it was earlier. Ian took the seat nearest the table where Mom and Aunt Beth had been playing rummy, so I opted for the cushioned one by the television where, due to the chip crumbs and empty plastic bottles of *Barq's Root beer*, I guessed Dad had been sitting. What is it about boring old men who watch other boring old men do things like fish or hunt or drive in circles? That's not television, it's *worse* than reading! That would be like girls watching shows with other girls painting other girls' nails or something...how lame!

Forty channels of nothing stared back at me as I

flipped through them. The first two channels were men in suits screaming at the television with bibles in their hands. They looked pissed! Then, just when they would finish, they'd smile real big and point their bibles toward the sky and say something like "but God is faithful..." or "but thank God we have Jesus!" No wonder people don't go to church...I would hate being yelled at too. The next channel was this huge concert. There were lights and about twenty people on stage. Everyone was on their feet, cheering, shouting, jumping, it was cool. For a second I was confused, because it wasn't anyone I knew, but then a familiar sound followed by familiar words came again.

"And now that you're near, everything is dif-ferent, everything's so dif-ferent Lord..."

"Hey, this is one of those songs we sang the other night," Ian said with a point.

We watched it for a second before I realized exactly what I was doing. I half-expected Sarah to walk in and clap that her diabolical scheme had worked, but I guess my mind can make up some really weird scenarios some times. The other thirty-seven channels were a bust. There were a couple of potential ones though; some movie about some kids on a Saturday morning detention, *like that would ever go over these days*, and another one with these guys who were beating a printer with a bat, but I decided to stop on a western. It was Nana's man, John Wayne.

From the corner of my eye I saw Ian look up at the

television and then look back at me like I was crazy, but then I think he understood.

That was when the frailest voice imaginable said, "Hub-ba Hub-ba..."

My eyes darted to the wrinkled smile of the old woman beneath the mass of blankets. Ian stood up like something had bit him, but then his feet shuffled and he couldn't move. For some reason my eyes were transfixed on her and I could only stalk toward her like she would die if I moved too fast. It seemed like forever before I finally reached the side of the bed. I could feel my heart pounding. I didn't want to be here, but I did. I didn't want to see her die, but something told me she might, and I wasn't sure how I felt about having that memory trapped in my mind forever. I saw Ian pull his phone out of his pocket, type a few buttons, hold it up to his ear, pull it away again, look at it, hold it up in the air, and then rush out of the room mumbling.

I didn't care about the reception in the hospital right then though, as I gazed into Nana's watery eyes. I didn't think to point to the phone in the room, so Ian wouldn't have to sprint to the down three flights of stairs to the lobby. I didn't think about Jake not calling or Ian's comment or the halter. My mind wrapped around Nana like my hands did her hands when I took the seat beside her bed. She smiled, but it wasn't that movie smile that the actors put on, you know, the one that shows their sadness in the midst of staring down death. It was a warm smile; the *'I'm so glad to see you'* smile, or the *'Here's some fresh chocolate chip cookies'* smile. I think the smile is what did it for me. I mean, how could someone smile like that, but yet be in so much pain and trapped in a hospital bed? As the tears started flowing down my cheeks she shushed me like I was a baby.

"Oh dear," she said sweetly, "it's alright.

I wanted to wipe my eyes and be stronger, but I couldn't. My hands wouldn't budge from hers. Something in her eyes told me she was the one who was being stronger than the rest of us, almost like she knew how much Aunt Beth and Mom were struggling. My mind began to churn. I tried to stop the words that came out, but I couldn't.

"Are you afraid?" I asked.

She smiled. "No dear."

"But I don't want you to go," I replied. The tears were streaming down my cheeks now and my shoulders were bobbing. I laid my head close to hers. She kissed me and stroked a few loose strands of hair out of my face.

"Everyone has a time on this earth to do with it what we choose..." she explained, "At first I made a lot of bad choices, but then once I was done wasting my time I starting making better ones, ones that mattered."

"What do you mean, Nana?"

"For a while I lived for me, for what I wanted, but then your Poppy died and I learned that everything I lived for was temporary: my house, my gardens, my westerns. When he died I learned that there wasn't anything I lived for that I couldn't lose or someone couldn't take from me. So, I started making better choices and living for things that *weren't* temporary...things that would stay with me forever. Do you know what I'm saying, child?"

"Kind of," I replied with a shrug.

"I started living for God. I started following his commandments and praying and reading His word. Soon, I realized the life I had been living wasn't half as great as the life God had planned for me."

I could tell by the look in her eyes that she believed wholeheartedly in every word she said, almost like they were rehearsed in her mind somewhere. I guess every old person comes to that time when they're so afraid that they just need something, anything that helps them understand life a little better. I can't imagine what it would be like knowing I'm going to close my eyes for the last time. What then? What happens once this life is finished? I guess I'd never really considered that until now. Will I close my eyes to the sound of the machines blearing the loud and final "beeeeep" and then wake up in a white room like in the movies?

A nurse came in a few seconds later and interrupted our time together. Soon, Mom and Aunt Beth came rushing in with Sarah and Dad and then Nana was bombarded with smiling, crying faces. I felt like I was standing still, yet sliding back from her as the bodies poured in, but somehow through it all I couldn't remove my eyes from her. I could still hear her words, her voice, and see the love in her eyes, the warmth that promised something awesome like fresh baked cookies or better yet...fresh bread.

Once the great couple of hours passed, Nana slipped into another deep sleep and the nurses re-stated the same things they had earlier that morning. "She could go at any time." Mom and Aunt Beth were a wreck all day. I think the moment of talking and tears must've brought some sort of a false hope that she might pull through again. Dad tried to tell some funny stories like he did on the ride out, but it was no use. At this point, everyone knew it was coming and no one pretended anymore. I'm not sure if it was that, or the fact that there was nothing he could do that made Dad so irritable all afternoon, but whatever it was took its toll. Whenever we asked him something or comment-ed about anything, he snapped at us. The pressure was starting to set in.

Sarah started praying. Aunt Beth and Mom were straddled on the sides of Nana's bed, each taking hold of her hands. Dad took turns growling at both us and thin air. I took it as a sign to steer clear for as long as I could manage. I had to go down to the lobby to even chance a call or a text, and even then it wasn't a guarantee. This time, I had to step into the gap between the two sets of doors to make my call. It wasn't nearly as cold in here as it was outside, but it was close. Jake didn't answer again. I thought about leaving him a really sweet message, you know, something to make him feel guilty because he hadn't even made an attempt to call or text, but something about Ian's comment struck true.

"Hey, this is Jake...leave me a message...Beep!"

"I've called three times now, and you still haven't called me back! No text, nothing! I guess we have a lot to talk about when I get back. I'm sure you're busy with everything and all and I'm sure I sound like a nagging girlfriend, but I really expected more from you, Jake."

I hung up the phone and shoved it in my coat pocket. I looked out the door to the parking lot just as snow flurries started to fall. The sight made me shiver a little and realize that a cup of hot cocoa would be nice. I turned to make my way back to the cafeteria with the hopes that their drinks were better than their foods, when my phone vibrated.

I gasped. "No way," I mouthed.

I slid it out of my pocket just in time to see the name *Whitney* flash across the screen.

"Hello," I answered.

"Hey...how are things? How are you doing?"

"Alright, I guess... Things could be better."

"Are you busy? Do you want me to call back later?"

"No, it's alright. I'm down in the lobby just hanging out."

"I tried to call Ian, but I guess his phone's silenced or something."

"No, there's just no reception up there is all," I explained.

She sounded a little more relieved that he wasn't

just ignoring her. Something in her voice was different than normal. She almost seemed scared that Ian hadn't answered the phone. Why would she be so worried? I mean, Ian was crazy about her.

"Are you okay?" I asked.

"Yeah," she replied, but I could tell she was holding something back.

"Are you sure?"

She was quiet for a second.

"I just... I heard you guys went to a party last night..." she said sadly.

I almost laughed out loud.

"I *guess* you could call it that."

"Was it fun? I mean, did you guys have a good time?" she asked. It was that sort of tone that had a plea in it that almost begged for me to say "man it sucked". She couldn't see me cringe and scowl. I think if the conversation would have been in person she would've understood without me having to say a word. Suddenly, it hit me why she was asking these questions.

"It wasn't the sort of party you're thinking it was," I explained. "It actually wasn't really a party at all...it was more like a concert."

"*Oh*," she sounded. By the tone of her voice she sounded even more scared. There were lots of things that happened at concerts. They were kind of like going to the club or school dances. A little bit of dancing starts and then suddenly people wake up places they shouldn't be or stumble into janitor's closets, forgetting they have cute, innocent little girlfriends like Whitney.

"Not like a *big* concert or anything," I explained, "but a small band performance type thing, nothing danceable. And there were only thirty people or so in the audience. It's a band my cousin plays in...not a big deal or anything."

"Oh, well that sounds cool," she replied. I could hear the relief in her voice again.

"Yeah, I guess, but it was Jesus stuff, so..."

"*Jesus stuff?* You mean, like Christian music?" she asked, her tone growing happier by the second.

"Yeah," I replied.

Suddenly, Whitney was restored to her old self.

"Oh, so it was like a church thing then?"

"No, well, I guess...I mean, all of her friends from church were there with us, so..."

"I guess that sounds kind of cool. Have you heard anything from Jake yet? I mean, has he called or anything? Ian told me he hasn't called you yet and that you've called him a few times, but he still hasn't returned any of your calls."

I felt smacked in the face again, but this time I really wasn't sure why it bothered me so bad. Ian had been right in what he said, but now I was hearing it from Whitney too. It was like they were teaming up on me to break up with Jake or something.

"Look, he's busy! Why are you and Ian bashing him just because it's been a day and he hasn't called?"

"I didn't mean it like *that*. I was just saying..."

"That he's a lousy boyfriend! Or in Ian's words, *a jerk*! Just back off and don't worry about it, alright? It's *not* big deal if he's called me or not." I hung up the phone. God, how bad can one day get? I'm stuck out in the middle of nowhere with no friends, a strange cousin, Jesus music, a snappy dad, a dying nana, and my boyfriend won't answer his phone at one o'clock on a Saturday. And to make things worse, my brother wants to bash my boyfriend and now his sidekick-of-a-girlfriend wants to jump in on the annoying questions too! Are they co-writing a book or something? Don't they have better things to talk about on the phone than me and my boyfriend?

I was on my way to get hot chocolate when my dad, Ian, and Sarah came out of the elevator. Ian's eyes were red, so were Sarah's, except her face wasn't nearly as somber. There was no need for them to say anything; I already knew what had happened. I guess I was wrong after all...my day *could* get worse.

We spent another hour at the hospital filling out paperwork before we left and headed back to Aunt Beth's house. We brought both vehicles today because Sarah said she had a couple of errands to run. I weighed my options and decided to go with Sarah instead of the adults. Thankfully, Ian decided to go with Mom and Dad. I really didn't want to be around him right now. When did everyone start getting so annoying? I think it was sometime around the whole stolen halter incident that people started losing their minds.

As I suspected, Sarah's errands were based around church and little Nazi-like chores her mother assigned her, but like a good little girl, Sarah didn't need to be told to do them, so she threw on her brainwashed smile and practically skipped around Clarence. I saw Nana everywhere. Something about old buildings made me imagine her standing on the sidewalk with a smile, waving. The flurries were gone now, replaced by full-blown snow. And the wind that had once made everything miserable was mixing with the snow to make the traffic even more unbearable. Not that there were wrecks, just *really* slow drivers. We drove past the coffee shop and the bakery. I noticed a woman in the window, peering out at the snow. She was an old woman, short and sweet. She was a Nana, someone's Nana…I almost started crying.

It seemed unreal that Nana had just died, almost like we were going to drive over to her house any second now and everything would be alright and she'd be sitting there in front of the television knitting something or tinkering on some little Christmas ornaments. We turned down another side street, old fashioned with lantern posts and cobblestone. Even the houses were three stories with spires and round rooms. It was pretty, especially with a layer of snow.

"I can't believe it's snowing before thanksgiving, again," she said, "that's the second year in a row!"

I thought to say something like "big deal" or "sucks to be you" but then something else made its way to my lips first.

"Where are we having thanksgiving this year now that Nana's gone?"

Sarah's expression went blank like the thought hadn't dawned on her either. "I don't know...our house?" she shrugged.

The thought of Christmas without her crossed my mind and my eyes started to water. Sarah cupped her hand over her mouth.

"What?" I asked.

"Thanksgiving's next week... What're we gonna do?"

The rest of the ride home was quiet. I'm sure we were both playing those memory movies in our mind and for once, Nana was the main character. It's amazing how easy it is to forget the little things, isn't it? The only thing that hindered the moment from being a full-blown one was the faint sound of Jesus music playing on the radio. This one sounded sadder than the ones I heard last night, which is still much better than Aunt Beth's. I tried to hear the words, but couldn't.

"Can I turn this up?" I asked. Shocked, Sarah quickly nodded. I gave it a little twist.

"Your ho-ly pre-sence liv-ing in me..." the girl sang, and man did she have an awesome voice.

"And I-I-I I'm desperate for you..."

I turned it back down a little.

"Do you like that song?" Sarah asked, a little *too* excited.

I shrugged, "It just sounded different than what you

guys were playing last night, so I was just seeing what it was about…"

"Her name is Rebecca St. James."

"She has a really awesome voice," I commented.

"I have a couple of her Cds if you want to borrow one or something," she offered.

I tried not to smile. "That's okay," I said.

"You can flip through my Cds and pick one out if you want to listen to any of them. I'm not sure how many you'll know, but there's a lot more upbeat stuff, if you like that. Not all Christian music is slow and worshipy."

I grabbed the Cd case and flipped through it.

"They're my favorite," she announced instantly. "We played a few of their songs last night," she added.

I nodded like I was interested, even though it sounded corny, but I'm sure Sarah was far beyond caring what people thought. I mean, who would wear the clothes she wears in public and then be self-conscious about her music choices? I ended up choosing some guy named Warren Barfield because he was remotely hot. For being such a big deal you'd think there'd be more hot Christian guys out there, but I guess only the girls are the hot ones. I finally saw pictures of that Rebecca girl and she was as hot as her voice. And then there's this other one named Natalie Grant, and she was hot too. The Warren guy had an amazing voice. Probably the most amazing voice I've ever heard on a guy before, especially a white guy.

When we walked in the door my Mom and Dad were

on their cell phones. Sarah and I carried everything inside and straight to the kitchen. Ian was washing dishes while Aunt Beth set the table. I could tell Ian wanted to say something, but he didn't. I forgot that I was supposed to be mad at him and immediately resumed my angered stare. A few minutes later Mom was off the phone and walking straight for me.

"I just got off the phone with Kylie's mom,"

"Really? *Why?* Is everything okay?"

Mom stared at me confused and then looked at Ian. "You haven't told her?"

"No," he replied, "I thought *you* might want to," he lied. It was obvious that he hadn't admitted to them his verbal bashing of Jake.

"We're going to stay the week here and go back next Sunday..."

"*What?*"

"So we don't have to make two trips and we can still be here for thanksgiving *and* the funeral," she added.

"What about school?" I complained. I wanted to ask, "What about Jake" but I was sure that'd sound really bad considering the fact Nana had just died.

Mom nodded, "That's why I called Kylie's mom, so she can have your teachers give me a call with your homework and assignments."

Great, another week away from Jake, *and* we get a taste of home-schooling. *Yippee!* So much for my personal life...

Chapter Twenty-Two ~
November 18th - Sunday

A ringing phone was the first sound I heard this morning. Ian answered it and slowly crept from the room with the look on his face like he was sorry...and he should be. Who in their right mind calls before nine on a Sunday? I tried my best to close my eyes and roll back over, but my mind was racing. There was no hope. I checked my phone, seven-forty-five, no voicemails, no texts. My temper shot through the roof and I had this gut-feeling that today was going to be a *horrible* day! I flung the covers away from me, grabbed my clothes, and walked to the bathroom. Hopefully, a nice hot shower would do the trick. *Wrong again!* The door was shut. *Great!*

From where I stood I could smell bacon cooking downstairs. I tossed my stuff in the floor beside the bathroom door to claim my place next in line and then followed my nose. Sarah and Aunt Beth were standing side-by-side with one of each of their legs cocked up to look like flamingos. Sarah looked rough. What was left of her ponytail was deformed and off to the side. I nearly laughed aloud. Aunt Beth smiled and ruffled Sarah's hair even more, a motion that did little to wake Sarah.

"Not much of a morning person?" I joked.

Sarah smiled a sweet, yet sarcastic smile. Ah-ha, there *is* life in there beneath all the Jesus stuff! She stopped turning the bacon and reached over to a cup of coffee and took a swig, allowing the black nectar to do its magic. My stomach growled and my throat started to close...I could *really* use a latte right now.

"Do you like French toast, Erin?" asked Aunt Beth.

"Yeah," I replied with a nod.

Dad walked in the kitchen a minute later and stopped in his tracks.

"Erin, are you okay?" he asked, almost scared.

"Yeah, why?" I asked, suddenly wondering if I was bleeding from somewhere.

"It's before nine...this has to be some sort of Mitchell family record or something..."

"Maybe it's a sign that you should come to church with us this morning," announced Aunt Beth.

I started to stammer some sort of excuse, but Dad took care of that for me.

"Of course she would!"

Wait a minute! Was I still asleep? Did I hear him right? I looked at Dad who was now sitting down with a smirk on his face.

"And so would Ian," he added, "I think it'd do them some good to go to church with you this morning. What do you think, Sarah?"

Sarah smiled another half-smile and continued to put her faith in her coffee cup for the time being.

"Breakfast will be ready in about five minutes, guys," Aunt Beth announced.

Well, no sense in waiting around here, I'll go in the living room and watch some... I opened the door of the kitchen and noticed for the first time why the living room seemed so bare. There wasn't a television. *What? Seriously?* Okay, I know they choose to wear skirts and stuff here, but where am I, the eighteen hundreds?

The women spent the next hour racing in and out of the bathroom, while Dad and Ian were stuck with the dishes. Thankfully, boys can take showers the night before and give women all the time they need in the morning. Unfortunately for us, there are four women who need the two blow-dryers, one curling iron, shower, and small bathroom mirror. But there's a reason why women are the smarter of the two species. Men would probably have had wars over these things in the past, but women are awesome. Leaving the water on, I jumped out of the shower, tossed the towel around me, and Sarah was right behind me jumping in. Aunt Beth was doing her make-up while mom finished blow-drying her hair. It was like an assembly line. Once Sarah was done with her shower, Aunt Beth was done with her makeup, mom was done with the blow-dryer and we rotated. Mom took over the makeup counter, I snatched the blow-dryer, and Sarah rushed out of the room to get dressed. Personally, I think we should make this a competitive sport, because we would rock.

We were all done in record time and out the door only ten minutes later than when Aunt Beth said they *normally* left for church. This excited me. Ten minutes late could mean a world of difference. On one hand, it could mean ten less minutes clapping methodically to some old country music hymn and on the other hand it could mean ten less minutes of watching all the people walk around with brainwashed smiles on their faces. It's what I like to call a win-win.

And of course there was always the boring old fat guy in a suit two sizes too small that stood up and talked everyone to sleep too; well, at least that's how it is on Easter Sunday. I wasn't too excited to see any of *those* people either, but it was only one day. I figured if Sarah and Aunt Beth could stomach it for four days a week, I could manage it for one.

Dad and Ian were dressed like they'd known all along we were going to be staying long enough to do something like this. I felt kinda grungy in blue jeans and a Hollister hoodie, but I guess that'd have to do... I mean, what were they gonna do kick me out for not having a dress? Sarah and Aunt Beth both had on dressy outfits; mom was wearing some of Aunt Beth's clothes, a nice skirt and a buttoned up white shirt. It looked really pretty on her.

"I was thinking about having mom's wake here," announced Aunt Beth, "If that's alright?"

"Sure," Mom replied. She nodded for a little while after she spoke. I do that sometimes. My mind will start to wander and have little flashbacks and I'll be in this dream world for a little while before I realize I'm still nodding along. It's embarrassing, but I'm sure she didn't care what others thought right now. It was obvious she had a lot on her mind.

"What about the burial?" Dad asked.

It sounded so odd to have an actual conversation about these sorts of things just after Nana died, but I guess that's what has to be done. I looked at Ian to see what he thought, but he only stared out the window, probably bummed out that he had to be another week without Whitney up his butt. Unintentionally, my hand reached for my cell phone and I remembered that Jake still hadn't called me back. *Maybe he would've if you wouldn't have left him such a crappy message!* A voice screamed in my mind. I hate it when I argue with my-self. I wanted to call him about four thousand more times, but I couldn't bring myself to do it. Then I would seem like the obsessive Whitney-ish girlfriend and I didn't want to seem like that... Another thought came to mind. What if he left town too, but only he forgot his cell phone? I mean, that would make perfect sense. His mom and dad *were* always going out of town on little business things. Maybe they were taking a trip to Vail to go skiing and since I was out of town, he thought he'd pass his lonely time by spending it with his folks? My stomach suddenly crept its way up to my throat. What if he gets home and listens to my message? It'd be like I was just another nagging girlfriend like all of the others; the ones he broke up with before me, the one's he said I wasn't like. What if he realized that I'm nothing special?

Our first date came back to mind. It felt like so long ago when we were sitting at Giorgio's and he was confessing his love for me. The images of the past few months rushed through my mind. He was so patient and sweet. He never pressured me into anything. Even after all the hang-ups and setbacks, he was still right there for me. He even sided with me against his friends and I nagged him over the phone because he hadn't called me...some girlfriend!

The sign read *Lakeview Assembly* and beside it was a man wearing a suit waving at everyone. How exciting! I could just tell that this was going to be a morning full of action and adventure. I got out of the blazer with a huff. I didn't want to be here anymore. I wanted to be with Jake. I wanted to tell him I was sorry and that I was stupid for treating him that way. Every step I took toward the door was getting more and more annoying; all the smiling faces, all of the laughing and dresses and suits. I know it's important to do these sorts of things and to support family and blah, blah, blah, but Jake needed me too. He needed to know how sorry I was for acting like all the other girls and that I didn't mean to be so whiny. Maybe he'd understand that I just missed him and that Whitney and Ian were being ridiculous and it was weighing on me? I was suddenly mad at Ian and Whitney all over again for being so dumb. Why was everyone smiling?

I must've heard "Good Morning" about five thousand times before we even made it to the front door. What makes them think it's such a good morning? Why do Jesus people seem to think it's okay to be annoying at church, but then when you see them in the mall they're just like everyone else? Well, except for their lack of fashion...

The building was "L" shaped and formed to the land that overlooked Grover's lake and Hammond Falls below. Inside the main room where I was preparing to be bored to death for the next hour and a half, there were large windows that had an amazing view. At least I'd have something to look at all comfortable in my blue jeans and hoodie while the overdressed guy sweated through all three pieces of his suit and blabbed on and on about stuff I didn't care about.

We used to go to church when we were younger. At least, I can remember having those little princess dresses that I'd wear every Sunday. Mom's family has always been about that sort of thing, which is why we're probably here today, for Nana. Mom and Aunt Beth grew up a few hours south of here through high school. Right after graduation, Aunt Beth got married, and mom moved to Davis-Buckley and met my dad. Dad's not too churchy though... Whenever we flip past the church channels on television he just shakes his head and makes some sort of comment about how they're

all about money or how fake they are, or something...
I never really understood what he meant, but I guess
now I kind of do. Everyone around me either has a nice
dress, highlights, or at least flashy jewelry. And then all
of the men have suits or at least something name brand
with a tie; most of them are old-man name brand, but
I guess if an old man were wearing Hollister I might
reconsider my fashion choices.

Aunt Beth sat with us while Sarah walked around
and mingled with some of her friends and the older ladies. At least I recognized a *few* people... Henry
and Lavender, the two kids from Africa, were walking
around with their mom and dad. Not too far from them
stood Savannah and Lisa talking with a few other girls.
Sarah made her way up front to the stage and talked to
Evan who was also sporting a suit-ish look: stylish jeans
with a blazer, fashionably churchy. Was she flirting
with him? She looked so excited and smiley, but then
again she always looked that way, so it was hard to tell
for sure. Of course, I'd like to think that goody-goody
church girls *could* have a bit of backseat fun sometimes
too, but I think that'd probably go against some of their
religious beliefs. And why would Sarah be all excited
about *him*? He wasn't even the hottest guy here! Nick
from the coffee shop was hotter than Evan! Maybe it's
some kind of Jesus thing, or something? You know,
something that says a hot Jesus girl can't date a hot Jesus
guy...

Church started a few minutes later. Surprisingly, the fat guy must've missed the memo and he was replaced by a skinnier, more excited, younger man. This guy gave a little speech about some kind of events and then asked everyone to bow their heads and pray. Once the prayer was done, about ten people made their way to the stage and took their positions behind their instruments. It seemed like there was going to be a little better music than the old country stuff Aunt Beth listens to... thank God! The man standing behind the keyboard started talking for a minute about a spirit... It all started getting so confusing after that. People started praying all around us and girls started crying somewhere in front of us. I've never seen so much chaos before. People were crying, others were laughing and some were even shouting things like "Praise you, Lord!" I couldn't make out if I was supposed to be happy or sad. Then the keyboard guy said something that seemed weirder than the usual weird.

"I know there's someone here today who feels like the world is letting them down; someone who feels like nothing makes any sense and that everything's falling apart all around them..."

Yeah!

"...well, I'm here to tell you can change that, if you want to..."

Oh really! I'm all ears!

"...I'm here to tell you that there is a world without limits waiting on you to make the tough decision..."

What decision?

"...a world without limits that's waiting on you to come to terms with the truth..."

What decision? What Truth?

"You see, right now you're a prisoner in a world of pressures and stress and pain, but I know a way out...I know a way to a key that can unlock every handcuff or shackle; a key that can unlock any prison door, all you have to do is make the choice..."

What choice? What decision?

"All you have to do is *believe*..."

What? Is that what it's really all about?

"All you have to do is realize what Jesus' life meant, what his death meant, and what his resurrection means to us all..."

Resurrection?

People all around the room were chanting "Amen" and "Preach it" and other things, but something was still bothering me. When was he going to answer all of his comments? What truth? What decision? What choice could I make to stop all of these problems? How could I make everything right? What did he mean by *realizing* what Jesus' life meant? And he came back to life? How? I thought he died on a cross...

"Jesus is the way, the truth, and the life..." he added as the band started to play, "and only the truth can set you free!"

So the truth *is* the key? Man, this church stuff is more confusing that Mrs. Prichard's English class. Why did it seem like everything was in code or something? I felt like I was trying to learn another language. Actually, Spanish was a lot easier than this...

The music was a lot like Sarah and her friends' style, except it was older people singing it. Their voices weren't *bad* and the beat was *alright,* but it was still this scrambled stuff about worshipping Jesus for who he was and all these names like Son of Man and Great I Am. Once the music stopped another guy came on stage and talking about the importance of giving with all of your heart.

"It's time to take up the offering," whispered Dad.

"Offering? What do you mean?"

"They always make a big deal about things when it's time to give the money... That's all churches are about anymore, money!"

I wasn't sure exactly what he meant, but I think he was right. I mean, this guy spoke for a while about the importance of giving in this season of thanksgiving and showing God how much you appreciated all he had done for you. I thought about that for a moment. Yeah, I really appreciate God for making my parents go psycho about a halter I *didn't* steal! Oh, and let's not forget the whole Carrie hurting my brother and becoming a skank incident either... Or the fact that Jake *hasn't* called me and that I'm stuck here in the middle of nowhere for another week. Oh, and my Nana died. Yeah, I have a lot to thank God for... I think he owes *me* money!

They passed around these little plates where everyone threw in their money. I can't believe how much it was… I could see green everywhere! Aunt Beth and Sarah put some in and Mom elbowed Dad with that look she gives me sometimes. After a silent argument that lasted a few seconds, Dad finally shook his head and caved and then did what she wanted him to.

Then something weird happened.

"The youth can be dismissed to their services," said the preacher-guy.

Sarah got up and grabbed my hand. "Come on," she said, "Youth…that's us!"

Ian stood up and walked with us down the small domed room until we came to another set of stairs that led down into a basement area. There were tables and chairs set up with a small thingy for the speaker to stand behind. There was a wall of shelves with tons of books on them on one side and then a painting on the other that looked like a knight getting ready to fight a dragon. The knight looked cool, but the dragon was kind of wimpy looking.

As we walked in, Henry and Lavender were setting out cups and pouring drinks. Evan and Savannah walked out from a storage closet with boxes of chips and cookies and passed them out to everyone. A guy who barely looked older than us told us to come on in and have a seat while we were being served. After a few seconds, everyone who wanted one had a drink and a snack on in front of them.

"Good morning guys and gals, I'm Brother Craig," he started.

Everyone mumbled something, either "good morning" or "we know who you are".

"I'm the youth pastor here at Lakeview Assembly and I'd like to welcome all of our visitors this morning...thanks for coming."

Pastor? Isn't that where cows graze?

"This morning we're going to be picking up where we left off Wednesday night, so if you'll all open your bibles to the book of Genesis we can get started. If you don't have a bible and you want to follow along, you can either share with a neighbor or borrow one of ours on the shelf. Take your pick, there's plenty!"

Suddenly I realized that all those books were bibles. There must be hundreds... Different shapes, sizes, colors, some leather, others harder like a school book... I didn't know they made all those kinds of bibles! I thought it was all old thou, thee, henceforth stuff...

I decided not to stand up in front of thirty kids I didn't know and simply leaned in close to Sarah. Ian did the same with Henry, who I noticed was smiling nearly as wide as he had been on the night we met him. He was such an awesome guy...always happy and positive. I remember when I used to be that way. It feels like so long ago now, but then again it's been a crazy past few months.

Brother Craig talked about this tower that people tried to build to get to heaven and he started drawing things out on a dry erase board and talking about how things were separated and how people were given different languages. It was sort of boring at first, but then it started to sound cooler the more he talked about it. It was like history, but magical and cooler. I always wondered how, if the earth used to be one big body of land like Mrs. Erickson says in Biology II, people had changed so much and started to speak and write and act completely different from one another. Of course, there were some *Jesus things* they had to throw in there that didn't make much sense, but the rest of it was pretty cool though. Now I had questions to ask Mrs. Erickson.

Before too long we were done and dismissed to go back upstairs. Brother Craig stopped us before we could leave and said, "Hey guys...before you go why don't you grab a bible off the shelf and take it with you... You know, make it your own! Give it a read sometimes?"

I shook my head. I really didn't care about having one, but then he shrugged and said, "I just want to get rid of them...and I saw how interested you two were with the lesson today, so if you want one, please, take your pick!"

I started to say, "Na, thanks anyway," but Ian walked past me and looked at the wall of bibles. I turned around to see Sarah waiting patiently, talking with Henry and the rest of her Friday night friends. Why not? I guess I can either stand in the circle of friends and feel left out, or I can hang out with Ian.

As we walked out of church and started to make our

way for the blazer, my hoodie pocket vibrated. I almost didn't recognize the feeling. The screen read, Message from Jake. I opened it, astonished.

"Hey baby, sry I hvn't clld snr. I'll call tnt & xpln."

I couldn't hide the smile on my face for the rest of the day. It had been a big misunderstanding just like I thought it was... take *that* Ian and Whitney!

Chapter Twenty-Three ~
November 19th - 21st
(The Week of Thanksgiving)

Sunday night was amazing. I talked to Jake for almost two hours...it felt so good just to hear his voice. It
reminded me of how it feels when you finally get to use
the bathroom after you've been holding it for a while, or
the moment a piece of Godiva chocolate touches your
lips. Anyway, it boiled down to this...

The same weekend we left to come here, Jake had to
work with his parents and deliver something for their
business. On his way to the warehouse in the company
truck, his cell slid down in the seat and he thought he
had forgotten it back in his truck, so... when he got back
to his truck and started home he realized that he didn't
have it. He checked his house, his parent's business, his
truck and finally the business truck, and there it was
under the seat. It took him a few days to find it thanks
to his parents working him like a dog all weekend, but
now he says I'm all his until I come back. I apologized
for the message, but he said it was no big deal and
that he would've been worried if I *wouldn't* have been

so worried? Ian has sort of avoided me ever since Jake
called Sunday night, which tells me that he's either being stubborn about what he said about Jake or that he's
worried I'm going to tell Jake and he's gonna get his butt
kicked or something., like I'd do that. I'd never call in
that favor. I'd just hold it over his head to get whatever I
wanted. *No dirty dishes for Erin next month, yes!*

Tuesday was the wake and funeral for Nana. I didn't
realize how loved she was by all the people around here.
Dad said it was probably just some of the old coots out
to get her antique jewelry and stuff, but I like to think it's
because she was well liked. The whole church showed up
and the young pastor guy gave a speech about her, it was
actually kind of nice. Afterwards, Aunt Beth said she
would have wanted them to have an actual church ser-
vice in memory of how much she loved church, so they
did. The band got up on stage and played for a while.
Everyone clapped and seemed to have a great time, almost like how they were on Sunday, except dressed in
all black instead of pretty frilly sun dresses and stuff.

It started to snow on the way to the cemetery. The
wind was cold and strong, but I was either beginning to
get used to it, or my mind was really distracted, because
all I could think about was what Nana said to me that
day in the room. She was ready. She believed in God.
As I looked around at the people who spent a lot more
time with my Nana than I ever did, I kind of felt jealous. What was it about God that was so much fun for
them and made her *"ready"*? What was it about God

that made everyone so happy? It wasn't the music... that's for sure!

After the burial, Dad walked up to Ian, Sarah, and I, and said, "Let's take a walk guys..." The look on his face told me something instructive or disciplining was coming.

"Listen guys," he started, once we were far away from Mom and Aunt Beth, "I know you're all going through a lot right now, but there's something I need all of you to do for me. Not just for me, but for your Moms' too!"

We all nodded, waiting...

"I know this might be a lot to ask, but I want you to take a few minutes to think about what I'm saying before you try to argue or say anything back. This is a life-altering thing your Moms are going through right now..." he stopped and looked to Sarah, "I know you already know what your mom's going through," he reached over and gave her a hug before continuing. "They need you guys right now...they need us all, so here's what I need from you. I need you all to put yourselves aside for a few months. Don't argue with them! Don't fuss about doing chores or any little thing they might ask you to do, okay? Just put yourself second for the next couple of months and focus on them, alright? Let your moms be the priority. Thanksgiving, Christmas, New Year's, those are big days out of the year and this'll be the first year they have it without their mom, so it's going to be like walking on eggshells around here, okay?"

Once he finished, we all looked at one another and nodded. There was no way I could even think of arguing with him. How could I? I mean, Nana was everything to Mom and I'm sure Aunt Beth depended on her a lot too... The three of us agreed almost instantly and I could see the stress rise off of my dad's shoulders.

That afternoon Ian and I sat with Sarah and made a list of things we could do for our moms to make things a little easier until they got back in the swing of things. Now that I really thought about it, it wasn't too much work, maybe even only ten more minutes a day of little things that weren't even really all that hard, and with Dad and Ian to help, it was going to be no problem. Sarah was having a hard time figuring out what she could do. After all, it was only her and Aunt Beth now. But then when I thought about it, I mean, what did Aunt Beth have to do? Sarah already did a lot!

"Maybe I could get a part-time job at the coffee shop or something?" she suggested, "That'd help out with gas money and things for me, so she didn't have to worry about that stuff."

I nodded. I mean, how much did Sarah really spend? She wore old skirts and clothes from the forties, for one; secondly, she could probably make a bedroom somewhere in the church and save hundreds in gas money. I almost snickered at the second thought, but something stopped me. She actually looked worried.

"Sarah, I'm sure everything will be fine... I mean, you already do a lot..."

"Yeah," added Ian, "You're like the best teenager ever, I think."

Sarah smiled, but I could tell this was really bothering her.

"It's just…a part-time job would mean that we're away from one another more and I'm sure it wouldn't be good for my mom to be all alone every night, but now that Nana's social security check isn't going to come anymore we're going to need the money…"

She started to cry. Ian leaned toward her and put his arm around her.

"It's gonna be fine," I said, "Maybe your Mom would want to get a little part-time job herself? Maybe you two could work together?"

"Or at the same times at least?" added Ian.

"At least you wouldn't have to be apart then…" I inserted.

Something we were saying was clicking because Sarah's tears started to disappear and her eyes started darting, as if something was coming to mind, something brilliant. Ian and I both waited on her to say something, but she didn't. Instead, she only nodded along.

Wednesday morning started out well, just like all the others had so far this week. Ian and I worked on our school work before mom asked us to and when she came upstairs to talk to us about it and saw that we were already doing it, she seemed happy. Seeing her happy about something like that made us both feel a little better about our promise to Dad. Besides, when you're only doing the school work it doesn't take nearly as long as it normally would spending the entire day at school. I can totally see why Sarah likes being home schooled now.

At lunch Kylie texted me and asked me how things were going out here. I texted her back and told her that things could be better, but at least they weren't as horrible as they had been. She said Carrie was still skank'n it up and that her new beau, Eric, was her greatest find yet. Drug dealer, user, and apparently he liked to hit girls, too. But according to Kylie, Carrie was clinging to his arm proudly sporting her bruises... Girls can be so stupid sometimes! The thought of how dumb Carrie was almost made me feel sorry for her, but then I remembered that she had practically asked for it all year. I mean, what sort of a girl has a Joe Gregory experience and then goes all psycho and starts seeking it out? If I let it, the thought of Carrie would've ruined my day, so I just shook the thoughts of how stupid she'd become from my mind and got back to my work.

It started snowing around two o'clock, when Sarah walked in from doing her work in her room.

"Hey, you guys about done?" she asked.

"I am," Ian said right away. They looked at me.

"I'm close enough," I replied, shutting my geometry book, "Why?"

"Wanna go into town for a few hours before our Youth tonight?" she asked.

Youth? I had forgotten all about having to go back to *church* before Thanksgiving.

Ian looked at me and shrugged. *Quick, think of a way out of it...Homework...nope! Important thing...nope!*

"It's a lot cooler...we do our own praise and worship on Youth nights..." she added.

I wanted to say, "Well, since it's the least *crappy* of the two," but I didn't. How could I tell those big, excited eyes that I just wasn't as excited about her music as I was mine? Why didn't she understand that her Jesus music wasn't for everybody?

"Sure," I blurted. I don't know what happened, it just came out! I would have to give myself a stern stare-down in the mirror for that one. That was worse than all the times I blurt what I'm thinking. Immediately, I realized why something compelled me to go along with her. I saw her eyes ignite, and that smile of hers that could light up a room, and I knew it was for a good reason. Sarah needed it. She needed us to be there for her as bad as Dad needed us to be there for our moms. Why? *I'm not sure*, because, I mean, she has *tons* of Jesus friends to hang out with, why would she need us? I guess it mattered a lot to her though because she seemed like a different girl when we left for town at three.

"What do you want to do, first?" she asked.

Oh, let's play some checkers down by the old soda pop store! Or have an igloo building contest! I'm sure my shrug masked my sarcasm, but honestly, what was there to do here?

"We could go to the Underground?" she offered.

My interests were peaked by the name of the place alone. "What's that?" I asked.

"It's a sort of hangout for the people who go to school around here," she said with a shrug, "kinda like their youth, but with secular music..."

I looked at Ian.

"What kind of music?"

"Secular; the kind *you* listen to. The stuff on the radio...MTV," she explained.

"Oh, so is it like a club or something?"

"No. Just a hangout; kind of like the coffee shop, but with a little of everything. There're games and tables, food...all kinds of stuff, it can be cool. I go there sometimes..."

Can be... I can't believe I hadn't heard of this place sooner.

We drove down Main Street first, and then took a side alley to a small lot where we parked and then walked. Sarah led the way back up to Main Street and then down the covered walkways to a place called *The Dandelion* in big neon letters. She opened the door and walked into a room with stairs going up and down. Music came from both ways.

"There's another place up top?" I asked.

"Yeah, it's sort of a bar and grill place," Sarah replied. "I hardly ever go there, only if it's late and we're hungry. The Underground's owned by the same people though, so it's all the same," she added with a wave for us to follow her. The stairs spiraled down into another room with a few doors.

"The bathrooms are back there; that door goes to the arcade room, and this one," she said, shoving the door, "is where the Underground is..."

The room reminded me of a Chili's but with more space and much more music and noise. With it being the day before thanksgiving, everyone was out having a good time before their long weekend. It was basically the same as any party I've ever been to, except there were people serving drinks and no one was throwing up. A small dance floor was off to the side where some lights were spinning and people were having sex with their clothes on. It has its purposes, but who wants to get sweaty and stinky if they don't have to? I guess if Jake were here, I would, but that's a different story.

Sarah led us to a table far away from the loudness of the speakers and the heat that seemed to pour from the dance floor. It amazes me how many people don't wear deodorant. I mean, thousands of years ago people took scented baths. Girls take hours putting on makeup, doing their hair, wearing deodorant *and* spray... Why can't a guy take two seconds to wipe some deodorant under his arms before he walks out the bathroom? *Disgusting!* They should hire a person to do sniff checks on guys before they walk into a place like this just to make sure. I mean, not a *girl* of course, maybe a homeless guy or something? I'd hate to have that job, but it's necessary!

No girl wants to get all bumped into by some sweaty mongrel who smells like onions! *Yuck!*

We sat there for a few minutes talking and looking at menus before a waitress came. It was relieving to hear real music for a change. I got to hear a few of my favorites before we looked at the clock and started to leave. It was like a breath of not-so-fresh, fresh air. On the way out a hand grabbed my arm and spun me around. It was a guy about Jake's size and suddenly he was really close to me.

"You can't leave yet," he said.

I looked at him for a second, scoffed, shook my head, and turned back around. He grabbed my arm again, but this time when he turned me around I shoved him in the chest.

"Back off!" I said.

He looked at his friends and they smiled and cheered him on.

"Oh, this one's feisty!" he laughed, "I like a feisty girl..."

Before I could blink, Ian's arm slid in front of me and put me behind him, but I don't think that did much good. He would get clobbered by this guy. I turned around to leave again, but when I did I saw that Sarah was having the same kind of trouble. There was another guy who was harassing her too, but worse. Apparently, they were all together, because from behind me I could hear the big guy cheering for his friend. Sarah was trying hard not to get mad. I guess it was some kind of

Jesus thing, but every time she would try to walk past the guy he would cut her off and then bump her back with his body. I grabbed someone's soda from a nearby table and walked up to Sarah.

"Back off, or get a shower, Jerk!"

The guy stopped laughing.

"What'd you say to me?"

"You heard me! Now back off before I make you smell better!"

He started to act like he was going to do something, but I brought my arm back to throw it and he lifted his hands as if to say that he didn't want a coke bath after all. We walked pretty fast through the rest of the club and just before we got to the door another hand reached out and grabbed my arm. I wasn't going to be harassed any longer. I turned with an open hand and slapped the guy harder on the face than I ever remember slapping anyone in my life.

Nick almost spun in a complete circle. The look on his face was horrifying.

"Oh my God, Nick, I'm so sorry! Are you okay? I thought you were one of those creepy guys... Nick, I'm so sorry!" I rushed up to him and put my hands on his face and then gave him a hug.

I must've said, "I'm sorry" about ten times before the shock finally wore off and he nodded and then said, "It's alright..."

"Erin," Ian called from the door.

"I've gotta go..." I said, still feeling bad.

"Is there any way I can make it up to you? I'm so sorry, I really did think..."

I stopped talking because his eyes lit up.

"What?" I asked.

"A kiss," he said.

"A kiss?"

"A kiss," he repeated, "That's how you can make it up to me..."

I smirked, but shook my head, "Nick, I can't..."

"Well, you asked if there was *any* way you could make it up to me..."

Suddenly, his cute face seemed cuter and I think the heat from the dance floor was starting to take its toll on me.

"I'll think about it..." I said as I turned. I made it to the door and looked back to see that he was still staring at me, holding his red cheek. Had Jake not called me on Sunday night I would have been all over Nick, but the thought of Jake kept me focused. *Only two more days, Erin... Keep it together!*

Chapter Twenty-four ~
November 22nd - Thursday
(Thanksgiving)

Mom, Aunt Beth, Sarah, and I spent most of the day in and out of the kitchen. There weren't a lot of people to cook for, but there was plenty of traditional food to make it a real Thanksgiving. We had to have the perfect turkey and stuffing, not to mention mashed potatoes and gravy, oh and green bean casserole, Nan's favorite. The smell of fresh bread filled up the whole house, thanks to Sarah. She taught me how to make it and wow! Its way better than anything I've ever bought from anywhere! I think I'll make that once a week until the day I die.

Jake called around noon and we talked for about thirty minutes. I asked him about Carrie and he laughed.

"Yeah, she's with a real winner now, let me tell you..." he said.

"How's basketball?"

"It doesn't start for another week or two still,"

"Oh,"

"So, when are you coming home?" he asked. I could

tell by his voice he was wanting something he hadn't had in quite a while; a present I was eager to give him after Nick's eyes had undressed me last night.

"Not soon enough," I whispered, "but when I do…"

I heard something shut and then Jake's hand slipped over the phone. He was saying something, but then he suddenly came back on the phone, "Sorry sweetie, my mom's been acting weird lately, just walks in on my phone conversations for some reason…"

"Welcome to the world of weird moms," I said with a laugh.

"Yeah, I guess…" he said, almost mad.

"Going to the cabin this weekend?" I asked.

He grumbled a little, "I don't know, maybe? I guess, just to hang out with the guys. Maybe I'll tell'm no chicks allowed just so I don't have to feel all alone," he added.

"Oh stop, you're making me feel bad!"

"Well," he said, "How would *you* feel if I left *you* all alone and all these hot guys kept hitting on you all day, but you had to keep telling them, 'No…my girlfriend's gonna to come home *some*day'."

"Oh really?" I laughed, "Hot girls, huh? All day long?"

"Well, maybe one or two," he chuckled.

"But of course you told them I'm way hotter than them, right?"

"Oh, sure," he said, "Yep, right after I said, *'Eww, are you serious? You girls are way too hideous!'*"

"Jake," I said, in my best motherly voice, "that's not funny! You told them you had a girlfriend right?"

"Of course, Erin," he laughed.

Once I got off the phone it was back to work for me. We had dinner around four, the traditional thanksgiving time. I think they originally started having dinner that early so they'd have room for more around seven or eight, but that's just my guess. As we all took our seats at the table, Aunt Beth stood up.

"Mom always wanted to go around the table and have everyone give thanks for something before we ate, but we never have, so I thought it would be a neat tradition to start now," she said. Everyone nodded along. Mom and Aunt Beth held hands for a second, both on the brink of crying, before Aunt Beth took a deep breath and started.

"I would like to give thanks for a great mother who raised us in a home of love, and who was always there for us."

Mom went next. "I would like to give thanks for a great family." As she said this she glanced at each of us, tears streaming down her cheeks. She swiped her napkin up to dab them as she continued. "I'm so thankful for everything right now."

Dad shuffled in his seat, nervous about what to say. I could tell he was probably going for the whole "great family" bit, but Mom had stolen his thunder. He leaned over and kissed Mom and then cleared his throat.

"I'm thankful for a job that allows me to take care of my family, and for a family that comes together when it needs to," he said with a smile and a wink to me and Ian.

I think it was during Ian's bumbling thanks when I realized that I should really prepare for something. What am I thankful for? Jake? No, I can't use that one when everyone else's using the whole "family" card. I am thankful for my Mom and Dad, but recently they haven't been very high-five supportive, if you know what I mean. Ian...not so much. Friends...no. What could I say? As I was thinking about it, I guess I had missed Ian finish, and everyone was staring at me.

"Erin," said Aunt Beth, "What are you thankful for, honey?"

"Well, I was trying to think about something you guys haven't already said...and I can't think of anything."

Sarah put her hand on my shoulder and stood. "I know there's been a lot that's gone on over the past few weeks, but I just want to thank Jesus for everything; for taking Nana home, for safety, and for my family. I know things are going to be alright because He loves us and He's in control."

Aunt Beth, Mom, and even Dad all said, "Amen".

Dinner was sooo good! Now I know why the women always do all the cooking; it tastes so much better when you cook it. Well, that *and* because the guys are lazy and would probably mess everything up, but still, it was great! We all sat around and grumbled for a little while afterwards, while Dad and Ian tuned the kitchen radio into the football game. It started snowing again once the sun went down and we all sat in the living room and played board games and ate cherry pie with ice cream on top until Dad fell asleep in the recliner. I think I gained five pounds since I woke up this morning, but I'm sure a few days' worth of leftovers will stop me from eating much more for the rest of the week.

I thought we might stay longer, but Dad's work week starts on Saturday, so tomorrow morning is apparently the time to go according to Mom. Ian and I got our stuff out of the dryer and folded it into our suitcases before Mom told us to. She probably thinks being around Sarah has influenced us. I hope she doesn't try to home school us hoping we'll turn into Jesus children or something because I'm not wearing a skirt and sixty year old fashions just for fun!

Chapter Twenty-Five

November 23rd - Friday

The ride home was a little better than the ride out to Aunt Beth's house, mainly because it was light out this time and we were able to see all of the things we hadn't seen on the way. Mom stopped at Starbuck's for us and we ended up stopping at some trucker place so the boys could get hot chocolate for a more *reasonable price*, or so they said. I think you get what you pay for, and I like the thought of drinking four dollars' worth of amazing Latte-ness.

Jake and I texted back and forth all day. He thinks I'm coming home on Sunday. I can't wait to see the look on his face when I surprise him tonight. He'll probably feel bad that he wasn't able to get the romantic stuff ready, but who needs romantic stuff when you've been away from one another for as long as we have? I just want him!

On one text he told me that he might be going to a party at Cheryl Sanford's house with Dyson and the guys. I'm sure Kylie will be there if Dyson is... Maybe if

I call her, she'll be able to let me know if he's still there or not? I'm sure she can keep a secret.

Dad drove the entire way this time and he even took a different route at one point just to bypass a few of the larger canyons. I thought to rush out the door right then, or at least act like I was tired and ready to go to bed so I could sneak out the back, but my Mom looked bummed out.

"You okay?" I asked.

She gave me a sort of half-smile and nodded. I wasn't convinced.

"You know, I never really noticed how much warmer it is here than there," I said.

"There's not as much wind here," she explained.

"Ah," I sounded. That's what it was, the wind! I noticed that my hair *actually* looked descent for the first time in over a week.

I wondered what Jake was doing and why Kylie hadn't text me back yet. If I hurried maybe I could make it to his house before he went to the party? The thought made me want to sprint down the railroad tracks, but my eyes wandered from the single light shining down on the distant crossing to the sad expression on my mom's face. I was almost positive there was nothing I could say to make anything better. It's so ironic that I'm torn between two situations, one where I can *completely* control the happiness, and the other where I can't. Yet, here I am struggling with the one I can't just take my shirt off for and solve.

But in all my excitement, my mouth moved faster than I wanted it to.

"Wanna go for a walk?" I blurted.

What are you doing? What about Jake? You remember that hot boyfriend of yours don't you? God, you're so stupid!

My mom smiled and nodded, "Sure."

Of course she would accept...

We stepped off the porch and started walking toward the junior college. Ironically, Jake's house was completely in the other direction. It's amazing how things work out sometimes, isn't it? If only my mom knew what I was sacrificing for her. Well, actually, now that I think about it, if she *knew* she would probably be acting completely different right now, and not to mention grounding me for life. I'd be the only eighty year old woman I know who can say they've only slept with one guy twenty-four times...in their life! But who's counting?

"I'm sorry I've been such a wreck lately," Mom said.

"What do you mean?"

"I've just been all scatter-brained and..." she waved her hands and stuck her tongue out.

I wondered suddenly if someone had looked out their window at that exact moment and what they might've thought. I know if it were me, I'd be dying laughing wishing I could've recorded it and put it on YouTube.

"Mom, Nana *just* died... How do you think you *should* be acting?"

She only nodded.

"I mean, I keep thinking how I would feel if I were you and had to face what you're facing, I'd be crazy. I can't imagine losing you! I don't know what I'd do."

Mom started getting teary eyed and so did I.

Quick, think of something clever! You don't want your eyes to be all puffy when Jake's kissing you!

"I mean, cause Dad sucks at cooking!"

Mom scoffed and slapped me on the shoulder.

"So that's all I am to you, huh, a cook?" she said, laughing.

"A *great* cook," I added instantly. Mom laughed some more. It was good to see her relax a little.

"And besides, Dad and Ian are too cheap to take me to Starbuck's, so you have to stick around a lot longer than them..."

"Oh, I should've known you'd need your coffee, too." she added.

As we walked, I turned down a street I hadn't walked down in months. I'd spent my entire summer up and down this street and it only felt natural to turn down the familiar sidewalk. My mom leaned in close and threw her arm around me. It felt like the old times again; the ones I thought I wasn't going to see after the halter incident. Apparently, the crazy pill had been accidentally passed around and taken by my parents, but now it appeared to be out of their systems completely and things were starting to get back to that odd place I like to call normal.

Another block and, once again, we turned right. I wasn't sure why we were walking this way, but the walk seemed to be doing Mom some good, so we kept going. My feet felt heavier and heavier the further I got from Jake's bedroom, but I guess it all boiled down to Dad's little talk that day at the funeral, and the look on Mom's face showed how well his plan was working.

"You know, this is nice," she said. "We haven't talk-ed in a long time, you know?"

I nodded.

"How come?"

I shrugged. "Just a bunch of junk, I guess..."

She nodded her agreement. After all, it *was* true. School had turned out to be so much more this year than I could have ever planned for it to be, starting with Jake. I mean, now that I think about it, everything had been about Jake in some way this year. The halter inci-dent, the cabin, the parties...

"So how are things with you and Jake?" Mom asked. I almost screamed out loud. Was she telepathic?

"Good," I said. *But with a little luck they'll be a lot better before I go to sleep tonight.*

"Can you believe Whitney and Ian are together?" she asked. She sort of made a face that told me she never expected that to happen.

I nodded and smirked to show her that I agreed with her puzzled expression. I knew that Whitney had this thing for him at the beginning of the year, but I never once noticed him notice her. It's amazing how things work out sometimes. It dawned on me why Mom asked that question as soon as we turned the corner. We were now on Carrie's street. After years of being friends it seemed unreal that I wasn't close to her anymore. We knew everything about one another. Well, everyone knew everything about me, too – thanks to her – but I guess that's a different story. Even Whitney and I had sort of fallen away from one another thanks to her little infatuation with Ian. Why did my friends have to date my brother? Kylie and I knew one another pretty well, but we weren't what you'd call best friends, close yeah, but not *best* material.

Mom snickered and I came from my daydream.

"What?" I asked.

"Oh," she said, laughing a little more before she finished, "I was just thinking about what Kylie did that night at the football game…"

"Oh, when she beat on Joe Gregory?"

Mom just laughed.

"I love that little girl to death," she said. Hopefully, she was talking about Kylie.

"You know, Carrie ended up dating him again anyway…"

"*Really?*" Mom scoffed, "That's a shame…that's such a shame, she's such a pretty girl to be into all the things I hear her being into these days. Poor Margaret doesn't know what to do with her now. I guess she's all sorts of wild now… Sneaking out… Going to parties…"

Mom shook her head sadly, but what she said made

me think. Nothing she named was what I'd consider *wild*. I'd think the fact she's slept with about twenty guys over the past few months and, according to Kylie, she's with a drug dealer and probably doing some drugs herself would be a lot *wilder* than sneaking out and going to parties, but maybe that's just because I'm sneaking out with Jake, or because I'm going to parties too?

"Well, I don't think her sneaking out is all that bad. I mean, as long as she's not doing bad things when she does."

Mom nodded slowly.

"Yeah, but think of it this way," she said. "Pretend you're a Mom, lying in bed, and you think your children are safe and sound in their rooms and then suddenly the phone rings and it's a sheriff telling you your child has just been arrested or something. How would you feel then? Do you think you'd be able to sleep the same after that?"

I wanted to have something smart to say back to show her that I knew what she was talking about, but let's face it, I'm not a Mom...I don't know those sorts of things. I don't have those sorts of feelings.

"I don't know...I bet I'd be pretty scared!"

"At least once a month your Dad comes home and tells me about some things he and the guys talk about at work. They talk about all the kids who die every year in drunk-driving accidents and how many girls get raped at prom and all sorts of junk. I'm always so worried for you guys and I know I shouldn't be, but..."

Her words fell away and her eyes widened. For a second I looked at the shock in her eyes and wondered if she somehow miraculously realized I'd been sneaking out. Did I say something that could've given it away? Why was I shaking? My armpits were starting to leak... I'm so glad I'm wearing a hoodie, but why is it suddenly so hot?

"Erin, let's go!" she said, grabbing my arm.

Something told me it wasn't about me sneaking out. She was still mortified and staring at something over my shoulder. I thought I'd turn to see a large man stalking toward us, or perhaps *Jason* or *Michael Myers* or something out of a scary movie, but it was something worse. It was Jake. I stopped in my tracks, my mouth fell to my knees. He was with Carrie...

"Erin, let's go!" Mom said, more sternly, "Come on honey, look at me! Erin!"

I yanked my arm from her grip and shook my head in denial.

They were standing beside the truck, his truck, in *her* drive way. I guess they thought they were back far enough that the street light couldn't reach them, but Mom didn't miss them and neither could I. He was kissing her the same way he kissed me, touching her the same way he touched me.

On our side of the street there were no street lights. I bet they didn't even know we were there. I stood in awe for a second. My mom kept begging me to turn around and she even tried to grab my arm again, but I think she realized I wasn't going to move. Something in my mind kept telling me it was a bad dream, that it wasn't real; it wasn't Jake, not my Jake. You'll wake up, just keep staring. No, this was some sort of misunderstanding. Yeah, maybe she's choking and he's... Maybe he's checking for a heart beat on her chest? Maybe she dropped something down his pants?

As if the knife could go no deeper, her front door burst open and out stepped Michael and T.J. as well as Brittany and Ashley. That wasn't the part that hurt though... it was the couple that followed them, Dyson and Kylie.

"Come on you two," Michael blurted, "You need another five minutes or something? How many times are you guys gonna *do it* in one night?"

My hand rushed to cover my mouth, tears brushed my cheeks. My mom was suddenly right beside me. "Come on honey, let's go," she whispered, "Erin, you don't need to see this..."

But she was wrong. I *did* need to see this! I needed to see how Kylie had betrayed me. I needed to see how low Carrie would stoop... And most of all, I needed to see Jake be the guy everyone said he was, but I wouldn't believe. I heard Kylie's voice in my head. "Just make sure you're his only dealer..."

She knew all along.

"Yeah, Jake, man, what're you gonna do when Erin gets back?" T.J. laughed, "You can't screw them both, you know? I mean, that'd be hot, but I don't think little miss princess would go for that!"

"You could always try though," Michael added, "there's no harm in trying, right girls?" he said with a smack to both Ashley and Brittany's butts.

I wondered what he would say back to their comments. I was at least hoping for the line you always hear in the movies, you know, the one where the guy says something like, "this isn't easy for me" or something like that, but he didn't. He only finished kissing Carrie and then grabbed her butt in a sexy way and shoved her toward her front door.

"When *does* she get back?" she asked. I didn't miss her evil grin. I imagined her porch collapsing on top of her.

"Sunday," Jake answered coolly.

"I'll see you tomorrow then?" she asked.

"Definitely!" he replied with a smile.

Something about his tone spelled it all out for me. *Definitely!* It was so deep and sure. It was more than just a response, it was his emotions behind it. He enjoyed whatever she had given him, a lot. More than he ever had with me. There was something about the way he stood there staring at her as she walked away that told me how everything had played out. Suddenly, I realized how lame his excuse had been for not calling me. Who loses their phone like that? He probably left it at her house or something? I wonder if they were having sex when I called? Why would she do that to me? I thought of Nick and how easily I could've had him if I would've wanted to, but the thought of Jake stopped me.

I couldn't do that to Jake. How could he do that to me? There was only one thing I needed to know.

Against my mom's complaints, I tugged away from her for the last time and walked out into the light. I was halfway across the street before Kylie and Dyson saw me. I never thought a black person could go pale, but I guess I never thought Jake would cheat on me, either. Jake's back was to me now. He was talking to T.J. and Michael who were apparently in front of his truck. I couldn't see them from where I was; I could only see Kylie and Dyson. I heard car doors shut. Brittany and Ashley were already in the backseat of Michael's car.

Jake opened his truck door and started to get in just as Michael walked around the trunk of his car and saw me. His eyes went huge.

Kylie was right beside me trying to talk to me.

"Erin," she said, but I ignored her and kept walking.

At the sound of my name Jake turned around and his jaw dropped. I wondered for a second if he'd say anything at all. He reached for me to touch my shoulders, probably to restrain me.

"Baby..." he said.

My expression must've shown how disgusted I was that he would even call me that after what I'd seen. I couldn't control the tears that streaked down my cheeks. I fought to hold them back for a second. I wanted to slap him harder than I did Nick, but that wouldn't take back the hurt; it wouldn't fix what had already happened. At this point, it wouldn't even make me feel better. He kept trying to touch my arms, but something, maybe it was the thought of how he had just been touching Carrie, wanted his arms to fall off; I wanted them to do anything *but* touch me! Part of me wanted to know how long it had been going on, but the better part of me told me not to ask. Some things were just better left unsaid... I've heard that saying my whole life and now I finally know why.

He was stammering to say something, anything, but I made it easy for him.

"Did you *ever* love me? Did you mean any of that – that *crap* – you said to me? When you said I was different and that you wanted something *real*?"

I saw the nervousness leave his eyes. I think he thought I was going to do something else, but then my questions showed him how weak and desperate I was just to know the truth; I needed to know that he had at least loved me and that I wasn't just a game. The silence was broken by a low laugh from T.J. He was shaking his head slowly. That was all the answer I needed.

"You're cold man!" T.J. said with a smile, shaking his head. "I'm gonna start calling you Iceman or something..."

Michael's expression lightened up. I think he thought I was gonna pull out a gun and start shooting. His face loosened, his eyes regained their normal size as they shot back and forth to catch how everyone was reacting; he even managed a slight chuckle at the comment.

Jake only looked at me, his face starting to show how little he cared. He had gotten what he wanted and now he was moving on. It had been the game Ashley and Brittany said it was, only they forgot to tell me that it's not a game when your heart is into it; they forgot to tell me how cruel the game is and how much it hurts.

"You can be my wingman anytime, Maverick!" Michael joked as I walked away.

Tears streamed down my face. I felt so worthless, so... like such a...

Chapter Twenty-Six ~
N^ovember 26th - Monday

Kylie tried to call about seven times over the week-end. Even her mom called and talked to my Mom, but still I didn't want to talk to her. As a matter of fact, I didn't even come out of my room for most of the time. I threw all the notes away, all the little gifts, the dried up roses, and of course I did what all girls do, cried my eyes out. Mom tried to talk to me all the way home, but I couldn't find anything to talk about.

Why couldn't her porch have just collapsed? Where was God when you needed him? Why did this have to happen to me? What have I done to deserve this? I went to church all week with Sarah, doesn't that count for something?

The worst thing of all was that my mom was there to see it. All of my worst secrets were out in the open now. It would only be a matter of time before she walked in my room, turned Hitler, and started my lifelong pun-ishment for the crime of being a teen.

"You can't screw them both..." T.J. said. I know she heard *that*!

What am I gonna do? Should I even bother going to school again? Suddenly, home-schooling didn't seem so bad. Who needs friends? I guess when I think about it I don't because I don't have any! Kylie's gone...forever! Carrie might as well fall off of something really high, and Whitney, well, she's too busy with Ian. They're probably talking about me right now anyway.

She'd probably say, "Man, I wish she would've seen how much of a loser Jake was like *we* did..."

Then Ian would reply with something like, "Yeah, I bet she's wishing she would've listened to me when I said he was such a jerk..."

My head felt like it could explode. My room was a mess. Since I was throwing away a lot of stuff, I decided to throw away a bunch more too, and well, that made quite a pile. What else did I have to do? It's not like I had friends anymore. Ian tried to act tough at first and say that he would do something, but I know he won't. He's too smart to think he can beat up Jake, especially with Dyson around. I can't believe I actually thought he loved me. I can't believe how dumb I am. They're all laughing at me right now, I can feel it! How many girls had there been? For how long? I should've asked him. *No*, I shouldn't have! I'm glad I didn't! Knowing that he cheated on me with one was enough. What if he would've said "ten" or something like "the entire time," how horrible would I feel then? How much worse *could* I feel?

Every smile flashed through my mind, every hug;

every patient moment where he waited and I thought he was so perfect. As a snow globe flew across my room, I wondered why I hadn't seen his patience as a trick? How had he been able to convince me into thinking he wasn't a jerk? Why didn't I see that he was just another Joe Gregory, but smoother and more evil? I guess he could afford to be patient if he was having sex with other girls at the same time. He wouldn't have to worry about being told *no* when there were hundreds of girls lined up to say yes. And Carrie had been line the whole time...

This is the part in the movie where every girl has an awesome best friend who slashes his tires and ruins his life by framing him or something; a friend or two like that would be nice right now, but I'd settle for a *regular* friend or two...

Dad brought home some Oreos and a six pack of little Nestle milks for me and slid them in my door with an empty coffee cup. They're my favorite, but I still didn't feel like eating. If my bathroom wasn't so close to my bedroom, I probably wouldn't do anything.

How could he do this to me? I did everything for him, everything he wanted me to do, everything he had planned right from the start. I snuck out to meet him. All the times we had sex crossed my mind and I couldn't close my eyes tight enough to block them out. I turned on the television, but everywhere there's either people in love, people cheating on one another, gay people, or the news. I guess I'd rather hear about another school shooting than the others, so news it was...

Maybe I should shoot up my school? There'd be Jake, Michael, T.J., Brittany, Ashley, Dyson, Kylie, Carrie...who else? And they'd all be in the same spot too... I wouldn't want to get anyone else though, so it'd have to be... *What?* What am I doing? I'm not going to shoot up my school! Maybe I could collapse Carrie's house? She could have any guy she wanted, why mine? Why Jake? What did she have that I didn't? Besides, a gorgeous body and a lot more experience in bed? She wasn't smart! I guess you don't have to be smart when you look that good naked though... I'm sure guys would pick some nerd over a supermodel any day to have sex with... Guys are such pigs! I mean, don't guys care that she's slept with like five hundred other guys?

Did you care that Jake had slept with like five hundred other girls?

Touché mind, touché...

I can't believe he'd do this to me... What did she do to lure him in? I thought back to all those lessons Brittany and Ashley taught me. Maybe they took her under their wing and turned her against me? Maybe it's been some kind of plan from the start?

No Erin, this isn't a movie!

Why the hell are you so smart all the sudden, *voice*? Where were you when Jake was smoothing us over? What...no reply for that one, huh, smarty?

Guys are jerks! Flash some boobs at them and their mind goes blank. It's like the red flashy thing on Men in Black. Once they're flashed all you have to do is give them a new memory and they're yours, but there must be something wrong with the system because apparently Carrie's flashy thing worked better than mine.

Why did he even pick me in the first place? Why me? What did I do to deserve this? What about all those stupid Jesus songs that said '*love*' and '*mercy*' and '*hope*'? Why me? Where's my love? Where's my hope?

Monday morning came fast. I guess that's what happens when you sleep all weekend. Well, sleep, pee, and cry... My legs hurt. Now that I think about it, my whole body pretty much aches all over. I wish I could just be invisible or something. It couldn't be that bad though, could it? I mean, two weeks ago guys were drooling over me, right? It won't be a big deal, will it? I'll just dress normally and try and act like nothing's wrong and see what happens. Maybe I can make Jake jealous? After all, it won't be hard for me to get another boyfriend. Do I want another boyfriend? *No*, guys are pigs!

It had only been two days, but I guess since I was out of town all week too, down stairs looked completely different. I looked at myself in the mirror. I felt so weak, like I could shatter or something. How could he do this to me right after my Nana died? A thought occurred to me...

While my Nana was dying! Man, he's such a jerk! I hope he wrecks on the way to school this morning! I hope he hits Carrie on accident with his truck or something...that'd teach him!

Mom and Ian were in the kitchen eating breakfast.

Mom made bacon, egg, and cheese sandwiches, but I wasn't hungry.

"I made you one, sweetie,"

"I'm not hungry, Mom,"

"Erin, you need to eat. It's not good for you to keep doing this to yourself..."

"What would *you* do?" I asked.

My Mom just sort of nodded.

"Just promise me that you'll stay away from them, okay?" she said. She leaned in close and gave me a hug, "please..."

If she only knew how far away I wanted to be from Davis-Buckley right now she wouldn't have even thought of saying something like that. Why would I want to be around *him*? Or any of them?

I nodded. I still didn't feel like talking too much. Something inside of me told me if I started talking that might trigger my eyes to leak and I wasn't excited about that right now. Mom gave us a ride to school today. She must feel really bad for me because I can count on one hand how many times she's given me a ride to school in my life. She probably didn't think I could make the walk. Now that I think about it, I probably couldn't have made it. Once I stepped foot out of my mom's car all eyes were on me. Everyone was either glancing at me or staring, almost waiting for me to crumble or shatter or burst into tears. My body temperature warmed up. I felt like I was under a microscope. Didn't they have better things to do than to stare at me?

I kept looking around with a death grip on my books. Please stop staring at me! Just look away, talk about something else. Stop whispering and pointing! Don't look at me like you're sorry for me and you just spent the past weekend on the phone with me. Talk about the recent school shootings in Pennsylvania or the drought in Texas, or the bird flu epidemic in China, or how the Dow is down! Okay, too much news for Erin... Next time I'll go with the gay shows, at least *they're* funny.

How could celebrities live like this? I wonder if they'll roll out the red carpet for Carrie and Jake when they pull up? They'll probably call a pep rally for everyone and give them all awards for best performance by a crew of deceivers. Kylie would win the Best Supporting Actress award, I'm sure. I mean, it takes a special kind of person to make you think they're your friend and then turn evil at the last second to twist the knife a little deeper. Amazing acting! I mean, I was shocked and *I* was in the movie! Great, now my life is a thriller.

I walked through the front doors and the scene didn't change: stares and whispers, giggles and sad faces, I saw every expression that could be seen all the way to my locker. For some reason I looked at Ian. He looked pissed! Why was *he* so mad? I grabbed his arm when we got to the locker and he gave me a one-armed hug while he undid my combination lock for me. I didn't want him to hold me like this in front of everybody. It showed them the weakness I wanted to hide; how horrible I felt and how vulnerable I truly was inside. So much for my thoughts of acting strong or bouncing back! But I guess I didn't care anymore. There was a time when I would've shrugged him away and just turned my face into a growl and stomped around like the meanest girl in school, but that wasn't right now. Maybe next week? Right now I was done pretending. I didn't want to be here anymore. It'd only been three or four minutes, but when everyone's looking at you it feels like an eternity. I felt like every stare, every whisper, just drained me. I think if Ian wasn't holding my shoulder I might collapse.

He opened my locker and then started on his when Whitney walked up. They did their best to look sad – or mad in Ian's case – while I was around, but I'm sure they were happy it wasn't them. I mean, what couple really cares about the problems of others? People always just point and say, "Man, if they would've been in love like us..."

I know, because that's what *I* used to do. I would weigh everything against what I thought Jake and I had; turns out, it wasn't a fair comparison after all. I guess we'd *always* outweigh people when there's about five or ten girls standing on the scale behind me.

Ian offered to walk me to Mrs. Prichard's English class, but I shook my head. After all, there's no need. I mean, he can't sit through the class with me too. I'll just have to get used to the stares or something. Maybe by lunch someone will get in a fight and I'll be old news?

Not likely...

Great, you again!

I didn't have anyone to talk to, so I arrived early at Mrs. Prichard's room. Her expression told me that I was the last person she expected to see walk into her room five minutes early.

"Good Morning, Miss Mitchell," she said.

I faked a smile for a quick second and walked past.

"I'm sorry to hear about your grandmother dear," she added with a whisper, "Please, let me know if there's anything I can do for you."

I nodded and then something came to mind.

"Mrs. Prichard?"

"Yes, dear?"

"Is there any way I can be moved away from Kylie?" I asked.

She looked at me confused and then said, "Perhaps, but why?"

"Something happened this weekend and I don't think we should be around one another,"

I could tell by her expression that she was expecting more of an explanation than that, but I guess she felt sorry for me because she nodded and told me I could sit in the back.

Thank God! Finally, somewhere where no one can stare at me! I felt so low and pathetic, like pond scum. It was now four minutes until class started and here I sat, all alone. I had absolutely no one now. I could even hear Jessica Gentry out in the hallway snorting and laughing with all of her band geek friends, but yet I, the girl who had just dated the most popular guy in school, had no one. Life isn't fair. How can Jake have friends? Don't they get tired of being stabbed in the back? I'm sure he stabs them, too.

Michael and T.J. walked by the door and saw me and with an evil grin Michael held his hands out in front of him.

"Teej! We've got a bogey, dead ahead!" he said and then acted like he was firing his guns at me.

"She's been hit! She's been hit!" I could hear him chant as they turned the corner.

Just before the bell rang I could hear them sing, "High-way to the danger zone" in unison and then burst into laughter.

I couldn't control the tears. I hated them! I hated all of them! I slid out of my desk and started to run to the door. Everyone would be coming through the front doors soon and into the halls to get their things. A couple minutes later, they'd be piling into the classroom. I couldn't let them see me like this. They couldn't see me look like a mess with my mascara running and my eyes all red and puffy. I had to go somewhere; I had to go to the bathroom. I covered my face with one hand so that hopefully no one would see me. The bathrooms were only a few feet away from Mrs. Prichard's door if I walked toward the Senior side of the hall. I could make it! Maybe no one would notice me? I just needed to get to the bathroom.

I rushed to the first stall and slammed it shut. I locked it, cleaned the seat, and sat down. I yanked a roll of toilet paper and blew my nose just as the door opened behind me. I thought it might be Mrs. Prichard chasing after me, but it wasn't. Two girls walked in laughing and joking.

"Oh-my-God, did you see Erin Mitchell this morning?" One said.

"She looks like a truck hit her or something," commented the second.

"Well, you heard what happened, didn't you?"

"Yeah, something about her gran, right?"

"Oh, no," commented the other excitedly, "Jake Cunningham dumped her because she wasn't any good in bed!"

"Shut-up! Are you serious?"

"Oh yeah," said the girl, "and there's more…"

The door opened and another group of girls walked in talking about something exciting.

As if she were uninterrupted, the girl continued, "I hear she's pregnant!"

"Oh-my-God!"

"Are you guys talking about Erin?" One of the new girls asked.

"Yeah, did you hear?"

"Yeah, but I heard she caught Jake screwing some other chick!"

"*Really?* Who?"

"I don't know, but I heard Erin went psycho and he pushed her down and made her have a miscarriage…"

"That's why she looks horrible!"

"Oh-my-God!" several voices said with a gasp.

I wanted to leap out of the stall and tell them all the truth. I wanted to yell at them and show them how psycho I could be, but all I could do was cry.

The rest of the day wasn't much better. Carrie and her new friends were around every corner smiling evilly, knowing they had single-handedly ruined my life, though the looks on their faces showed how little they really cared. By the time lunch came around I could barely keep my legs beneath me. I heard three separate groups say something about my stomach looking bigger on my way to the cafeteria. I just wanted to go home. Maybe I could go to the nurse and they'd let me just go home? After all, according to everyone else I looked like a truck hit me.

I couldn't disagree with them though; I mean, my mascara *was* practically gone. I looked like a raccoon for almost two classes before I thought to check my face. If I wasn't sweating because everyone was staring at me I was freezing in Mr. Harper's History class. My hair was greasy looking thanks to the sweat and constantly wiping it from my face to blow my nose or wipe the tears away. Makeup was all over my right sleeve on my hoodie from wiping my face in class.

Images kept crossing my mind of Jake and I having sex. My imagination didn't help. It carried everything away and made it three times worse. After a while, my imagination turned it into Carrie, not me. Everywhere

I looked I could see people smiling from behind locker doors and looking at me as I passed. I felt like the entire lunch hall was waiting on me to shrink into nothing or explode into a gush of tears like a human water balloon. I wanted to shout, to scream at them all; to tell them that I was a person who had feelings and that they were all evil for treating me like I was a zoo animal. As soon as the lunch bell rang I was back to fending the mob of stares and whispers. By the end of the day Ian was mad. I guess he had heard his fair share of gossip about me throughout the day; the look in his eyes told me that he honestly might punch somebody. Whitney seemed more upset than she did that morning, which made me consider maybe the two of them *were* thinking of my feelings and not just how it affected their relationship.

We walked home after school. The railroad tracks always had scattered groups that walked them after school, but eventually it was just the two of us. We heard a horn honk down the street and when we looked we didn't recognize who it was, so we kept walking. As it got closer it honked again, and again we looked, but this time we *did* notice who it was...

"Is that..." Ian started, confused.

"Sarah?"

Her blazer stopped at the next crossing. She rolled down the window, slid sideways in her seat, pulled her sunglasses low, and puckered her lips like she was jamming to some music. She looked so ridiculous that we couldn't help but laugh. I think it was mostly the thought of how un-cool she was that made it so funny, or maybe it was because I've seen her Cds and I knew that she didn't have any music worth jamming to.

"What are you doing here?" Ian asked as we walked up.

"Mom's pretty lonely...said she missed you guys a lot after you left. I think she misses having people around, so we decided to make a trip down for the week, you know, keep the streak going. Hop in!"

As soon as we took off, her gas light came on.

"Hey, where's the nearest gas station?"

"Right around the corner by the Baskin Robbins," Ian said.

As we pulled in she handed me a fifty and gave me a wink.

"Let's say...thirty," she said.

I nodded.

Something about her seemed different, almost like she was more carefree when she wasn't near Hammond Falls. As she hopped out of the blazer I noticed that she was wearing blue jeans. Thank God! Not that it mattered, I mean, I don't think my reputation could plummet much more than it already had, but I guess it's a habit I'll have to break. A shrill whistle stole my attention as I walked across the open lot to the building. My heart fell to my feet. I saw a silver Truck and a Jeep parked by the air pump.

Of course, why wouldn't they be here? They could be anywhere in the world, but right here is where they are...yep!

"Bogey at nine o'clock," Michael said with a laugh. I tried not to look, but I couldn't help it. I saw the long blond hair in the passenger seat next to Jake and knew who it was instantly. She was wearing her, 'look what I've got' smile. I *hate* her!

"Who's the hottie?" Michael cheered. Sarah ignored him and kept pumping gas. I stopped at the door and noticed that Jake and the guys were checking her out. Carrie's smile was replaced with a 'look what I could lose' grin; one she should know all too well by how easily she stripped him away from me.

When I came out they pulled up next to Sarah. I noticed that Brittany and Ashley weren't with them. They stopped just on the other side of the pumps.

"Hey there," said T.J., "I've never seen *you* before, have I?"

"Nope," she answered, not looking at him.

"So are you new here?"

"Yeah,"

"Maybe you could give me your number and I could show you around or..."

"Maybe you could hold your breath for a couple of years while I try not to think about it," she said.

"Ohhh," taunted Michael, pointing at T.J.

I walked up and got in the blazer. I tried not to look at them while Sarah finished pumping gas. I could feel Carrie's eyes on me. She wanted me to show her how jealous I was; she wanted to see me cry and wish I were her.

"So..." Michael started.

"Aren't you *boys* supposed to be riding the bus home or something right now?" she asked with a wave, "Go on...shew! Run away little boys! Go!"

Michael started to laugh and make a comment, but she interrupted him again.

"Get! I think I hear your Mommies calling!"

Their expressions showed how burned they felt. A hot girl had just degraded them. From the backseat I could hear Ian snicker. Neither of us expected Sarah to act that way, especially after she had been so different last week. She hopped into the blazer and shut the door with an aggravated exhale.

"Man, do you guys know them?"

"The guy in the truck *used* to be my boyfriend..." I said.

She looked at me, astonished. "*That* guy? The one with the blond?"

"And she *used* to be my friend..."

Sarah's face turned sad.

"When did all this..."

"Friday night when we got back," I answered.

She let out a gasp, "Erin, I'm so sorry!"

"Don't be! It's not your fault..."

I wanted to act tougher, like I did that night in the Underground when I threatened that guy and slapped Nick, but I couldn't be. Tears started falling again. I would've thought they'd all be gone by now, but no, apparently they love their job and don't mind working overtime. She leaned across the truck and gave me a hug. It was different than anything I'd ever felt. It felt like I had a big sister...it felt like I had a *real* friend.

"Would some ice cream make it better?"

I thought to say *no* immediately, but something about Baskin Robbins did sound appealing. "I don't know about *better...*"

"But the question you should ask is '*will it make it worse*'?" she said in reply, with an upraised finger. The answer was definitely *no*, but it *will* make me fatter, which will make the rumors of pregnancy look more and more true as the weeks pass.

Chapter Twenty-Seven

November 26th –
Monday Evening

We got home and immediately Sarah asked if I wanted to go and hangout for a little while.

"Just cruise," she said, throwing her arm out like a wave. Could she be any more un-cool? I wanted to tell her *no*, but something told me I shouldn't. It wasn't the fact that I knew I would spent another lonely night thinking about Jake, but it was something else. There was a look in her eyes, something was motivating her; she really wanted to be here for me. I couldn't say no.

When we turned out of the driveway I wasn't sure where we'd go. She took a left, then a right, and a few more turns before we talked about anything. It was obvious how nervous we both were, but why? I mean, why would *she* be nervous?

"So tell me something...," she started. Her voice was really cool and collected. Funny, I thought she'd be more nervous.

"Yeah,"

"Where are you right now?"

I looked around. I wasn't sure how to answer. Thankfully, she rephrased the question.

"Are you still bitter? Are you past the shock yet? Are you mad? Do you want revenge? Are you hurt? Where are you in the stage of things?"

The stage of things? So this is all a process now?

"I...I don't..." I started, but something stopped me.

Be honest! Don't just push her back and then complain that you don't have friends who care!

I sighed. "I'm not sure. I mean, I guess I still want to see him get what he deserves, but then at the same time I keep having these daydreams that Carrie's porch collapses on her, but then I'm still amazed how quickly everything disappeared. It's almost like this dream I had, but then I woke up. You know, like the ones where you remember every little detail so well that you think it was real?"

She nodded, "I know *exactly* what you mean."

"I guess I'm a little bit of everywhere..."

"Did it shock you to see how much I'd changed when you saw me over thanksgiving?" Sarah asked.

I thought to lie and act surprised that she would even ask such a thing, but her voice told me that she already knew my answer.

I nodded, "Yeah."

"Wanna know why?"

"Yeah," I said before I could control my thoughts. It'd been something that'd nagged my mind for weeks. Why would such a beautiful girl do that to herself?

"When I was a sophomore – the same age as you – my mom had me in public school. Anyway, I was in to all the latest fashions, music, you name it, I was all about it. If it was cool, I was there. If there was a party, Sarah was the first one through the door and the last one to leave. My girlfriends were jealous because they couldn't take me anywhere without a guy coming up to us and bothering us. They even made me start wearing a ring so the guys would just stare and not interrupt us."

I laughed.

"So what happened? Why the change?"

"Just like you, I started dating this guy my sophomore year and he was the light of my life. We did everything together. My mom trusted him, his parents were important people in the township; it was the making of something cool. Things led to other *things*. Lots of parties and drinking, and before I knew it, I found myself doing things that I didn't want to do; worse than that, things I *shouldn't* have wanted to do, but I did them for him because I thought that that's what love was. Before too long I was dressing different, losing friends, and losing my family to arguments. I kept sneaking out or just walking out the front door when my mom would tell me not to."

I couldn't speak. *There's no way she... I... There's just no way Sarah would...*

"We dated for almost five months before I saw what was going on in my life and started to try and slow things down, but by then it was too late. Things had happened and the hole was already dug way over my head. I guess it's kinda like being trapped in a well. Every time I tried to reach up and climb out someone would kick more dirt on top of me and keep me down there where I belonged. My *friends*, or so-called friends, were all talk. I tried to show them what we were all doing and how wrong it was and they pretended to understand for a little while. We all started to take it easy and not go to so many parties. We did more social things like dancing at the Underground instead of drugs and drinking, but after a while that only got us involved in the other drug, sex. Everything spiraled with my boyfriend from there. He started demanding more and more, it was like we were slaves to being teenagers. The next thing I knew I was on the side of the road with my clothes in my hands, practically naked, drunk and high on some drug that I didn't bother to ask what it was. I was used and left out in the cold like garbage. He was just like Jake!"

"Sarah...," My hand was fixed over my mouth, "I never..."

"No one did!" she said, almost begging me to stop, "not even my mom knew everything..."

"What did you do? How did you..." I tried to ask. I wanted to cry. It was like watching a talk show, or a really sad chick flick.

"I didn't," she answered.

My face must've shown how confused I was because Sarah smirked and then pointed to a small sign off to the side of the road. *Café Latte* it read.

She pulled her blazer into the small parking lot and we got out and started walking inside. What did she mean by 'I didn't...' and how could she be the way she is today if she hadn't changed in some way? We chatted a little as we waited to get our drinks and a small plate of apples with caramel dip and then made our way to a corner table. The place was quiet, nothing like the coffee shop in Clarence.

"Are you ready for the rest?" she asked.

I nodded, almost excited.

"Are you sure?"

Something about the look on her face told me that I should be ready for this before I agreed, but I couldn't help myself.

"What happened?"

"Well, there I was out of my mind, drunk, high, and stumbling half-naked, trying to put my clothes on when this guy starts talking to me."

"A guy? In the woods?"

"In the woods!" she nodded, sipping her drink.

My face must've shown how odd this was starting to sound.

"I stopped, pulled my shirt over my head and got ready to run, but there was something about him that made me feel like I could trust him. I don't know if it was his voice or how he was dressed? I think it was something in his eyes..." She dazed off for a second in that daydream-nodding state that my mom and I do all the time and then she finally came back.

"What happened then?"

"He told me that he saw everything that had happened and how my boyfriend left me out, practically naked, in the cold all drunk and messed up and that he would walk with me until I got somewhere safely, if I wanted him to."

"Weirdo!" I said.

"That's what I thought too. I remember thinking, 'this is how scary movies start', you know? But then those eyes were there again and that voice. It all calmed me and told me that if he wanted to rape me he could have easily done it without even letting me know he was in the woods to start with, you know?"

I nodded. That *was* a good point.

"So what happened?"

"We walked and talked about almost everything." She chuckled and then added, "Have you ever been drunk, Erin?"

"No,"

"Well, let me tell you something about being drunk...you talk about *everything*, even if you don't want to... It just kinda *gushes* out of you! All of the truth you have deep inside comes flowing out of you when you're drunk, and it did, and he was there to listen to it all."

"What did he say?"

She stopped and sipped her drink again with a smile. "I'll never forget it. He said he had been down a road similar to the same one I was on. He said he was popular, that he had a lot of friends once, but then one day he had this crazy idea in his mind to do something and when he decided to do it, his whole life changed. Suddenly, he found himself surrounded by people who didn't care about him at all. He left a wealthy family, tons of friends, and started hanging out with all of these people who liked the thought of partying with him and hanging out, but they never really *cared* about him."

"What happened?"

"Well, his so-called friends turned against him, just like mine did, *just like yours did*, and they even went so far as to deny that they were even his friends when others asked. When he looked around, he realized he was surrounded by people who didn't like him, people he had cared a lot for, but had only used him and then left him out in the cold and laughed at him, just like what happened to us."

"Man...that sucks! Why are people like that? I mean, how hard is it to get a good friend? How can so much change in such a short amount of time."

"Well, the bad thing about this guy's story was that he had these friends for years! He knew these people for a long time, hung out with them, went to parties at people's houses. He was there for them when they were down. He lifted them up when they'd let him. He was a great guy, the best friend anyone could hope to have."

I could only shake my head. How could someone do something like that to such a caring person? I mean, how could Brittany and Ashley blame me for snitching when they stole the halter and I didn't even know? Why wouldn't they just fess up and say they did it?

"So what happened then?"

"Well, his story is a lot like yours and mine, except his turned out a lot worse..."

"How?"

"Well, when the police came to arrest him for breaking the law, he found out that one of his own friends, a guy who had been breaking the law with him, was the one who turned him in."

"Backstabber!" I growled.

Sarah nodded, "And that's not even the half of it..." she said, "then they beat him up!"

"What?" I blurted a little too loud. I looked around, mouthed how sorry I was to a couple of people, and then looked back at Sarah, "Are you serious? How? What about the police?"

"They were in on it too. They turned against him."

"But couldn't the policemen lose their jobs for that? I mean, how could they get away with that?"

Sarah only shrugged, "Things were different where he was from," she said.

Crazy southerners!

"Then he told me that to make things worse, this gang didn't just beat him up, but they stole his clothes too."

"Oh, that's horrible! I can't believe he told you all of this. I'd be too embarrassed to tell a stranger about everything I've done."

"Yeah," she said with a nod, "I thought the same thing as you, but in just a second I'll tell you *why* he told me. But first, I want to tell you something else he told me, something that's stuck with me ever since."

I sat up in my chair, almost hugging the corner of the seat. I can't believe how I felt right now. It was almost relieving to hear a story worse than mine, it made me feel like someone had been there before me, like someone knew how I felt.

"He told me that every person in the world is that way..."

"What?" I blurted, "I don't know about that, I mean, *you're* not!"

"That's what I thought too, because I know a lot of good people, but when it all comes down to it Jake was born a baby just like you and me, Erin. He wasn't born evil he was just born into a world that doesn't care about things the way it should. I mean, have you tried to watch the T.V. lately? Look at all the sex and cheating and lying and nasty things that happen out there... school shootings...wars..."

She had a point. The world did seem to be full of people like that, but that doesn't mean that *everyone's* that way.

"Yeah, but that doesn't mean that *everyone's* that way!"

"Do you know what the definition of *possible* is, Erin?"

"I could guess," I shrugged.

"It's means to be *capable of existing, occurring, or being done.*"

She stopped and let the words hang in the air for a second before she continued.

"Don't you think that it's *possible* for every man and woman to be like Jake, even a little? I mean, I'm sure you never imagined something like that until you saw it with your own eyes and felt it with your own heart, but now that you know…"

I couldn't argue with her on that one. It *was* possible that everyone could have that somewhere deep inside of them.

"You see, every person in this world can and might betray you, steal something that belongs to you, or beat you up. If you can imagine it, I'm sure it can or already has been done to someone, somewhere."

I could only shake my head. How sick! My stomach and throat felt lumpy, like I was about to hurl. I could see Jake smiling and I hated him for it, not because he was smiling, but because he didn't care about hurting someone.

"Some *encouraging* words," I said with a scoff, "I can see he probably had a hard time finding good friends after that, huh?"

"Actually, he went back home and made-up with the old friends and family he left behind."

"They took him back?"

"Oh, sure, but the really weird thing is that he still tries to make friends with the people who beat him up all those years ago."

"What?" My mind seemed like it was baking. Why would someone do something like that? I mean, I could never just walk up to Carrie, hand her a knife and say, "Would you like another stab?" How could anyone do something like that?

"Why would he?" I asked.

"I told you, he's an awesome guy. When he puts his mind to something he never lets it go..."

"He sounds a little naïve to me, almost like he *likes* being beat up and lied to and cheated on."

"Well, I wouldn't say he *likes* it, but I know that what he wants more than anything is to have his cake and eat it too." She explained.

"What do you mean?"

"He wants to have the best of both worlds; he wants to have his loyal friends and family *and* then have the others too. He doesn't want anyone to have to feel like they made him feel, even the ones who betrayed him, beat him, stole his clothes, and left him for dead."

"If that were me I'd go back to my rich dad and start killing folks off!" I joked.

Sarah nodded with a smirk.

"It took me a while to realize that what he was saying was true though; I mean, it all goes back to how people are these days. Look at movies... How many movies do you see where after the guy loses his wife and kids, he goes and tries to help the people that killed them? Never! Life is all about number one and if anyone gets in your way or betrays you, you're supposed to cut them deeper or hurt them worse than they hurt you! It's like a world of pirates! It's cutthroat and ruthless!"

"So you think this guy is right for trying to just blow it off like nothing happened and make friends with these people? I mean, where's the punishment for what they did? Isn't there supposed to be some kind of punishment for doing such a hideous thing?"

"If you and I were friends and you betrayed me for some reason, but instead of hurting you back, I constantly kept trying to help you over and over again, for no reason, do you think that eventually you would see that I was your only *true* friend? Do you think that you'd eventually see what you'd done to me and that you didn't deserve me to be your friend?"

"Well...yeah," I replied. "But who'd do that?"

"*That's* where part of the punishment is... in knowing that you're not even close to being good enough to deserve a friend like him! Have you ever heard of the saying, *kill them with kindness*?"

"Yeah,"

"That's kinda the idea. He just shows them he would never do the things they did to him and slowly they see that he's telling the truth and they see things for what they really are deep down."

It took a few moments of thinking before either of us said anything else. There was just one thing that kept repeating over and over again in my mind.

"I can't believe he told you all this on just one little walk."

"It was a really, really long walk, Erin…" Sarah said with a frown.

Something told me that her walk was a hard one to take all drunk and high and heartbroken, but this guy…

"What happened once you got to where you were going?"

"Well, I got to the end of the dirt road and I guess I made it to the first house when I passed out. They rushed me to the hospital and did all these tests on me. They pumped my stomach and made me drink some disgusting charcoal stuff…" she made a face that explained all too well the nastiness of it before she continued, "and when I woke up I was in a hospital bed with my Mom beside me, crying.

"What about the guy?"

"Well, the doctors say I was lucky to have run into somebody way out there, because they don't see how I would have ever made it if I hadn't. They said the drugs mixed with the alcohol should've killed me, but somehow talking with the guy kept my brain functioning and got me safely to where someone could call an ambulance and rescue me."

"So did you ever see him again? Do you still talk to him?"

Sarah smiled and nodded, "All the time. He's the *new* light of my life."

I gasped, an image flashed across my mind and I knew instantly who she was talking about.

"You love him, don't you?" I asked.

She smiled, her eyes tearing up, "You have no idea."

"Why didn't you say anything when I was there?"

"I tried, but I guess I was embarrassed," she said, almost sadly as she wiped the tears from her eyes. "It's hard to tell people this kind of stuff sometimes, you know?"

"I would've never guessed by looking at him that he'd been through so much."

Sarah's face suddenly scrunched up. "What do you mean?"

"Well, when I met him..." I explained, "I just would've never guessed that he had been through so much?"

She smirked, "Who do you think I'm talking about?"

"Well..." I suddenly second guessed myself. For once, my secret agent skills felt like they were letting me down. "Evan, right? He's the guy you're in love with, right?"

She started laughing in a way that reminded me of how I would reply if someone asked me if Ian and I were dating.

"I'm not in love with *Evan*!"

"Then who's the guy?" I asked, intrigued. *It couldn't be Henry...or could it? It's definitely not Nick!*

"It's Jesus, Erin... Jesus is the man I've been talking about."

Chapter Twenty-Eight ~
Nº vember 26th - Monday

The look on my face must've been amusing, but Sarah only sipped her drink as if she hadn't just said the weirdest thing I've ever heard in my life. I could tell she was absolutely, one hundred percent serious, but for some reason as soon as she said the name *Jesus* the whole story seemed to not make sense anymore. How could he have walked with her two years ago if he's been dead for centuries? How could she be in love with someone who's dead? That's as intriguing as it is weird, and maybe even a little sick, but I guess that's another thing. I stammered for words for a minute and then gave up. I tried to say something else, but those words were hard to find too. For some reason the only thing I could ask was, "How?"

"Before you get too wrapped around everything you've heard your entire life, let me finish the story that *he* didn't get the chance to. You see, he left off the most important part, and I realize now that he did it for a reason. It's kinda like when you go to the food court in the mall and they give you those little samplers of food. That one little bite is sooo good that it makes you want to go get the whole meal so you can enjoy it all. Erin, he gave me a taste of something and it was up to me to choose to buy into the whole meal or not; a choice I'm glad I made because that one *free* sample has changed my life. I know that when you see me you don't see the same preppy, cool, fashionable girl I used to be, and I might not be as popular as I used to be, but he wasn't any of those things either, and he's the most caring and loving person who ever lived."

"But how do you *know* that though? How do you *know* that he's the most caring person who ever lived?" I asked. "How do you know that he even lived at all?"

"Do you mean beside the fact that he walked with me down that dirt road and saved my life?" she asked. One of her eyebrows rose, she smirked, and I suddenly realized how I was acting. I mean, how could I be so intrigued one minute and so doubting the next?

"The important part of the story is that he didn't *just* get betrayed, beat up, and robbed, but he got humiliated and killed by the same people he wanted to help. And today, thousands of years later, he still reaches out to people and gives them the same free sample he gave me, but this free sample is the difference between life and death, Erin. What Jesus said about the world is true. It's made up of people who only want what's best for themselves. Jake and all those other guys, you, me, we're all self-centered and focused on our own goals, but Jesus is focused on *us*! He built us a bridge to heaven and he wants nothing more than to share that with us, but we have to make that choice, he won't *force* us to make it."

I felt my head shaking as I thought of the reasons why something seemed so wrong about all of this. It didn't make sense. It seemed so far-fetched, like a sci-fi movie or something. All I knew is that I was happy with who I was and the only things I wanted to change were the cruelty and meanness in other people. There's nothing wrong with me! I haven't done anything wrong!

"Why are you telling *me* all of this? Shouldn't you be telling people like Jake and your old boyfriend? I mean, what did *I* do wrong?"

"We've all done *wrong*, Erin, but the important thing to think about is what you can do *right* from now on? Being a Christian is a tough, tough life that has a purpose instead of an easy one of fashion and possessions, that doesn't. It would be so easy to just do what everyone else does and fit in, but that's not always what's best. Sometimes, there're movies that shouldn't be seen, songs that shouldn't be heard, and fashions that shouldn't be worn and it takes a lot of struggling for me to remind myself that I shouldn't want those things anymore."

"But why? What's so wrong with dressing fashion-able or seeing a bad movie from time to time?"

"Because God gave us our own specific qualities: beauty, intellect, whatever...and he wants us to use them for him and to be thankful for them, not to flaunt and show them off for our own benefit. We're supposed to be humble... Do you know what that means?"

I didn't, but for a second I thought to act like I did, but something forced me to be honest. I shook my head.

"It means that we're supposed to want to think of ourselves less and think of others and God more. It's a concept that's completely against the world today; it's one of the hardest things to do as a Christian."

"Yeah, but why should we be forced to change? I mean, if God's so full of love why does he want us to change?"

"I never felt like God *wanted* me to change who I was. I never felt like he didn't like the way I dressed or what I was doing. I changed those things because I felt that God deserved more *from* me. After all he's done for his people, after all the love he's shown – the horrible punishment on the cross – I feel like the least I can do is represent him the same way he would represent me, the same way he *did* represent me when he lived. Think of your own Dad, do you think you'd rather dress like you are now, or would you rather dress skanky for him?"

The question seemed absurd. I'd never show my boobs around my dad!

"I think you'd rather dress one way for your dad and then another for the boys at school, right?"

"Well, yeah..."

"But why do you think that is?"

I couldn't think of an answer, so I shrugged.

"Because deep down you know that it's not who you

are and that it's only a game you play for attention. You already know that you don't have to dress a certain way, or say certain things to get the attention of your Dad, so you don't. God's the same way."

We were quiet again, but this time it was a little tenser. I could tell that she wanted me to say something, but nothing was coming to mind. It was all too much. It was kinda like watching Peter Pan and then being told that if I just thought a happy-thought I *really could* fly. It was just one of those imagination things that didn't seem to line up with reality.

"What made you decide to do all of this?" I blurted suddenly. *I've got to stop doing that!*

Sarah shrugged slightly and then looked off for a second as if she was trying to remember exactly and then shrugged again.

"I think I was laying the hospital and then it dawned on me that everything Jesus went through, he went through it for me. Well, not *just* for me, but for all of us. He lived this blameless, caring, loving life to show us how to be; walked a path that we're supposed to try to walk every day; did things we're *supposed* to do, and when it was all said and done, he was treated horribly just so he could die and hang on a cross for you and me."

"I don't understand. Why did he have to do all that? I mean, if he was God why couldn't he just snap his fingers and make it all suddenly possible?"

Sarah nodded slowly, thinking of how to answer my question.

"I guess there're a couple reasons – probably a *whole* lot more – but I can only think of a couple... On one hand, it was the ultimate chick flick; a man who would die for love. You know, kind of like Romeo and Juliet. Then, on the other hand, I guess it was because he was tired of seeing the people he created failing and doing things wrong over and over and over again. You see, back in the days before Jesus everyone was held to the standards that God gave Moses, the Ten Commandments, but when God sent his own son to the earth to save all mankind, it was a new standard to follow. Not a written one, but a living, breathing one that actually *showed* God's people firsthand what to do, how to do it, and why. It was kinda like a mother duck walking with all of her cute little ducklings in line behind her."

"So Jesus came to show us how to live?"

"Yes! How to live, love, pray, everything."

"So because Jesus did all of this for us, he expects us to do all of this in return? Is that how you go to heaven?"

"No!" Sarah answered, shaking her head, "That's another thing that people misunderstand. He doesn't *expect* anything from us, only faith in him."

"What do you mean?"

"In the bible it says that, "For God so loved the world that he *gave* his only begotten son..."

"*Okay?*" I didn't understand what she was trying to say.

"*Gave*, not traded... *Gave*, not exchanged... For God so loved the world that he *gave*... When you give something you don't expect anything in return. Besides, what could you or I give God that he doesn't already have?"

Hmm. "So he did it for nothing?"

"No, he did it for you! He did it so that you could be with him forever if you really wanted to be, and that's what it all comes down to, Erin, whether or not *you* want to be with God when our lives end here. After all, there are only two alternatives and the bible talks about them both. And I'd choose heaven over hell any day!"

"So what is faith then? If faith is all you have to have... I mean, how does it work?"

Sarah smiled. I could tell by her expression that this one was going to be another hard one to explain.

"Faith is kinda like...um... Well, what are you doing tomorrow?"

And I thought *my* attention span was short..."Well, I'm probably going to go to school to suffer again... why?"

"So you have five or six classes?"

"Yeah"

"Homework, schoolwork, lunch...?"

"Yeah"

"So would you say your day is pretty planned out before you even wake up in the morning? I mean, breakfast, shower, blow-dry your hair, makeup, school, homework, etc..."

"Yeah"

"Well, that's *kind of* like faith..."

I was suddenly confused again, but it was something I had been getting used to over the past hour.

"You see, you're so sure that you're going to wake up in the morning that you already have your day planned out. You're so sure that you're going to be alive and well tomorrow that you don't even think about it. You don't even consider the possibility that tomorrow might not come at all. You see, you know that you know that you know that it's going to happen so much that you can picture it in your mind. You believe in it… That's complete, one hundred percent, faith."

I was speechless.

"Faith in God is no different," she continued, "Just a lot harder than it sounds. There are two bible scriptures that I always remember when I pray, and I use them all the time. One of them is 'I can do all things through Christ who strengthens me' and the other is 'Whatever you ask for in prayer, believe that you have received it, and it will be yours.' If I know that I can do all things because Jesus gives me the strength and I believe that I have already received what I'm asking for, God will give it to me…"

"So you've done this before? And it's worked?" I asked a little more skeptically than I should have. *I've got to work on that too!*

"Almost every day," Sarah replied instantly, nodding.

"So you've never prayed and God *didn't* answer your prayers?"

"Well, of course I have, but that's a different story," she replied.

"Why?"

"Well, because you and I are only human. We don't see everything like God sees it. You see, he sees the big picture. He's seen that picture since long before you and I were ever born. God is only going to answer your prayers according to what's best for you and me. He loves us! He doesn't want to see us fail or get something crappy when we could have gotten something great if we would've just been more patient or faithful and waited on it. You know what I mean?"

"I guess..." I replied with a shrug.

"What do you mean?" she asked.

"So he doesn't answer our prayers sometimes because he knows what's best for us and we don't?"

"Basically..."

"So if I pray for a certain car and I don't get it, but then I go out and buy it myself, what happens?"

Sarah shrugged, "I guess anything could happen, but maybe that car will break down in a week or maybe a better car would have come tomorrow if you'd just waited a little longer? I don't know for sure, but what I do know is that what you just said is the real beauty behind God's love for us..."

"What? That I can buy it myself?"

"Yep, that you still have a choice to do something even if it's not what God wants for you! You see, he gave us the ability to choose for ourselves. That's what makes it so awesome if you really think about it. I mean, he's done so much for us and after sending his own son to die for us, he *still* gives us the choice whether we want to follow him or not. If that's not love, I don't know what is."

"But why doesn't he just *make* some people..."

"Because if he made us worship him, it wouldn't be love, it would be slavery! And it wouldn't be the way God meant for things to be. That's another reason why he sent Jesus. See, Erin, we're almost like slaves to our own selves. I know that doesn't make too much sense, but we are! We spend all of our time doing things for us, or for others so *we* look good, or to impress other people with how smart or beautiful *we* are. When we do that we're making gods out of ourselves! We're saying that we're the most important things in our world and that's the number one thing God hates..."

"But God can't hate if he's all love and hugs and stuff, can he? I mean, doesn't that kind of go against itself?" I asked.

"No," she answered plainly. "Do you think your dad liked whipping you when you were growing up? Do you think he likes grounding you when you do something wrong? No! But when you do something wrong there's still a punishment for the crime, isn't there? God's no different."

I had no idea this Jesus stuff was so deep. I mean, who would think that it's more than sitting around listening to people talk and singing some crappy old music? Once our coffees were finished and all of the caramel dip consumed, Sarah and I drove back home.

The Jesus conversation eased up once we left the coffee house and returned to more casual talk about how much warmer it was here than in Hammond Falls and how our deals with my dad had been going. Needless to say, I think my mom's stress level had risen thanks to Jake and Carrie.

After everyone went to bed, I was still awake. Headlights flashed across my bedroom walls. It was windy out. I guess the weather up where Sarah and Aunt Beth are from must've followed them down to Davis-Buckley. I could see the shadows of the trees dancing in the yard. It was quiet. I hate it when it's quiet and I'm awake. If the house were empty I'd just turn on a radio or something, but right now I can't. I'd put on my headphones, but that would require me getting out of bed and let's face it, that's not happening. Maybe I could call Ian and get him to do it? I laughed. For a second my mind started to wander, but then I laughed again because I thought of how funny I would look to someone lying in a bed in the middle of a dark, silent room laughing for no apparent reason. Sometimes I really do think I need professional help!

My eyes were tired, my body was tired, but my mind...*that* was a whole other story. The first thought that came to mind was Jake. I almost growled like a rabid animal, but something told me deep down in the back of my mind that I needed to wrestle this thing, this aggravation; that I had to let him go and move on.

To what? How? How could I just let him get away with it? He needed to be taught a lesson! I heard one thought shout.

What are you going to do, kill him? Neither of you are going to move away anytime soon, are you? There's no getting away from this, just face it and be done with it! Another thought argued.

I suddenly felt like I had a front row seat for the soap opera in my mind.

I should make him jealous... Yeah! I have to make him see what he's missing! blurted the first thought.

But what will that prove? You'll only end up hurting someone else like he did you, or turning into a tramp just like Carrie, then who's the idiot? argued the second.

Voice number two, one point... Voice number one, zero!

Desperate times call for desperate measures... chimed number one.

Are we desperate? I think the better word is confused... countered the second voice.

Oh, sure, make sure you baby yourself...it'll help fix everything, I'm sure! spat the first voice.

The voices went at it for a while before I couldn't stand it any longer and changed the channel inside my mind. It was all too much! Jake, Carrie, everyone's stares, the rumors...

Sarah showing up and giving me this explosion of Jesus stuff didn't seem to help either. It *did* take my mind off of how bad things were for a while, but yet here I am with the same old problems that won't seem to go away. But still, the Jesus grenade had its moments that sounded like they *could* make sense. I guess it's inevitable... I mean, how do you dodge an explosion like that without getting at least a few things on you? In my mind I saw Jake again and almost instantly I pictured some handsome guy leaving Sarah stranded on the side of that dark dirt road she told me about. It was hard to picture her all drugged up and stuff, but I just imagined Jenny from the movie Forrest Gump and it made it easier. I guess I'd see Jesus too if I had all those drugs in me...

It's amazing to me how far things had come from what they were in the beginning. Is this how life really is? Change after change after chaos? Only four months ago we were a close group and now it's decimated. It's like another type of explosion wiped us out or something. I call it the High school grenade. How had it disappeared so quickly? So easily? At first, I thought no one could possibly understand, but somehow Sarah – the last person I would have ever expected – just showed up with this hidden secret. She had been through what I'm going through and much, much more. How weird? She abandoned her real friends and then her new friends abandoned her, just like me. I guess what goes around really does come around? And she seems happy about her choices... I mean, she didn't act like she regretted leaving fashion far behind along with everything else that was cool. I guess sometimes she wears normal clothes and dresses like she's from *this* century, but otherwise she's all skirted up and happy-go-lucky. It's all a part of that humble thing she was talking about in Clarence.

Another thought popped into my mind. I'm not self-centered, am I? I mean, I do things for people and I don't *always* think about just myself. I think about Ian and other people too! I used to think about Jake all the time and what I could do to make him happy! That's not selfish!

But why were you thinking about Jake? A voice in my head prompted.

I stewed on my own question. Is that pathetic or what?

Is it because you were expecting something in return? A little thing called love perhaps? Maybe popularity? Recognition? A chance to step out of Carrie's shadow and prove to someone other than your mom that you can be pretty too?

The accusations were harsh, but far from shocking. All the words, every comment the voices made were the cold, hard truth. I sat up in my bed. I felt like my face had just been slapped. How could I argue any longer? I *was* selfish. I *was* just doing those things for me. How had I not seen that before now?

Chapter Twenty-Nine

November 27th - Tuesday

After the worst night of sleep ever, I woke to the sound of chaos. Pots and pans screamed as they clashed together and then to the kitchen floor, each chiming a different tune. For some reason my bedroom door was open, or at least cracked, otherwise I don't think I would have heard more than a distant muffle. The sun shined through my multicolored drapes. I looked at my clock. I must've turned my alarm off because I was forty-five minutes late.

"Crap! As if I needed *this* too!"

I threw the covers back. My feet hit the floor, but I didn't get out of bed. Perched on my bedside table was something interesting, something unusual, something delicious, a latte. Simply because no girl in her right mind would dare question such a miracle, I quickly grabbed the divine nectar and huddled myself around it like it was a small fire in a cup. I could hear voices through the cracked door and after nearly a minute, I decided to explore further.

Everyone was downstairs huddled around the table,

some sitting, some standing. As I walked into the kitchen Mom raised her hand toward me and Dad shook his head somberly.

"I told your father that you'd wake up," she said, "but he seems to think you'll sleep through anything."

"I might've if my door would have been shut all the way," I replied.

"Ha!" countered Dad with a point back to Mom. She only rolled her eyes.

Aunt Beth smiled. She looked like she had been awake for hours, so did Sarah. Aunt Beth's hair was still wet, but Sarah looked more than ready to start her day. It was obvious where my latte came from.

"No school?"

"Two hour delay," chimed Mom and Dad.

"Oh,"

"But I don't see why you just can't take the whole day since it's not going to be worth it anyway," shrugged Mom.

I watched for Dad's eyebrows to clench, or for the lines to wrinkle on his forehead, but nothing happened. Did he agree? I shrugged as if it was a cool idea, but deep inside I was screaming *yes!* After a day like yesterday I think Ian and I deserved a good break. Thank God Christmas vacation was coming soon too.

"So why are *you* home?" I asked, looking at Dad.

He shrugged. "Don't know, thought I'd just take a day. We've been kicking around the idea of going and doing something, if you want..."

Unintentionally, I glanced around at everyone. Their faces were mixed.

"Like what?"

"I don't know. We were thinking about taking a ride up into the mountains," he said.

I guess my face showed how crazy I thought that was because my mom and dad quickly looked to one another and smirked.

"...on the Yellow Brooke Express," he clarified.

I tried to fight the smile that came to my face, but I couldn't. The train into the mountains that used to connect Tisdale to Yellow Brooke was probably the coolest thing around, well, next to the mall. It was one of those things the tourists usually did all year long, but especially during this time of year the views are amazing, ridiculously cold, but amazing. The tickets were usually pretty steep too, which is another reason we hardly rode it, but during the winter months they went down because only half the track was open. I don't think they wanted to chance taking an entire train full of people through the Rockies this close to Christmas.

The train conductor walked around, shook everyone's hands, and took tickets. The old fashioned railcars were still bare and rickety. The seats were old wood booths, but padded. The full nine hour ride would eventually become uncomfortable. It's a good thing my Mom's side of the family comes equipped with a naturally padded butt. Ian and Dad on the other hand...

After the conductor collected the tickets, he sat down and radioed the front and a few minutes later we were slowly starting to pull away from Yellow Brooke station. The first thirty minutes or so were boring. The train cut through the streets. Passersby waved at the dumb tourists on the train about to freeze themselves to death. I'm sure the locals were thinking, "What idiots would pay to be miserable for four hours?"

We followed along the river for a while before we started our climb into the mountains. The houses grew with the openness of the land; the smaller townhouses replaced by large four and five bedroom houses, which were replaced by the large mansion-like houses up near Briar Ridge. So beautiful... One house had a waterfall right next to it that spilled into a small pond and started its own little river that eventually ran into the larger one. We crossed a few antique looking wood bridges with the arches and neat designs on them. It's so cool how some things can be preserved or at least replicated and made to look like the old days. The thought of old times made me glance and wonder what Aunt Beth and Sarah were wearing. Both of them were smartly sporting blue jeans with boots. Ian and Dad came back from the concessions car with mugs of hot chocolate and man was it good! It's got to be the best hot chocolate ever!

Sarah and I were the first ones out on the observation car. It was so cold, but not as bad as I thought it was going to be. We both brought scarves and hats and gloves, *the works*, so it wasn't too bad. Sarah had a huge camera that even made the cool camera sound when she took a picture.

"Wow, where'd you get that?"

"Well, before I got into all that stuff I told you about, I used to want to be a photographer, so for Christmas one year my brother and Mom came together and bought me this camera."

"Wow, that must've been a fortune…"

"Well, I had to save up for the extra lenses, but yeah, it was a lot of money for them to spend on one present," she said with a wide-eyed nod, "but it was worth it," she added.

We spent a few minutes admiring the view. The town of Yellow Brooke was beginning to look like a distant anthill. Soon, we'd curve and start into the mountains toward Tisdale and all the really pretty stuff.

"Do you think that's what you're gonna go to college for?" I asked, "Photography?"

Sarah shrugged. "I'm not sure yet," she replied. "Things change. *I've* changed. I guess it's just hard to say right now."

My mind immediately started sorting through everything we talked about the day before; about her ex-boyfriend and her encounter with the stranger on the dirt road. She could've died that night if she hadn't made it to… How *did* she make it to that house? Who had she talked to all that way? Was she just walking by herself?

"What's wrong?" she asked.

I fought for an excuse or a lie, but the only thing that came was, "How did you make it to that house?"

She seemed shocked that my mind would have wandered off like that, but before she could answer I was speaking again.

"There's no way you could've made it there by yourself, right? I mean, how did you get there drunk *and* high? It was over a mile to the nearest house, right? I mean, you had this whole conversation about stuff..."

Sarah stared at me like my Mom does sometimes when she wants me to sort out my thoughts. Almost like she was patiently waiting on me to come to the conclusion that I was supposed to, but nothing else was coming. How did she get there? Why was she alive when everything pointed toward the fact that she should be dead?

"Here's something that will really get you thinking. It's kept me confused for over a year now. There are two things I want you to think about. Whoever it was, and I personally believe it was Jesus, told me the exact life of Jesus in a story. People say I was hallucinating. Well, if I was just hallucinating, how did I suddenly know the story of Jesus' life? Another thing is, like you said, how did a drunken teenager, messed up on drugs, *walk* all the way back down that dark dirt road without a scratch? Erin, I was in the hospital for about a week. I was so messed up on drugs that I couldn't even see straight. The nurses said that a person with that much in their system shouldn't have been able to function.

How could I have walked all that way without someone helping me? Better yet, how could I have walked all that way without falling or stumbling or..." she flailed her hands and shrugged.

She was right. She should've been worm food.

"So you're kind of like a walking miracle then, huh?" I said.

She nodded, "And I remind myself that every day!"

"So that's why you chose to," I started, but couldn't finish, so I just waved my hand up a down.

She nodded with a smirk.

"I meant everything I said, Erin. The story he told me, the story I told you, the answers to all of your questions. All of that stuff is really important, and trust me, you're not asking anything I didn't ask myself when I started down the road that I hope you'll be starting down soon."

"What road is that?"

"The road to truth. The road that leads to a future, not a...not some...inescapable bowl of pain..."

Inescapable bowl of pain... The words echoed in my head for a while. I pictured the world being this big bowl with these impossibly steep walls, too slick to really grab. If I tried to climb out I'd only make it so far before I would lose my grip and slide back down into the middle of Jake and all his mean friends; back into the middle of all the drama and the lies, to all the fakeness and the pain, and the next Joe Gregory; back into the rhythm of the dance where everyone is following along in repetition, almost chanting "Sex, drugs, and lies" or "Look out for number one and screw everyone else!"

An inescapable bowl of pain…

Then the story of Jesus as Sarah told it to me stood out. How he left heaven just to be with us and we did nothing but beat him up and kill him. How could someone still love someone like that? How could he still love me after everything I'd done to him? If lying to my mom means lying to God, and if every mistake is somehow against him too, then everything I've ever done wrong has only broken his heart over and over again. I'm no better than Jake or Carrie or Kylie!

I felt miserable. My heart sank to my feet and my stomach rose to my throat. Somewhere along the way as they passed one another a huge hole opened in my chest. I felt like the old man standing next to me would take a picture and send it in to the Sci-fi channel or something.

Then, Sarah asked me a question, one I had heard used in phrases, mostly in jokes or on T.V., but I never truly understood what it meant, until now.

"Erin, would you like to be *saved* from all of that?"

From the emptiness of the hole inside my chest, something started to flutter. *Was it nervousness? Why would I be nervous?*

Because everything's about to change, a voice replied. I saw Jake and all of the others; I saw how selfish I'd become, and I knew I didn't want to be a part of the bowl anymore. I didn't want to feel that way ever again.

I wanted to be a part of something more, a group of friends, *real* friends.

The cold wind assaulted my face and burned as we stood there. I couldn't reply, but that didn't stop Sarah from seeing my choice. She leaned in close and hugged me. "Repeat this prayer after me," she said in my ear, so I did, every word...even the *Amen*. She stepped back with tears streaking down her rosy cheeks and snapped a few quick pictures of me.

"What did you do that for?" I asked, wiping my face. "I look horrible."

"No," she said, shaking her head, a wide smile on her face. "You look better than a model...you look like a *re*-model." She leaned in close to me and took a picture of us together.

"I want to remember this day, forever," she said. "I know God will..."